MY W
nymysteries.com

The Lemrow Mystery

Mary Jo Robertiello

eBook ISBN 978-0-9888850-1-1

Chapter 1

10 p.m. Thursday, January 29

"Rita told me to keep the answers short and sweet."
Detective Steve Kulchek referred to the prosecutor,
Rita McCarthy, and to their warm-up session for the
last day of the trial. He nodded at his iPhone as if he
were talking across his desk to his partner,
Dominique Leguizamo.

After clicking off, he flattened his aching
back against his customary booth at BOLOS,
rotating his right shoulder, then his left. Steve
pushed back the dingy calico café curtains and
stared out at the rain beating down in the alley. The
cozy bar was housed in one of the last remaining
one-story brick buildings on First Avenue. It
squatted between a fifty-two story glass and steel
high rise and an under construction skyscraper.

Life was good. No, life was better. He licked
his lips over their tight murder-felony case. Arson
with three dead. He figured the building owners,
owing lots of money, arranged the fire. Taking

down the perp, a twenty-four-year-old Mexican-American, was their first step.

They had a witness. Reluctant but a witness, an ex-con who was working security at a nearby building on 86th Street and Third Avenue. He had taken photos of the perp pouring gasoline and then lighting it. Steve's team figured that their witness was interested in blackmail, but they got to him and his cell phone first.

All wrapped up except for the lead detective's testimony in court tomorrow. Steve was ready.

He left his phone on the table. Let Carmen call him. He was sick to death of their seesaw affair: one minute, fighting, the next minute, make up sex. He inhaled deeply, hating her. Why isn't she here? What's the point of a girl friend if she can't celebrate with you?

Steve gazed at his second home, soaking up its cracked fake leather stools at the zinc topped bar, year-round Christmas decorations slung on the mirror facing the patrons, neon signs advertising beers that were long gone into bankruptcy, deep wooden booths, dim lighting, a twinkling juke box. He raised his bourbon to the plaintive Sinatra rendition of Sinatra feeling sorry for himself.

It was the scene of celebrations: cases won, promotions, weddings, you name it. It was the scene of defeats: cases lost, demotions, divorces.

Steve signaled the bartender/owner/ex-cop for another Jack and inhaled the stale smell of booze and babes. From the wooden bar's past life, his olfactory nerves picked up the scent of unfiltered Camels. He couldn't retire. He had to make enough cash to buy them.

Steve ducked out the side door for a fix. He stood under the overhang, shivering and listening to Johnny Cash walking the line. He blew a smoke ring and considered giving up smoking. Go to a clinic? Be hypnotized? Wear funny things over his ears? Acupuncture? Steve shuddered at the thought of needles.

All for Carmen. Carmen the tall, proud, passionate, opinionated woman he adored. Fire, that's what she was. So, giving up smoking and getting married. That's what she wanted. Giving up smoking? Maybe. Getting married? Steve's stomach did somersaults. Not for him. Once around the block had been enough. The one good result was his nineteen–year-old daughter.

What's this? The slamming of a taxi door and then a good-looking woman running out of the rain toward BOLOS. For a second, he imagined it was his Carmen. In your dreams. He liked her legs and her short tight skirt. By the time he took a deep drag, ducked back into his BOLOS booth, and slipped a lozenge into his mouth, she was seated on a bar stool. Her curly chestnut hair glistened with raindrops. He studied her ass then signaled to the bartender to give her a drink on him.

In a stage whisper laced with a fruity tone, the bartender said as he placed Makers Mark straight up in front of her, "The gentleman in the third booth would like you to accept this with his compliments."

She swiveled around to give him the once over.

No competition for Carmen but not bad. The legs were great. The face was heavy on the blush.

"Join me?" He knew his lopsided smile got them, at least initially. The red light in Steve's brain was blinking on and off. He ignored it. He wanted to celebrate almost winning the case. Any excuse to get laid. He tucked his phone into his pocket.

"Why not?" She grinned and slid off the stool, grabbed her drink and her bag. She flung her Armani knock off into the booth and plopped down next to it. She gave him a fleeting smile as she rooted in her bag for a Kleenex. She didn't wipe off her face or run the tissue over her hair. Instead, she stroked her purse, working the tissue down the fake leather.

"Armani?" Steve said.

"Yeah."

"Very classy." Steve's tone and look included the woman. He didn't mention that his three years in Robbery had honed his skills at identifying any up market knock offs from heels to bags to jewelry.

"You smoke?" She took a sip of her drink.

"Why?" *Not another female minding his business for him.*

"Maybe I can bum a cigarette." He knew she smelled it. Who's picking up who?

"I'm Steve."

"I'm Kimberly."

"Classy name."

Kimberly smiled. She looked vaguely familiar. The gap between her two middle upper teeth reminded him of a model who had a minor acting career. "You're a model? An actress, excuse me, an actor?"

She giggled. Her breasts rose invitingly above her low cut satin blouse.

"What do you do, Kimberly?" Steve signaled the bartender for two more.

"I'm resting." She raised her glass and drained it.

The second round arrived. The bartender set the drinks on the table and gave them a thumbs up.

Steve and Kimberly laughed together, their eyes signaling what a jerk the guy was. Steve held up his Jack and clinked his glass with hers. They both drank deeply. In the background the room was warming up with some folk music.

Steve tilted his head toward the jukebox. "I hate that shit."

She leaned across the table, her breasts resting on the surface like rising dough. "I'd love a cigarette."

"We can stand outside. Not get too wet. Not get too cold." Steve stopped. "I have a better idea." He stopped again. He couldn't suggest they go to his place. Carmen's photos were scattered all over the place, not to mention some of her clothes, make up. Nah.

As soon as they were out the door, they lit up. Both blew the smoke any which way, not having to care about annoying other people.

Steve stood in front of her, shielding her from most of the rain. Kimberly inhaled, "God, this is good." She smiled and, shivering, came close to him.

It was cozy, them against the non-smoking world being splattered by the raindrops hitting the alley and pinging onto their legs.

"What was your better idea?" she whispered.

"I thought we could go to my place, get to know one another better, but I just had it painted."

"Painted?" She gave him a knowing grin.

"Honest." He held up his hand as if he were taking an oath. "It stinks. I'm sleeping on my brother's couch tonight."

"No girl friend? A good looking guy like you?"

"Not at the moment." Steve reached down, cradled his right hand in her curly, scented hair and drew her close for a long kiss. "I've wanted to do that ever since I saw that sexy mouth."

"My place hasn't been painted in years."

"Live alone?"

"At the moment."

Steve used his special parking medallion to get as close as possible to Kimberly's building, a high rise on Second Avenue and 56th Street. As they ran through the rain, Steve played the gentleman and held his coat over her head. Up they went to the tenth floor, cuddling in the elevator. Once inside the studio, Kimberly clicked on the lights, then lowered them. Without asking, Steve went to the window overlooking Second Avenue, and lowered the blinds.

When he turned around, Kimberly was standing like a modeling agency's idea of a little girl. Head to one side, hands behind her back and her pampered feet, pigeon toed. In record time she had stripped down to a black satin slip. He felt a twinge of disappointment. How he loved to undress women.

"Catching up," Steve said as he unbuttoned his shirt and tossed it toward the night table, narrowly missing a cat-shaped clock whose mechanical eyes rolled back and forth.

"Watch out." Kimberly's sharp tone surprised him. "Sorry," she whispered, coming close and running her right hand down his side. "Let me." She pulled him by his belt to her bed. It registered in his fevered brain that her apartment was neat, even her bed was made but not for long. They sunk on to it. Part of the rush, he realized later, was the smell of clean sheets.

Steve woke up about four a.m. He looked across at Kimberly who opened one eye and rolled over away from him. He turned on his side, giving himself a three-minute snooze. Without warning, she wrapped her arms around him. "Hey, big guy…"

He turned over to face her. She planted a big kiss on his mouth.

He ducked. "Honey, I have morning mouth."

Kimberly kissed him any way.

Steve struggled between a quickie and Murder-Felony. Murder-Felony won. He threw the upper sheet toward the bottom of the bed and swung his legs over his side.

"Kim, I'm out of here."

"Kimberly."

"Kimberly, I'm out of here."

"Annoyed because I want you to remember my name? What's the hurry?" Anger fringed the hurt tone. "I thought you liked me."

"You're great but I gotta go." He reached for his underpants and trousers.

She moved up behind him and hugged him, covering his upper back with kisses and playful strokes with her nails. Then, she wrapped her legs around his waist.

What a pain in the ass, he thought but didn't say. He pretended to play along by tickling the bottom of her feet.

She giggled. He pulled at one of her legs, then the other.

"Come on, baby." He kept his voice soft.

He was surprised by her strength. "Come on, baby," he said again. Then, he pulled her legs apart and stood up, yanking up his underpants and trousers.

He looked down at her. She glared up at him as she rubbed her legs.

"Come on, Kim – Kimberly - "

She put her hand under her rumpled pillow, pulled out her black slip and pulled it on.

"I'll call you," he lied.

Still examining her legs, she looked up only to glare.

"Any bruises?" Steve buckled his belt.

"You'll be sorry."

He opened the door and took the elevator down to the lobby. *Why did she turn like that?* He shrugged his shoulders. By the time he was at ground level, he was concentrating on the big day ahead. Outside, the air was fresh, the rain had stopped and the birdsong surprised him on Second Avenue. Steve felt great. As he headed to his car, he figured he'd get home to Stuyvesant Town in time for a few hours sleep before showering, shaving and putting on his seldom worn business suit, just back from the cleaners. Then he'd head downtown to court.

At 9 a.m. Steve stood in the crowded hallway outside the 100 Centre Street courtroom. Assistant District Attorney Rita McCarthy and one of her aides flanked him. They were surrounded by Latinos. Not surprising, since three Ecuadorians had died in the fire and the defendant was a Mexican-American. In addition to the victims' relatives and friends, Steve recognized reporters from Telemundo and Univision.

The defense lawyer, a guy Steve had seen around the courts but didn't know, smiled at Rita and passed by. Why? Calm down, Steve said to himself, but his inner detective worried about that smile.

After the crowd was ushered into the dingy courtroom, Steve scanned the room for the newest addition to his team.

He saw King standing at the back of the room, a tall, good looking black guy with a shaved head. He had been brought on board during one of the department's multicultural sweeps. This case was as important to him as it was to Steve.

Dominique Leguizamo, Steve's partner, wasn't there, but he knew she was checking her iPhone. This was her last case before moving up to Lieutenant.

Rosaria, his buddy, wasn't there either, but she'd called him early this morning and given him an account of what a homeless person, Bettylisha Moishabisha, had said on the witness stand. Bettylisha claimed she'd seen a security guard photographing the perp, Jorge Sanchez, pouring some smelly stuff on the corner of the 203 East 86th Street building and then lighting it.

The evidence was in. The perp was responsible for the Ecuadorians' deaths. Convict him and sooner or later he'd reduce his sentence by implicating the building's owners.

Promptly at 9:30 a.m. Judge Michael Feingold entered the courtroom and stepped up to the bench. He was a no nonsense judge with a tired expression who was facing retirement in two weeks time. His black robes, shiny with age, hung lopsided on his stooped shoulders. Without expression, Judge Feingold's beady eye swept over the well, the area in which the defendant, his lawyers, the prosecution lawyers, the court clerk, and the court stenographer were seated at adjacent tables. He then nodded at the court officer at the back of the courtroom before seating himself under the In God We Trust sign.

As soon as the court sat down and the judge thanked the jury for its attentiveness and punctuality. The defendant, Jorge Sanchez, gabbed into his lawyer's ear. Like Detective King, Sanchez had a shaved head. Unlike King, he had a tattooed snake slithering out of his orange regulation uniform, ringing his neck and then slinking up the back of his head. Since it was a criminal trial, two security officers sat behind him.

As soon as Steve was sworn in, ADA McCarthy led him through his background: John Jay College of Criminal Justice graduate, three years on Robbery, two years on the Anti-Crime Unit and for the last eight years Detective second grade.

The ADA addressed the jury, "Detective Kulchek was awarded a Medal for Valor and an MPD Medal."

"Wear your medals," McCarthy had ordered during their warm up session.

"And resemble a South American dictator? Never."

Then McCarthy wanted Steve to wear his uniform, but the minute he reminded her that juries hate cops, she desisted.

The ADA didn't waste time. "Detective Kulchek, please describe what you did on July 11 of last year."

"Fire Marshall Ross called me at 5:10 a.m. at the 19th Precinct, 153 East 67th Street."

"What, if anything, did Fire Marshall Ross say?"

"A building at 203 East 86th Street was on fire. Three burned bodies had been found in the basement."

"What, if anything, did you do?"

"I left the precinct and arrived at the scene at 5:25 a.m."

"Describe what you found at 203 East 86th Street."

"The 19th Ladder Company had put out the fire, but I saw the burned bodies of three people in the cellar." The ADA had told Steve to look at the jury when he said this. He singled out a man who looked Latino.

"Do you know how the cause of their death was determined?"

"Yes, the forensic and the coroner's units determined the victims had died from smoke inhalation and burning."

Although the jury had seen the photos of the fire and of the burned bodies, Steve paused, as instructed, to refresh the gristly memory.

"What was your first action at the scene?"

"I inspected the scene with Marshal Ross. He showed me a gallon can at the building's northeast corner. A substance I identified as gasoline, had been thrown around the area. There was evidence of gasoline in the can."

"What was your next action?"

"I had the scene photographed. My team found a witness who'd seen a person taking photos of the gasoline being poured out of the can."

"Describe what, if anything, you did upon learning that…," the ADA glanced at her notes and stated the homeless woman's name carefully, fully aware of the jury's desire to pounce on a snotty attitude, "Ms. Bettylisha Moishabisha had witnessed Mr. Iggy Martin, the security guard at the adjacent building, 205 East 86th Street, photographing the defendant as he poured gasoline…"

"Objection, your Honor," said the defense lawyer.

"Sustained. Watch your step, Counselor," Judge Feingold eyed the ADA.

"Yes, your Honor. Detective Kulchek, describe what, if anything, you did upon learning that Ms. Bettylisha Moishabisha had witnessed Mr. Iggy Martin photographing the defendant."

The prosecution didn't mention that Mr. Martin, their only witness, had done time. This would be hammered home by the defense.

"We interviewed Ms. Moishabisha." Steve had plastered his standard issue altar boy look on his face before making eye contact with a heavy set black woman he knew was the jury's spokesperson.

His subconscious kicked in with a replay of the reek of urine, cheap booze, her dog's feces and the remains of give-away food that had been emptied from Bettylisha's unspeakable Goodwill sleeping bag before his crew found the 86th Street All Night Bagels to Go receipt stamped with the time 4:55 a.m. placing Bettylisha near the burning building.

"For the record, your Honor, I would like to replay Ms. Moishabisha's testimony."

Being the head detective who was going to testify, Steve was not in the courtroom when Bettylisha took the stand. Steve recalled his buddy, Rosaria, describing in their early morning phone call how the witness, a homeless woman, bathed and dressed courtesy of the prosecution, had been articulate to the point of loquaciousness and had to be pried out of the witness box.

"Approach the bench," Judge Feingold said to the two lawyers. "Ms. McCarthy, what's the point?" he said.

"To refresh the jury's memory. We have the witness, the security guard who shot the photos and the defendant."

"What do you think, Counselor?" The Judge said to the defense lawyer.

"Waste of time." This was a savvy answer. Judge Feingold was known for his speedy trials.

"Request, denied, Counselor McCarthy. Lunchtime approaches."

"Yes, your Honor." The ADA moved back to her table and leaned against it before addressing Steve. "Detective, you stated that you interviewed Ms. Bettylisha Moishabisha."

The ADA paused to let the jury remember Bettylisha's account of the defendant being photographed setting fire to 203 East 86th Street.

"What if anything, did you do then, Detective?"

"We interviewed Mr. Martin who corroborated he took photos on his cell phone. We confiscated his cell."

"Objection, hearsay, your Honor," the defense lawyer said.

"Granted," Judge Feingold said.

"Yes, your Honor," ADA McCarthy said. "We want to show the photos of the fire again."

"Objection, your Honor. Repetitive. The jury has already seen those photos," the defense lawyer said.

"What's the point, Ms. McCarthy?" Judge Feingold said.

"To give the jury the opportunity to study the photos."

"Overruled."

"Yes, your Honor." McCarthy had expected this. "May we approach the bench?"

The judge nodded, rose from his chair and stepped down from the bench on the far side of the jury. He was joined by the lawyers for the prosecution and the defense, the law clerk and, in the middle of the huddle, the court stenographer.

"Well, Counselor?" The judge eyed McCarthy and crossed his black bat-like arms.

"May the People show the photo of the gasoline being poured near the building?"

The judge beat the defense lawyer in objecting because the jury had already seen it.

"The jury saw a blurry photo," McCarthy said. "It's been made clearer. Not any alteration, simply made clearer."

"Show me the original and the second version," the judge said to the court stenographer. She and the law clerk shuffled through evidence envelopes like poker pros and handed one to the judge. He held the encased photos so the defense and prosecution could see them. After the judge studied them, he said, "Okay, but only this one photo."

"I object, your Honor," the defense said.

"Noted, Counselor," the judge said and then climbed back to the bench.

After copies of the clearer version of the photo were distributed to the jury and to Steve, ADA McCarthy said, "Describe what's in exhibit Number One A and B for the People, Detective Kulchek."

"They're the same photo of a man pouring a liquid near a corner of a building."

"What's printed on the bottom of the photo?"

"The date, the present year and the time: July 11, 2011, 5:02 a.m."

"Can you identify the man?"

"Yes, it's Jorge Sanchez." Steve kept his tone neutral but noticed three of the four women on the jury were glowering at the defendant.

"How do you know it's Mr. Jorge Sanchez?"

"He's the one in the photo." Out of the corner of his eye, Steve noticed three jury members nod. "He has a record."

"The prosecution rests, your Honor. Thank you, Detective Kulchek."

"The Defense will present after lunch." Judge Michael Feingold looked at the defense team. He then addressed Steve and the jury. "We caution the witness that he's still on the stand and not to discuss his testimony. Ladies and gentlemen, we

will take a lunch break and resume at 1:30 sharp."
Bang went the gavel.

Still seated, Steve noticed the defense
lawyer with the curious smile glance back at the
courtroom's entrance. The door opened and a young
woman bustled to the rail that separated the well
from the rest of the court and handed the lawyer a
9" x 12" envelope. The defense lawyer opened the
envelope, slid out a few photos and let a grin escape
before assuming a poker face and shoving the
photos back. He rose from his desk and walked the
three feet between his space and ADA McCarthy's
desk. "These just arrived. Sorry about the short
notice."

Rita McCarthy put down her leather brief
case and opened the manila envelope. She slid out
the photos, caught sight of them and pushed them
back into the envelope. "I'll look at these in my
room."

From the witness box, Steve watched Rita
and the other lawyer.

"Detective? Lunchtime, " said a court
officer.

"Forget about lunchtime, Detective. Follow
me. Now," Rita said in a crisp tone. The muscles in
her left cheek were pumping.

Rita McCarthy closed the door of her
assigned room and locked it.

"What the fuck is this, Steve?" She kept her
voice low, but he noticed her right hand shook
slightly as she reached into the manila envelope and
pulled out three photos. She spread them on the
scarred desktop.

Steve looked down at a photo of him sleeping like a baby, a naked baby. In the corner of the shot was a nightstand. On it was a cat-shaped clock. A shirt, his shirt, partially hid the dial. On the bottom of the photo was 12:30 a.m. 01/30/12.

Photo number two showed bruised legs.

Photo number three showed Steve's buffed, muscular back and arms.

The ADA's cell's tone, a blues number, pierced the tense atmosphere. Steve glanced down at his business suit and wanted to rip it off.

Rita McCarthy listened. Her left cheek was twitching. "I'll call you back in five minutes."

"Where were you last night?" She eyed Steve.

"Obviously, you know. So?"

"So you were set up. She's the perp's girlfriend. She's claiming you threatened to beat her up if she didn't testify that her boyfriend set the fire."

"Meaning?"

"Don't play dense with me, Steve. Meaning she was forced to sleep with you."

"You believe her?"

"Frankly, no, but the defense is going for a mistrial. The fact that you had anything whatsoever to do with one of their witnesses…"

"Who knew? I saw her in BOLOS and picked her up." He thought that over. "We picked each other up."

"She's claiming you smacked her, bruised her."

"Bull shit."

"Go on."

"This morning she wrapped her legs around me to keep me in the sack." Steve was bright red. "I had to part her legs with force, but honest, Rita, I didn't hurt her."

"I'd like to kill you," she muttered. "Do you know how this is going to sound in that courtroom?" She pointed toward the door.

"Who is she?" Steve said. Something rattled around in his brain. He recalled in the bar that he had thought she looked familiar. He'd assumed she was an actress he'd seen in a skin flick.

"What are you thinking?" The ADA said.

"I'd like to know who's accusing me of beating her."

Rita McCarthy reached into the manila envelope and pulled out a photo of a woman with long straight blond hair and a closed mouth smile. "Kelly Smith, makeup artist and runner up in the Hooters International Swimmers Pageant," Rita read from a print out. "She has those bruises on her legs."

"Self-inflicted."

"She's the long-time girl friend of Jorge Sanchez. The perp. In case you forgot," said through clenched teeth.

"I was set up."

"Tampering with a witness."

"How did she know I was at BOLOS?" He said more to himself than to Rita McCarthy.

"Since you practically lived there, it's a no brainer."

An insider, he figured. Did Carmen betray him? He dismissed the shameful thought. Another one popped up. Oh shit, Carmen will find out.

Rita held up the photo. "Didn't you recognize her? This shot was hanging with the other possible defense witnesses." She was referring to the precinct's bulletin board of recent cases.

Steve didn't want to admit she'd looked familiar. "I didn't know who she was. She said she was an actress."

The ADA turned her back on him and spoke into her cell.

At 1:30 p.m. Judge Feingold entered the courtroom and seated himself. Previously, a court officer had delivered a message to the judge stating the lawyers wanted to speak to the judge without the jury being present.

"Counselors?" He looked at the prosecution and defense lawyers who approached the bench. With a solemn air the defense lawyer slid out the three photos and handed them to the judge. After Judge Feingold examined them, he shot a look at Steve who was seated at the prosecution's table. "Now what?" he said, still looking at Steve.

"My witness claims Detective Steve Kulchek threatened to beat her if she didn't testify that the defendant set fire to the 86th Street building," the defense attorney said.

"Detective Kulchek assures me he did not threaten or hurt the defense's witness." The ADA's voice was low. "He claims he was set up."

"The photos say another story." The defense lawyer pointed to the bruised legs photo.

"No proof, Counselor," the judge said.

The defense lawyer shifted to the nude, sleeping Steve photo.

"He admits to having slept with the defense witness last night." Ms. McCarthy's ears were red with rage. "Consensual sex."

"Not according to my witness," the defense lawyer said.

"Spare me, he says, she says, Counselors," the judge said. "We're wasting time. Put him in the witness box or are we talking mistrial?"

ADA McCarthy took a deep breath. Mistrial meant officially the prosecution department could start again from scratch. On paper it was still possible to get a guilty verdict - in about a thousand years. Unofficially, mistrial meant the case was dead in the water. Not only did the perp walk having killed three people. So did the building's owners. To make it worse, McCarthy realized the insurance company would have to pay out.

"Can I speak to Detective Kulchek?" she said to the judge. He nodded. The defense lawyer permitted himself a pitying smile.

The ADA walked to her table, leaned across it and said to Steve, "Jigs up. It's a mistrial. Three people died, Detective." She glared into his sad, embarrassed face. "What does this do – what do you do – for the prosecution of criminality in the state of New York?"

Chapter 2

9 a.m. Thursday, July 31

Captain Dick Holbrook stuck his turkey head out his door and announced for the whole room to hear, "Kulchek, my office now."

Steve stalled. Finally, after ten minutes of half listening to his daughter, Jessie, wishing him a happy birthday he said, "Gotta go." Steve shoved his cell into his pocket, drank the cold dregs from his coffee container, toyed with the idea of a quick smoke then marched across the room ignoring his former team and the rest of the dysfunctional NYPD family.

A sneer spread across Holbrook's crumpled face as he rocked back and forth in his executive chair. Everyone in the department knew that Dick Holbrook was a born bureaucrat who hated the street. Most of them knew that Dick Holbrook, Junior hated Steve as much as his father, the late Richard Holbrook, Senior, had hated Con Kulchek, Steve's uncle.

"Sign here." Holbrook shoved a piece of paper toward Steve. Steve picked it up, walked over to the window and turned his back on Holbrook while he read the latest authorized humiliation. Underneath the office jargon he was being told he was being transferred from desk duty to the Art Squad. He had hoped, without much hope, that after six months of punishment, he'd be reinstated to Homicide. Who was he kidding? Himself, as usual.

Steve placed the paper against the dirty window and scrawled his signature. Then he walked back to the desk, reached into his shirt pocket, yanked out his NYPD Homicide ID and pushed it and the signed paper across the desk.

Holbrook reached into his top drawer and pulled out an Art ID. He threw it across his desk. It made a soft thud on the metal surface.

The union rep had warned Steve this might happen. Then she said maybe Holbrook would cut him some slack, let him keep his Homicide ID.

Steve had known better. *It's too juicy. Holbrook Senior sacked my uncle and forced him into early retirement. Now Junior reassigns me.*

Steve ducked automatically to avoid hitting his head on the doorframe of the tiny third floor office. At 6'4", he felt as if he were incarcerated in his daughter's old dollhouse.

Detective Erica Moreau had moved from Human Relations, the softest of all units. Her main qualifications were getting along with Holbrook and a few college courses in art history.

He leaned against a poster of Van Gogh's sunflowers, Moreau's vain attempt at introducing culture to the Art Squad's newly formed Art and Antiques Provenance Unit.

Erica had given up saying hi to Steve since his only response was a grunt and a scowl.

"Get over to the Lemrow. It's a museum. Some woman knows you. She'll fill you in on the Chinese documents, insurance forms, stuff like that." Erica Moreau looked up from a P.A.L. flyer she was designing and pointed her magic marker at him. "AAP includes you review security."

"Since when do we supervise art exhibits?"

"Since we're tiptoeing around anything Chinese."

On a hunch, Steve checked with Stolen Property before leaving for the Lemrow. They informed him about a scandal involving a Met donor who claimed he had been lending, not giving, the museum a Quing landscape and now wanted it back.

Not expecting anything, Steve told Stolen Property to keep him informed about anything to do with the Chinese.

Steve knocked on the glass window to catch the guard's attention. The woman looked up from the rows of surveillance videos monitoring the museum's various locations. A plump man in a business suit stood behind her. Steve saw his own dour expression in the second video to the left. He flashed his new ID. The guard pressed a button and the double doors clicked open.

At the same time, Mary Lemrow Culpepper stepped out of the nearby elevator. Her expensive scent engulfed the area. "Steve Kulchek! Am I glad to see you." She greeted him with arms outstretched, reaching up and giving him a chaste embrace coupled with a peck on each cheek. Having met Mary L. on one of his first homicide cases, Steve knew her Auntie Mame pose had nothing to do with affection.

The man in the business suit came out of the guards' office. He extended his right hand to Steve who shook the sweaty paw and let go fast. "Kenny is the head of security," Mary L. said. "This is Steve Kulchek, the best homicide detective in the world."

"Homicide?" Kenny's tone gave the word rock star status.

"Art Squad," Steve said.

"Kenny, I want you to give Steve a Lemrow tour. Meet us in the Water Court at 11:30," Mary L. dismissed him by waving her hand.

"Let's grab a cup of coffee." She led Steve into the cafeteria. A few members of the staff were finishing their break. Mary L. and Steve headed to a quiet corner. After they were settled at a table, Mary L. said, "We're having our first Chinese exhibit. Eight beautiful Ming statues. You've heard of Wellington Chen?"

"Big in Hong Kong real estate?"

"I'm impressed."

"Why?"

"You actually knew about Wellington."

"I probably read about him in the sports section," Steve said, deadpan. "Why have someone from AAP?" He waited a second, enjoying the blank expression on her face. "Art and Antiques Provenance." Savoring his petty triumph, he got down to business. "Anything to do with that Chinese statue at the Met?"

Mary L. hooted at the thought of the Met in deep doo-doo with one of its benefactors. Steve figured her love of life's battles kept her fighting fit in her mid-seventies.

"We hope Wellington will bequeath his entire collection to us," she said. "He's made it clear that he chose the Lemrow because of its unblemished reputation."

"And you thought of me?" He didn't hide his puzzlement.

"I asked that nice Captain Holbrook if we needed someone to check out the exhibit. Everyone's so nervous about China, between their restrictions and ours, but you know this, being in provenance."

Steve didn't bother to contradict her.

"I mentioned your name and said what a pity you were in homicide."

"When was this?"

Mary L. pulled out her i-Pad and checked her calendar. "A few weeks ago. When I said your name Dick Holbrook laughed and said you'd switched out of homicide and into the Art Squad. Things work out for the best sometimes, don't they?" She looked very pleased with herself.

"How do you know him?"

"Dick and Harry Ross, our trustee chair, are buddies." Mary L. took a deep breath and looked to either side of her. "Elliot, Harry's son," she lowered her voice, "had a drug incident about a year ago. Dick Holbrook heads some anti-drug thing. Harry made a donation and Elliot did some community service."

"Who do I get the documents from?" Steve changed the subject, having had enough.

"The documents. All yours." Mary L. reached into her tote and scooped out a thick folder. "The director, Monika Syka, asked me to give these to you."

Too important to do it herself, Steve thought as he placed the folder on the table and glanced through the papers detailing the recent history of the different statues.

"Wellington Chen's niece, Phoebe, is one of our interns. One of the reasons he's lending us part of his priceless collection is that she loves the Lemrow. Also, it doesn't hurt that his old friend from Harvard, C. E. Stowbridge, was head of the Renaissance Wing." Mary L. wrinkled her nose at him and stirred her coffee. "We're an incestuous lot. Phoebe is engaged to Elliot Ross, Harry Ross's son." A cell phone tinkled. "That's mine. Sorry." Mary L. cupped it to her ear.

Steve thought over all the information that had been thrown at him. In homicide you had a web that branched out from the victim to the suspects and perp.

He leaned on his excellent memory to recall the people Mary L. had mentioned: Wellington Chen, the Hong Kong real estate guy who was lending a collection to the Lemrow where his daughter – no, niece – Phoebe was an intern. At first, Steve had been surprised to hear Dick Holbrook mentioned, but he figured sucking up to the rich and prominent was Holbrook's true vocation. So Harry Ross, the Lemrow chair had contributed to Dickie's drug fund when Harry's son, Elliot Ross, had skirted the law. Elliot was engaged to Phoebe Chen, the Hong Kong guy's niece. What was the director's name, he wondered. Got it - Monika Syka. Mary L. mentioned some guy, C. E.?

"Sorry about that," Mary L. got off her cell.

"Who's the guy with the initials?"

"What are you talking about?" Mary L. arched her eyebrows. "Do you mean C. E. Stowbridge? He was the head of the Renaissance Wing but had to retire because of a major heart attack. Wellington and he have been friends since their Harvard days. I'm sure C. E.'s influence was another reason why we're getting the Chen collection. Not to mention that C. E. pushed and I mean pushed, for Monika's appointment."

"The director?"

"Very good, Steve."

"Harry Ross is Holbrook's buddy?" Steve hated himself for circling around Holbrook.

"Who knows? I guess so." Mary L. shrugged her shoulders. "Harry's my successor as head of the board. I'm staying on to keep an eye on things." She lowered her voice. "My family is funding the Renaissance Wing's renovations. By the way, there's a meeting about the exhibit this coming Tuesday at 11:30. I hope you can make it.

You'll impress Wellington." She studied his blank expression. "At least, I hope you will."

Steve checked his Blackberry and tapped in the meeting's date and time. He figured that in the five days before the meeting he'd have a handle on the workings of the Lemrow and the Chen exhibit. "I want to check out the statues."

"I have a few minutes," Mary L. said.

Steve caught the patronizing tone. Homicide, the best word in the language, flicked on and off like an old neon sign in a B movie. Men respected you and it sure didn't hurt with the ladies.

He followed her up a marble flight of stairs and into a vestibule. Noticing other people coming in through the swinging doors, Steve figured this was the museum's main entrance. The muted lighting reminded him of the upscale funeral parlor one block east on Madison.

Mary L. turned left. Everything changed.

They entered a large space encircled by columns. Light streamed from the glass arched ceiling. At the room's center was an oval pool with a muscular statue of a seated creature raising a shell to his lips. Water shot from the shell drenching the statue.

"Ever been to Rome, Steve?" Mary L. eyed him.

"No," Steve said without taking his eyes off the half-man, half-fish statue. Jesus, how does the poor guy screw?

"Bernini's Triton. A copy, unfortunately. This is the Water Court." Mary L. raised her right hand and swept it conductor-like around the room at the merman fountain, the pink and white water lilies edging the pool's borders and the vaulted skylight. Her gaze rested on a pair of Ionic columns. "It's neoclassical. That's the style, Steve," she added gratuitously.

The fountain's gentle splash and the pockets of greenery relaxed Steve in spite of himself. He inhaled the faint greenhouse smell. The chip on his shoulder teetered but didn't fall off.

The security staff, mostly dark men in maroon uniforms, stood at various doorways leading to other galleries. Steve noticed how quiet the room was in spite of the presence of at least forty visitors. He strained to hear the, reassuring but faint, sound of Fifth Avenue traffic.

On the right, a door opened and a woman and two men entered. The woman was in her early forties and her buff arms were evidence of hard gym time. The only sound was the quick, light step of her heels. At the moment, her pretty features were distorted by suppressed rage. She flung her dark hair back with such force that the older man at her side flinched and swayed.

On her left side was a Chinese man about her own age. Like the woman, he was slim and like her he was wearing top of the line clothes that screamed Italy by whispering it. She murmured something to him. Steve was wondering if the men shared her anger. They didn't show it, but Steve sensed tension.

"Monika, wait," Mary L. said, rushing up to the trio.

The three stopped.

"I want you to meet the world's greatest homicide detective."

Steve cringed. He noticed that the Chinese guy cringed too.

The angry woman's expression changed. She studied him with interest. Her unblinking gaze reminded him of a fox he had, at the age of nine, unwisely tried to keep as a pet. The Chinese coughed, put his hand over his mouth and said something to the woman before he vanished down a corridor.

Steve thought he might be Wellington Chen but realized the man who had just disappeared was too young.

The older man raised his eyebrows, smiled in amusement and said, "A homicide detective? How exciting." The strong, authoritative voice was a surprise coming from this fragile appearing person whose clothes engulfed him.

"Steve Kulchek. Art Squad."

Both the woman and the man laughed. Then the man recovered his manners and said, "I'm C. E. Stowbridge and this is Monika Syka, our director. You don't look like the people we know in art. Isn't that so, Monika?"

She ran her light blue eyes from the top of Steve's hair to the tip of his cop's shoes. "Too true." She managed a tight smile.

"We're waiting for Kenny," Mary L. glanced at her watch. "He's taking Steve around."

"You're here to check out the Kuan-yin exhibit?" The director said to Steve, then looked at Mary L. "Give him the documents?"

Mary L. nodded.

The director said, "I'll let you get to it."

"That's the boss?" Steve asked, watching the backs of the shapely woman and the shapeless suit walk down the corridor.

"Director Monika Syka. Appointed six months ago. Our first woman director and our first authority on Chinese art."

Steve nodded, encouraging her to talk.

"C. E. Stowbridge, the gent with her, is the one I was telling you about. He was very instrumental in getting her hired." Mary L. lowered her voice. "Recently, had a heart attack. Had to retire. As I mentioned before, he and Wellington Chen go way back. In fact, C. E. is Phoebe Chen's godfather."

"What's the director angry about?"

"Angry? Maybe she's anxious. It's quite a job."

Steve changed the subject. "Who was the young Chinese?"

"Sami is a curator from the Hong Kong museum that sold Wellington two of the statues. This Chinese exhibit is a big deal. If Wellington likes the reviews, if his niece Phoebe continues to love us, who knows how much he'll contribute." She looked up as the portly head of security approached. "Here's Kenny. Steve, give me a call if you have any questions."

No sooner had Mary L. walked back through the Water Court and disappeared behind a pillar than Kenny said, "So you were in homicide?"

Steve ignored the question. "Let's check out the exhibit."

Without saying another word, Kenny led the way out of the Water Court into the Central Gallery, then turned left and walked to the end of the room. He unlocked one of two double oak doors and slid it neatly into the wall to reveal a rectangular room with a cathedral ceiling. He flipped on a light switch.

Steve saw six statues on wooden pedestals. Four paintings were mounted in individual niches. He walked from one image to the next. Both pictures and sculpture looked alike to him: exotic, foreign and vaguely religious. From his stint in burglary, he figured the gilt, ornate frames were very valuable.

"What about the paintings?" Steve said.

"They belong to the Lemrow," Kenny said.

Steve examined the statues. Mounted on pedestals about three feet high, they varied in height from five to seven feet. They reminded him of the Virgin Mary grottos that dotted the Long Island of his childhood.

"This is it?" he said. Resignation filled his voice. Why wasn't his daughter with him? She had inherited the artistic gene from his ex-wife.

"Worth millions. Millions," whispered Kenny.

When Steve didn't answer, Kenny said in the same tone, "Injured? That's why you transferred?"

Steve scowled at him.

"Sorry." Kenny threw up his beefy hands.

Steve opened the folder Mary L. had handed him and started matching the statues with the documentation.

Beside two empty pedestals were two airfreight packs. Steve squatted and checked the labels against his papers. "Guangzhou? That mean anything to you?"

Kenny shrugged his shoulders. "Not a thing."

"I don't have any records of these," Steve said.

Behind him he heard someone enter the room. Looking over his shoulder, he made eye contact with the Chinese guy who'd accompanied the director.

"I'm sorry." The man stared at Steve, then bowed and backed out of the room.

"What's his story?" Steve said to Kenny.

"A curator. He's installing the exhibit."

"Sami?" Steve said.

"Right, Sami." Kenny's expression showed surprise that Steve knew the name.

"First or last name?"

"He's always referred to as Sami."

What's he running from? Steve looked back at the statues, particularly the wrapped ones, with renewed interest.

As he was checking the written information, his investigative DNA clicked in: who benefits from selling these pieces, why did Sami disappear twice, and I don't know shit about provenance.

"What's the layout of this place?" Steve said, feeling more at home discussing security.

"This floor houses the museum and the research library. Above us are the offices, the board room and the restoration department," Kenny said. "On the bottom floor, where you entered, are the cafeteria, my office and the locker room. This place used to be the Lemrows' residence. According to Lemrow's will, after his death it was turned into a museum. "

"Mary L.'s father grew up here."

Kenny couldn't resist. "How did you know that?"

"I know Mary L. from another case." Steve changed the subject. "How many people work here?"

Kenny thought for a moment. "We have about fifty full time employees. Fifteen to twenty people are part time."

"Can I get a list of all the employees and what they do?"

After Kenny nodded, Steve said, "Lemrow made his money in banking?" Steve said, recalling the earlier case.

"Banking." Kenny studied him.

Steve ignored him and looked around at the exhibit.

"You don't know anything about these?" He pointed to the two wrapped bundles.

"Nothing." Kenny threw up his hands. "That stuff arrived yesterday."

"I'm finished here for now," Steve said.

"We'll start with the library. It's on the east side of this floor. You can use it."

"Use it?"

"People use it to check out stuff. It's a reference library."

They walked across the Central Gallery to the east wing in silence.

Kenny opened one of the oak paneled doors and stood to one side so that Steve could enter. Instead Steve stood in the doorway, transported back to the Bayside Children's Library built and maintained by a rich spinster. The spinster's own portraits of her beloved cats Fluffy, Cottontail and Muffins had looked down at the children from the gentle blue walls.

Returning to the present and to the Lemrow reading room, Steve noticed that two marble busts of dogs' heads flanked a long table at the front of the room.

For the first time in six months a feeling of peace welled up in Steve. Memories of his Aunt Bess, a sweet woman with a great sense of humor, swept over him. After his parents were killed in a boating accident, he was adopted by his mother's sister, Bess and her husband, Con, a NYPD detective who had taken Steve on surveillance for his tenth birthday. What a present. He was hooked for life.

Leather bound volumes filled cases that lined the four walls of the room. The two men walked past the ten rows of rectangular tables. Studying books and documents, about a dozen people sat at different tables on cushioned Windsor chairs. Steve laughed aloud, as he recalled grinding out fourth grade book reports under Aunt Bess's vigilant eye. He smiled at Kenny. "This is great," he said without lowering his voice. Several people shushed him.

"Let's check out the top floor offices," Steve whispered as they left the library.

Kenny opened an oak door. "Take a look at the Renaissance Wing."

Amidst paintings and statues, Steve noticed a large desk.

"That's Mr. Lemrow's original desk. The Renaissance Wing used to be his library and those stairs," Kenny pointed to a sweeping staircase, "lead to the top floor – where the offices are, but since we're here, let's take the elevator."

A young man, reeking of cigarette smoke, joined them at the elevator bank.

"Geoff, don't tell me," Kenny said, waving his hand in front of his nose. "You're coming from a cigarette break. Don't forget. No smoking after October 11."

Steve gave the guy a sympathetic glance. Geoff shrugged his shoulders, causing a Canon slung around his neck to swing like a pendulum.

After they entered, Kenny held his ID over a sensor in the elevator. "Before you leave, I'll give you yours."

"Only staff use the elevator?" Steve said.

"That's right. The collection is on this floor only."

At eight p.m., after his two cigarette daily allotment, Steve was sitting in BOLO's, mulling over the day. For half a year he'd been hiding from everyone. Tonight, his fortieth birthday, he returned to his old drinking haunt. He was in a dark alcove, seated in a small booth with his back to the wall. He looked out at the entire room. Unless someone was looking for him, he wouldn't be noticed.

In homicide, even his enemies conceded that Steve was methodical. He kept lists of all the people he met. With the help of the employees' list Kenny had given him, Steve had entered the different people at the Lemrow into his Blackberry: Mary L., Kenny, Monika Syka, C. E. Stowbridge, Sami, the Chinese curator, Geoff, the smoker.

Again, because it was his habit, he thought about them. Monika Syka was permanently bad tempered or she was deeply disturbed about something. What's she like to work for?

Steve read the next name on his list: Sami. What's with him? Steve thought back to meeting Sami, Director Monika Syka and C. E., the recently retired curator. After Mary L. revealed that Steve was a detective, Sami had covered his mouth to prevent lip reading, then left the group in a hurry. Later, he disappeared when he saw Steve in the Chen exhibit.

Steve Googled Guangzhou, the name he'd seen on the wrapped parcels in the exhibit. He learned it was a Cantonese city in southern China.

He thought over Mary L.'s talking about Dick Holbrook in familiar terms as he checked his notes. She'd been introduced to Holbrook through Harry Ross whose son had been caught taking or dealing drugs. Steve made a mental note to check it out.

Signaling to the waiter for another Jim Beam, he ran his eyes over his copy of the Chen exhibit's documents, feeling like an accountant instead of a detective. Everything seemed in order except the papers for the two airfreight packs.

He and Kenny had spent the afternoon prowling around the museum so Kenny could demonstrate the various functions of the up-to-date Lemrow system. He conceded that Kenny, with his relentless commitment to the fine art of security, was good at his job.

Steve took a sip of bourbon and mused on NYC's curious practice of converting residences into schools and museums. Taking a deep, relaxing breath, he opened his briefcase and pulled out the Lemrow's floor plan.

In the center of the museum was the Water Court. That's where they had run into Director Monika Syka, C. E. Stowbridge and the slippery curator, Sami. The three of them had come out of a room to the right.

Monika Syka. He Googled her name on his Blackberry. Her birth date confirmed what he had guessed. She was forty-one. Educated up the wazoo: B. A. from Reed, M. A. and Ph.D. in Chinese Studies from Berkeley.

Steve thought about the director's buff and refined exterior that couldn't hide her seething fury. Had something happened in that room she'd just left or was it her personality?

What happened next? That's right. Kenny took him to the Chen exhibit, a small room at the west end of the Central Gallery. Sami had stuck his

head in the door, looked uncomfortable? alarmed?
Steve figured his homicide training was kicking in.

He slurped some bourbon and reminded
himself he was in provenance.

Then he and Kenny walked back through the
Central Gallery to the east wing to inspect the
reference library. The library – he recalled how it
make him think of his sweet Aunt Bess.

A wave of shame spread over him. Thank
God she died before he was demoted. He looked
down at his Blackberry. Time to call his Uncle Con.
He'd been avoiding him for six months.

"Hey. Happy Birthday." His uncle picked up
on the first ring. Con, a retired cop, ran through a
mental list of why his nephew had been re-assigned.
Six months ago, Steve had slept with a perp's girl
friend, check. Case declared a mistrial, check.
Suspect was acquitted in spite of the fact that three
people had been killed, check.

"What's up?" Con said.

"Transferred to the Art Squad," Steve said.

"What?"

"To be exact, I'm in Art and Antiques
Provenance."

"Huh?"

Con's confusion made Steve laugh in spite
of himself. "I keep track of valuable stuff. Check
out the owners. Make sure it's not stolen or forged."

"You know anything about this?"

"I don't know shit."

"Holbrook behind this?"

"Yeah." Steve imagined his uncle's reaction
to that name. Holbrook Senior's last achievement,

before dying of a heart attack, was to dump Con into early retirement.

"What's the rep say?" Con said.

"She says I'm lucky. That's what Dom said too." Steve's boss, Lieutenant Dominique Leguizamo, had come to the NYPD from the Third Battalion, First Marines.

"Your ex-partner said what exactly?"

Steve heard the note of respect in Con's voice.

"She said she was really pissed off because Holbrook was right." Steve had heartburn over almost derailing Dom's climb to lieutenant. "I'm quitting. Set up my own shop. Join Hazmat. If only."

His daughter Jessie's Rhode Island School of Design tuition bill was waiting for him on his Ikea desk back home in Stuyvesant Town.

Besides, he'd never give Holbrook the satisfaction of quitting.

"Look at the bright side - off weekends, no emergencies," Con said.

"Like a dermatologist instead of a surgeon."

"Jessie know?"

"That I'm off desk duty? Yeah. She thinks me being in art provenance is great. Says we can go to museums together."

Con guffawed. In spite of his self-pity, Steve joined in.

He looked down at the last drops of bourbon and resisted ordering another. He knew too many cops who crawled into the bottle at the end of the day.

"You in BOLO's?" Con said.

"Yeah. Time to go home and feed the fish." His daughter's aquarium had become his responsibility when she moved up to Providence for college.

Shirley Horn's "I'm Old Fashioned" was playing. Steve noticed a woman backing away from the jukebox. Pink shimmers in her red brown hair had caught his attention. Some guy pulled out a stool for her.

The guy was Holbrook. Even worse the woman was Carmen. My Carmen with Holbrook. First date and it better be their last.

"Gotta go," Steve said.

Two years ago, Steve recalled, he and Carmen had had their first date here.

It ended six months ago. His sleeping with the witness's girlfriend had been the final straw. In addition his long hours, fear of commitment and smoking had contributed to the end.

Holbrook was flapping his gums. Steve couldn't see Carmen's face and he was too far away to hear her. Maybe she's thinking of us.

While Holbrook was flashing his platinum and making a production out of paying the tab, Steve slid a few bucks on the table and headed out of the restaurant ahead of them, then stationed himself in a dark corner of an alley between BOLO's and the next building.

Here they come. Holbrook holding the door for her, droning on about his diet. Steve caught his breath. What a sexy bitch.

Losing her and destroying that case were twin sores that didn't heal. And both were his fault.

Carmen and Holbrook walked toward a Lexus. How'd you pay for that, bro? Suit wasn't bad, either, part of the endless new wardrobe since fat boy had shed a ton.

Steve remembered who Holbrook reminded him of, in spite of the fancy clothes, the scarecrow in *The Wizard of Oz*, a movie he and his daughter had watched at least eight thousand times.

Holbrook, quite the little gentleman in his new suit, held the door while Carmen slid into the passenger's seat.

Steve ached to hear her laugh. While the Scarecrow was prancing around to the driver's seat, Steve thought he'd cheer her up.

Any excuse to text her. "Don't sleep with little dick, Carmen. B. O. and bad breath." He watched her, expecting her to laugh. Instead, after a second's shocked recognition, sadness swept over her face, dimming the brightness. She clicked off her cell.

Chapter 3

7:30 p.m. Sunday, September 3

On an early fall evening, Charles Edward Stowbridge was having the best fun he could with his clothes on. His childhood nickname, C. E., fitted in neatly with his present position, curator emeritus of the prestigious Lemrow Museum.

C. E. was nestled in his E-Z Boy recliner, the one incongruent note in the room. He smiled at the empty French art modern chair favored by his boyfriend, Yoshi, who was returning tonight from a business trip. The room was cloaked in dense olive curtains that were always drawn. It was as dark as a Caravaggio, and its furnishings reflected C. E.'s hedonistic and catholic taste. The museum quality thermostats and humidity controls were adjusted for the needs of the furnishings.

C. E. relished the sounds of himself pouring wine, munching fine French cheese and crackers, and Michael Feinstein crooning "Night and Day" in the background.

He ran his practiced eye along the collection
of salt and pepper shakers prancing across the
surface of an eighteenth century French table.

Then, he gazed lovingly at the small
Renaissance statue in his lap. C. E. wouldn't have
dreamed of touching the Riccio with bare hands. He
took one of his large, gloved hands off the bronze
statue placed between his legs, and waved at the
perky Little Boy Blue with holes in his head.

Never having had the slightest desire to
sleep with a woman, C. E. nevertheless liked to ogle
the newest addition to his salt and pepper collection,
the saucy girl salt shaker who had her back to him
and was looking coyly over her right shoulder. Her
little hands held her permanently uplifted skirt to
expose holes in her plump buttocks.

"So pre-casino Atlantic City," he murmured,
his practiced curator's eye always working. He
winked at her. She's the only good thing I found in
Scranton, he thought. She winked back, or maybe it
was the second bottle of Chateau Montrose.

He fondled the hard wings of the Riccio
putto, a chubby little boy angel, he'd determined
was bronze and scribbled a note on a pad on the
side table. He glanced back at the girl salt shaker.
Next to her, he'd placed a photo that cute boy
photographer had given him.

As he studied the photo of himself holding
the Riccio with gloved hands, flanked by two other
people, intense anger tightened his jaw. Gently, he
placed the Riccio on the side table, lumbered out of
the recliner. Steadying himself, still not up to speed
after the heart attack, he picked up a pair of sharp

scissors from the side table. Flicking them open and shut like Edward Scissorhands, he approached the photo and stared at the two figures. Looking over at the Riccio, he said, "We look good." Then he cropped the photo and, with relish, sliced the discarded portions into tiny pieces and flung them in the direction of the barren fireplace, placing the altered photo of himself and the Riccio next to the girl salt shaker.

Contented, C. E. picked up the Riccio again and sank into his chair, took a slurp of the Chateau Montrose and doodled a little sketch of the Riccio on the note pad.

God's in his heaven, all's right with the world. Well, not *all* is right.

His cell phone rang. C. E. grabbed it off the side table and put it to his ear. It was his beautiful, self-centered goddaughter, Phoebe Chen.

He listened to her whimpering. "Elliot's driving me crazy."

C. E. recalled Phoebe's fiancé's body and attitude.

"He's awfully good looking." C. E. stroked the hard, curly head of the statue between his legs.

"Cristobel thinks so," Phoebe said in a little girl voice that made C. E. grind his teeth. How Wellington spoils her, he thought.

"Cristobel?" C. E. said.

"She's a research assistant. Come on, C. E. you know who she is."

C. E. recalled a sweet young thing in the library. Mentally, he returned to the Chen family saga. Wellington's only sibling, Phoebe's mother, had died young. Wellington himself, in spite of three failed marriages, had no children. No time for them, he'd told C. E. Phoebe was the only heir to the vast family fortune.

"Darling, I'm not crazy or senile, am I?" C. E. said.

If only she'd say, "You mean about something awful going on at the Lemrow? I'll rush right over and we'll talk about it."

In your dreams.

Instead, she whined about sexy but stupid Elliot.

"Poor baby." C. E. was deeply bored. He hoped his goddaughter didn't hear it in his voice. He waited a respectful second before continuing, "About that matter of the irregularities at the Lemrow…" his tone beseeching her to help him.

"I've done something so stupid," Phoebe interrupted him. She was breathing hard. "Have you ever done anything for love? I mean have you ever hurt someone you love for someone else you love?"

Trite questions from the young and beautiful usually drove C. E. to tears – of laughter.

"C. E., have you ever been unfaithful?"

Surprised by the personal questions, C. E. hesitated. "Well…"

"I have to see Elliot. I have to cancel," Phoebe said in her little girl voice.

He ached to cry out, "Get over here. I have to talk to someone." Instead, he said, "Of course, darling."

Always leave them laughing, he thought. Always present the witty charmer, not the needy old fart.

The call over, he flung the cell phone onto the side table and staunched his thoughts by taking a deep slurp of his favorite med. Then, very quickly, before his heart knew it, he shoved the rest of the Saint-Andre triple crème into his mouth.

The phone rang. C. E. checked the caller ID. It was Yoshi, his partner who was as angular as C. E. was round or had been round before the heart attack. They once had gone to a costume ball as the World's Fair 1939 obelisk and sphere. Some snot had said the costumes were superfluous.

"What's in your mouth?" Yoshi demanded. Before leaving on his business trip five days ago, he had searched their apartment for C. E.'s favorite, cholesterol soaked goodies.

"No one you know."

"What did you eat for lunch?"

"Salad," C. E. lied.

"If you want another heart attack... You sound worried."

"Maybe a little."

"I'll be home in an hour. I couldn't stand being away from you."

"Cut short a business trip for little old me? I'm so glad you're back." C. E. gulped wine. "We'll talk about it when you get home."

"What did I just hear?" fox-eared Yoshi said. "How much have you drunk?"

"O.J., dear boy. Phoebe was supposed to have dinner with me. Thank God she canceled," C.

E. said. "Boy trouble. If only. We'll have a wonderful din din."

"I'll bring in something."

"There's a Colonel Sanders…"

"Absolutely not."

"The leech called for another loan." C. E. was referring to his twin brother. He scribbled something on the pad.

"Keep your hands in your pockets," Yoshi said.

"*Your* pockets."

They both giggled.

C. E. smiled across the room at the cropped photo. "The Lemrow's boy photographer took a rather nice picture of me."

"Whatever for?"

"On Thursday I was in the Green Room with Monika and her smooth friend, Sami. I agreed to take a look at the most darling little statue I have between my legs."

"I don't understand. You have a piece from the Lemrow in our apartment?"

"Perfectly legit. Monika arranged for someone from the museum to deliver it, a chatterbox we all call Ms. Mouse." C. E. sighed. "You know, darling, I have the oddest concern. I'm not crazy or senile?"

"I love you anyway," Yoshi said.

"I have to discuss something about the museum, very serious. Promise we'll discuss it."

"I promise, as long as it's not about Scranton. Let me get off the phone and get home."

"None of those fucking veggies, okay?" C. E. hung up.

Within two seconds, the phone rang again. He picked it up without checking the caller ID and said in a falsetto voice, expecting it to be Yoshi, "Now what?"

Then, his voice hardened. "*Oh*, it's you."

Instantly sober and once again the head of the Renaissance wing, he said, "What's your decision?" His left hand circled the Riccio to protect it from falling. His right hand, holding the cell, shook, but not his voice.

He expected the caller to say, "I'll resign."

C. E. listened, horrified. Then, he shrieked as he looked down at the little statue, "Stealing the Riccio. Me? Steal the Riccio?"

It dawned on him he'd been set up. "You shit."

Pain blinked on and off in his left arm. He'd known that horrid feeling before. He forced himself to brace the Riccio between his knees and breathe deeply. Then, he clutched the cell. He gasped for breath, then, with his right hand, clasped his heart. The pain raced up his left arm. "Please help me," he whimpered. "Don't shout at me, please," he gasped. "Please call…" He dropped the cell.

Trembling, he patted his body with his gloved right hand, feeling for the medical alarm button he was told never to take off. He saw it – across the room where he'd dumped it on the Louis Quatorze chair.

Chapter 4

9:45 a.m. Monday, September 4
At 9:45 a.m. Geoff, the museum photographer, was
standing in the outside corridor that led to the
employees' entrance. He leaned against the notice
announcing that on Monday, October 11, smoking
would no longer be allowed anywhere at the
Lemrow. Geoff was smoking one of his ten daily
cigarettes. His pal, Cristobel, swung open the ornate
iron door that separated the Lemrow from the rest
of the world and walked down the corridor as if it
were a runway. Her fooling around was usually
good for a laugh. Not today.

Geoff moaned, "I can't find my new Canon.
I can't find my bag. I've looked everywhere."

"Not again?" But Cristobel was an easy
touch and immediately took on the older sister role.
"Penthouse? Stacks? Reading Room? Chestnut
Room? Basement? Cafeteria?"

Shivering and sweating, Geoff shook his
head. In spite of his distressed denim jacket and his

vintage aviator sunglasses, he resembled an abused waif.

"Where was the last place you used the camera?"

"How fucking original," he snarled.

"Careful."

They had both been warned about using profanity on the premises, so their conversation was remarkably chaste. Without saying a word, she brushed past him.

"Don't be mad, Cristobel."

"It's an obvious question, but it makes sense." She turned and faced him, making a big deal of waving away the cigarette smoke. "So when was the last time you used it?"

"This morning. Walking through the park."

"What time did you get here?"

"Around nine. I went to the john and that's it."

"Did you take it into the bathroom with you?"

"I think so."

"A camera is usually around your neck."

"True, True." Geoff took a deep drag on his cigarette. "After I shot in the park I put it in the satchel. I didn't take it out again."

"Check with Kenny," Cristobel said.

"Him?" Geoff groaned. "He's such a tight ass. He's always lecturing me about smoking and now he'll get on my case about losing my camera."

"The guy is head of security. If someone stole it, he has to know."

At that moment Geoff and Cristobel stopped talking. Kenny, waving his large right hand in front of his face, passed them along with several other employees.

"I'm not saying anyone stole it," Geoff said. "Maybe someone picked it up for me."

"Would this someone put it in your locker?"

"I didn't check there." Recovering somewhat, Geoff blew a smoke ring to say thanks, then ground out his cigarette.

She put her hand on his wrist to keep him from running off. "C. E. died last night. Another heart attack."

"Oh, yeah?" Geoff said, vaguely interested. "I gave him a print on Thursday."

"You knew C. E.?"

"No, not really. I was shooting some Renaissance statues in the Green Room. I had a photo of C. E. and one of the bronzes I didn't want so I gave it to him and a copy to Theodora. I got a great one of Theodora looking battier than ever and Phoebe looking as beautiful as ever." He didn't notice how Cristobel stiffened at the mention of Phoebe's name. "And our dear boss, Hilda, but I can't show it to you," Geoff whined. "Where's my camera?"

"C. E. hired me. I'll miss him. Knew his stuff," Cristobel said.

"If he hired you, he had to."

She smiled, pleased. "Lunch?"

"Oneish. Gotta go. Gotta find my Canon."

Cristobel emailed Geoff at eleven:thirty, and he texted her back. "STILL MISSING. Now what? Offer a reward?"

At one-thirty they were sitting in the cafeteria. "What do you think?" Geoff showed Cristobel the e-mail reward poster. Under a computer drawing of a camera with a shoulder bag and the caption Canon and Shoulder Bag, he had written in caps, each on a different line: missing, reward, no questions asked.

Cristobel studied the poster for a moment. "Don't put 'no questions asked'. The first thing you'll say is, 'Where did you find them?' Is the camera insured?"

"I think so."

"Stop sweating. That old satchel needs to be replaced."

Geoff lowered his voice so the nearby lunch crowd couldn't hear him. "Some things I don't want anyone to see."

"Like what?"

"Shhhh. Never mind," Geoff's olive skin had turned pea green.

"Speak to Kenny?"

"Yeah. He's the one who told me to distribute the poster."

Instead of teasing him, Cristobel said, "Run it past Hilda, too."

Hilda was the senior research librarian and the self-appointed guardian of good manners. She was their immediate superior and the one who had told them to watch their language.

Always difficult, Geoff said, "Jesus, this place is worse than a prison."

"Hello, Mr. War Correspondent? It's a museum, remember? Suck up to her."

A cell buzzed. They patted themselves down, then Geoff jumped up and pulled his out of his hip pocket. He listened. Then he said, "Yes, thank God. Can I get them now? Great."

"Fabulous," said surrogate older sister, Cristobel, beaming at her friend's good fortune.

Then, her cell rang. It was Hilda. "We had an appointment five minutes ago."

"Two minutes, max." Cristobel leapt out of her chair and headed out of the lunchroom.

At 4:35 p.m. Cristobel dropped by the cafeteria for tea. The photographer was sitting at their table.

"Still here?" Cristobel said. "Don't you ever work?"

Geoff was sitting as still as a stone. He had on his sunglasses and his jacket's collar was turned up, hiding the lower half of his face. He glanced to the right and left. The few people in the room were engrossed in their own conversations.

"What happened?" She looked around for the Canon but saw only the shoulder bag in his lap. He was gripping it like a small boy shielding it from a bully.

"Geoff, have you been smoking?" She didn't mean cigarettes. "You look crazy. Take off the shades and go wash your face and comb your hair."

"Why hate me so much?"

"I don't hate you."

"I don't mean you."

"Where's the camera?"

Geoff shook his head back and forth, his long hair swinging like a cartoon floor mop.

Chapter 5

9:15 a.m. Tuesday, September 5

The early morning sunlight streamed through the windows of the Lemrow offices. Phoebe Chen stretched her supple body before sitting on a chair and wrapping her legs around each other. She continued to talk to eccentric, sweet Theodora, a long time photo archive-and-cataloging assistant. No cubicle in the Lemrow offices was tidy. Even so, Theodora's stood out. Her Mac was covered with tiny cut-out reproductions of dissolute, white wigged counts, sweet Virgin Marys, and Theodora in one of her homemade, queen mother hats. Suspended from an overhead cabinet were mobiles made of old rosary beads and crucifixes. Perched on top of the cabinet were three busts of forgotten royalty decked out in religious medals and Mardi Gras beads.

Since her salary was ladylike rather than substantial, the museum turned a semi-blind eye to Theodora's entrepreneurial fantasies. Theodora had her own little business. She fixed, or as she said, mended jewelry. Theodora was repairing the clasp of Phoebe's pearl necklace which Phoebe wanted to wear it to the following night's opening of the Chen exhibit.

Imagine having an uncle, like a fairy godfather, who would lend his priceless statues because you liked your little intern job. Theodora was in awe of Phoebe's beauty, social prominence and wealth. Even so, she wished that Phoebe would stop touching the mobiles suspended over the desk.

Even more, she wished Phoebe's lovely hand wasn't so near the scrapbook.

As Phoebe touched the whirligig objects and emailed her friends, Theodora's photo archive eyes studied the red mark on Phoebe's swanlike neck. She wondered if that awful boyfriend had grabbed the necklace she was mending but, of course, didn't say anything.

Looking up and seeing Theodora staring at her neck, Phoebe put her hand over the mark.

Theodora said, "Hurt yourself?"

Instead of snubbing her, Phoebe put her index finger on the cut. "It's nothing. I should say, he was nothing."

"He's so young, so callow," Theodora dared to say.

Phoebe's beautiful eyes widened in confusion. Her rosebud lips parted in a smile. "You mean Elliot Ross? I wasn't talking about him. You're right though. He is young and callow. That reminds me. I have to text him."

Theodora's idol was talking to her about her private life. She couldn't wait to tell Hilda, her beloved companion of many years and the Lemrow's head librarian.

"I miss C. E. so much. Don't you?" Phoebe didn't take her eyes off her iPhone.

"Yes," Theodora said, not meaning it. She recalled the snooty curator emeritus who condescended on occasion to say good morning.

"So lovable. He was fat and loved to drink," Phoebe confided. She looked up from texting. Theodora's magma-like shape overflowed the chair. Embarrassed, Phoebe burbled, "Your office reminds me of *The Old Curiosity Shop*. I've never read it, but I like the name, don't you?"

Without listening to Theodora's muted yes, Phoebe fiddled with an overhead papier-mache creation.

Theodora put down a small sharp tool and tested the clasp a few times. Phoebe turned her head so that the repaired necklace could be placed on her neck. Theodora, slipping into the seventeenth century, became Phoebe's personal maid and fastened the necklace ever so gently without touching my lady's neck. She took her time, sneaking a peek at what Phoebe was tapping on her iPhone. "Don't - statues."

Phoebe thanked Theodora as she patted the pearls. The northern morning light shone on her satin black hair arranged in a stylish, sloppy ponytail and on her long, graceful fingers, beautifully manicured without a speck of lacquer.

Theodora studied her handiwork around Phoebe's lovely neck, flawless except for the tiny red mark. Then Theodora reached behind her, burrowed through a mound of papers and pulled out her camera.

"May I?" Theodora held it up.

Used to being gawked at and never having taken a bad photo in her life, Phoebe said, "Of course."

As Theodora clicked away, Phoebe couldn't resist staring at the scapula and rosary beads draped around Theodora's fleshy neck. They cascaded down her matronly bosom, peeking out of the frilly folds of a Pepto-Bismol pink blouse, overlaid with a chartreuse chiffon scarf.

What did she wear to her first job interview, Phoebe wondered. Then, feeling a little guilty, she said, "You're so clever. Let me pay you for this."

Theodora shook her head.

Phoebe nodded, used to people serving her. She checked her watch, 9:45, but didn't get up. There was something cozy about this cluttered corner.

Who could she tell? Who could she confide in? She smiled sweetly at Theodora, inwardly dismissing her as a harmless dingbat who repaired her jewelry.

On a shelf bulging with green folders annotated in Theodora's spidery handwriting, Phoebe noticed two salt and pepper shakers. Salt was a coy girl snake and Pepper was a manly boy snake. She reached over, oblivious to Theodora's grinding her teeth, and with her index finger followed the curve of the girl snake's eyelashes. "C. E. would have loved these."

Phoebe's eyes traveled to a deck of Tarot cards. The stern armored figure on the cover made her shiver. "Is that Death?" she whispered.

"Yes," Theodora said cheerfully.

Phoebe lowered her voice. "Could there be a thief in the museum?"

Theodora's long nose twitched. "I suppose so, but he'd be caught by security. The bells would ring."

"I mean someone who works here."

"What are you suggesting?" Theodora's professional paranoia and love of gossip were in a photo finish.

"I don't know if the word thief is exactly what I mean." Phoebe wrung her lovely hands, talking more to herself than to Theodora. "C. E. wanted to talk about it, but I canceled our dinner date the night he died."

"Talk about what?" Theodora's goose-like neck shot out of the frilly blouse. She couldn't wait to tell Hilda.

"I feel so guilty – about lots of things." Phoebe whispered. Her hazel-caramel eyes were pleading. "Please don't tell anyone."

At that moment a very syrupy version of "Ave Maria" filled their little corner. The other occupants didn't turn from their computers, but everyone had been listening to Phoebe and Theodora ever since Phoebe in her latest Bergdorf outfit had entered Theodora's cubicle.

Theodora flipped open her cell and punched a button. "Ave Maria" was replaced by someone crying. It was Hilda.

"What's wrong?" Theodora's whisper hissed around the other cubicles. Heads were turned imperceptibly toward her corner. "My God." Theodora crossed herself. She held tightly to the cell. "I have to go." She stood up, not noticing the miniature pliers falling to the floor.

"What's wrong?" Phoebe had caught Theodora's anxiety. Everyone in the outer room was openly staring at them.

"I have to go. I have to go. I have to go to the Green Room."

"Well, I'll go with you." In an impromptu gesture, Phoebe arranged Theodora's green chiffon scarf around her plump shoulders, then linked her arm through Theodora's as they walked to the elevator. Once in it, Phoebe flicked her ID card over a light and pushed the first floor button. As the elevator creaked to its destination, Theodora whispered, "Geoff."

"The photographer?"

Theodora nodded. "Poor Hildy found him."

"Found him?"

Theodora sobbed and hid her face in her hands. "He's in the Green Room."

Phoebe managed to guide distraught, weeping Theodora out of the elevator, flash the card at a little red light in the wall, open the door, unlatch the velvet guide rope, and head down the corridor to the Green Room.

The second lieutenant for security was standing in a military pose in front of the closed doors. A few guests walked by, intent on finding a Caravaggio or sitting in the adjacent Water Court.

Phoebe waited until the guests were beyond earshot then she looked at the guard, Jean Pierre, a very serious Haitian. "What happened?" In reply, Jean Pierre rolled his shoulders and kept his hands clenched behind his back.

"What happened?" Phoebe asked again, a little too loudly.

The guard frowned. If Phoebe had been anyone else, he would have told her to lower her voice. Phoebe sidled nearer to him.

The Green Room door opened a sliver. Phoebe and Theodora watched Monika Syka, who was removing some latex gloves. At that moment the director looked up and saw the two women staring at her. She stopped removing the gloves and came toward them.

She put her gloved hands on Phoebe's shoulders. "Something terrible has happened. Geoff has killed himself."

Stunned, Phoebe turned to Theodora.

Several staff members were clustered at the far end of the colonnade. Seeing Hilda, the librarian, Theodora let go of Phoebe's hand, ran to Hilda and threw herself into Hilda's arms. "What happened, Hildi?"

"I opened the Green Room door and saw Geoff. I couldn't go in. I couldn't go near him. I called the director."

Three policemen were rounding the corner.
One stopped and stood in front of the group. The
other two walked toward the woman who was
shoving gloves into her pocket. "I'm Director
Monika Syka."

The police and the director walked back to
the Green Room. They spoke in low tones to Jean
Pierre who opened the door for them.

Twenty minutes later, the police and the
director came out of the room. She turned toward
the small group and gestured to the matronly
woman who was holding Theodora's hand.

"The Lemrow is sealed," the director said to
the staff. "Hilda, announce over the intercom that
guests and employees will meet in the Music Room
immediately."

The police had blocked the entrances and
were escorting people to the Music Room. People
were being allowed to use their cells. This allayed
some anxiety, but a few of the patrons were
threatening to call their lawyers.

Hilda blew her nose which was red from
constant wiping. Beside her, Theodora clutched her
own hands then gripped Hilda's under the fold of
her voluminous skirt. Phoebe sat across the room,
alone. Her usually smooth brow was wrinkled. She
was tapping on her iPhone.

At 11:30 a.m. in a room designed for
classical concerts and literary talks, the director
stood on the stage's podium. She was flanked by
two men in business suits who were turned toward
her, thereby directing all eyes in the room to her.
With all the ochre damask seats filled, a mixture of

visitors and employees lined the silk upholstered walls. Patrolmen were stationed around the room.

"I'm Monika Syka, the Lemrow director," she said. Her voice was low and crisp. "One of our staff was found dead in the adjacent Green Room." She waited while her audience gasped. "I apologize to our guests for your shock and anxiety. I'm sure you understand that we are as horrified as you are. We'll work together to get to the bottom of this. The New York Police Department will be collecting the addresses of all those present in the museum. Allow me to thank you for your cooperation and to introduce you to some of the people who will be   . working with the police and me to get to the bottom of this."

She looked to her left. Harry Ross stood up and nodded to the group. "This is Harry Ross, chair of our board of trustees." Harry, for once, was silent. His gravitas floated across the room like a dark cloud. After nodding to the group, he sat down.

Monika looked to her right. Kenny jumped up. "Kenny O'Malley is the head of our security." Kenny's eager puppy eyes studied the crowd before he sat down.

"Harry Ross and Kenny O'Malley join me in thanking you for your co-operation. I will now turn this over to the Nineteenth Precinct."

Four hours later, everyone had filled in the questionnaire and had their IDs examined by the police.

Chapter 6

10:10 a.m. Tuesday, September 5

Steve flicked his ID at the Lemrow's sensor and nodded to Kenny who was waiting for him. Earlier, Kenny had phoned Steve and told him about Geoff's suicide.

"That guy who killed himself - we met him in the elevator on Thursday?" Steve asked.

Kenny thought a moment and then nodded. He mopped his sweaty brow with a damp handkerchief. "Horrible sight – Poor guy. He left dirty photos of himself. I guess you're used to it."

At the same time, Mary L. stepped out of the elevator and spoke to Kenny. "Don't forget. You're expected at the meeting. Be there at 11:30 sharp." She dismissed him with a tight smile.

Kenny crept back to his cage, and Mary L. hustled Steve into the tiny wooden elevator.

He expected her to say something about Geoff's suicide. She surprised him.

"I'm so glad you're doing the provenance for the Chen exhibit." Mary L. punched in the floor number, and Steve put out his hand to pull a gate across the elevator door. "Don't touch that," she commanded as the gate closed automatically. The elevator shuddered upward. "I'm delighted you're here."

Steve couldn't bring himself to say, "Me too," so he mumbled, "How's your brother?"

"Harrison's hanging in there. Hanging." She splayed her manicured right hand across her large chest. "How could that photographer kill himself here?" The elevator jolted to a stop. The gate snapped back, Steve ducked his head, and they shuffled out of the elevator.

Mary L. led him down a paneled corridor. The light streaming in from the north side warmed up the rich oak. Flowered, silky drapes flowed to the floor, held back by thick bands of the same texture. Fortuny fabrics flashed in Steve's burglary memory bank. Each pane of the framed windows glistened from rubbing.

"I have to tell you. Harrison's never been better." A year and a half ago, Steve had put away Harrison Kahn, Mary L.'s feckless brother, for shooting his now ex-wife's lover. "He's teaching the other inmates all about finances. Hope they're not listening."

Steve's noncommittal look hid the surprise he felt at her cheery manner. He didn't understand the rich, but he didn't understand the poor either.

Without slowing down, she glanced at the artwork hung on either side of the corridor.

"Millais. So sentimental. There's a Corot. C. E. wasn't fond of him so he's not on view. That's all changed, hasn't it?" She looked at Steve for confirmation. "Of course, you didn't know him."

"C. E. Stowbridge? I met him the other day."

"He'll be greatly missed."

"I want to ask you something." Steve stopped in the middle of the corridor.

Mary L. spun around.

"I got the impression that you'd met Captain Holbrook."

She thought for a moment. "Yes, of course." "Where?"

"At our annual Lemrow benefit. Harry, our board head, had to fill a table."

"Who else was at the table?"

"Moi, Harry of course, Monika, Wellington Chen, Dick Holbrook and a few other people."

Steve sensed she was hesitating. "Come on. You can tell me."

"Well, Steve, that girl you were going out with. You know when you sent poor Harrison to jail."

Christ, it was a body blow. Thursday night wasn't a first, boring date.

"When was this?"

"I love being interrogated," Mary L. cooed. "About five months ago, a month after Monika was appointed."

Steve and Carmen had split up six months ago. She couldn't wait, could she?

"May I proceed, sir?" Mary L. said coyly. They walked to the end of the corridor in silence.

Steve was concentrating on the present by telling himself how much he hated Carmen even though he knew it was his fault that they'd broken up.

Mary L. tapped on one side of a double oak door and opened it without waiting. They walked into a large, square room with windows overlooking Fifth Avenue. It reminded Steve of a genteel club he had inspected in connection with a homicide. With its upholstered sofas and easy chairs arranged in small clusters around stone fireplaces, all that was missing were elderly billionaires. Oil paintings were hung on the robin's egg blue brocaded walls. An agreeable if surprising note was the trombone solo playing softly in the background.

At the far end was a large partners desk laden with folders, art books and a Mac. A photo of the late curator, C. E. Stowbridge, was placed on a corner of the desk, angled so that people who entered the room could see it. A small, dark haired woman was seated behind the desk. Although her back was turned to them, Steve recognized Monika Syka. On the wall closest to the desk, he was amused to see a small mirror in an ornate frame placed at the director's eye level. She could watch her own back and freshen her lipstick at the same time.

Steve screened out Mary L.'s chatter and listened as the director said into her Smartphone. "I'm taking care of it," clicked off the cell, slid it into her pocket, and swiveled around to face them.

From the stern tone of her voice, he had expected a hardened expression. He was wrong. Her face, with its air of innocence and mischief, was definitely a nine. He recalled the angry expression the first time he'd met her.

The director glanced at her computer before standing up and coming around the desk. Then she extended her hand. "Hello, Mr. Art Provenance. Please… " She indicated a leather chair.

Steve smiled in spite of himself, amused by the smoky softness of her voice, in sharp contrast with the way she had sounded on the phone.

"The first woman director of the Lemrow," Mary L. advertised. She then looked Steve up and down. "I ordered a handsome one, brains as well."

Embarrassed, Steve ran his right hand through his thick, graying hair.

"Shooo, but be back in twenty minutes." The director waved Mary L. out of her office before sitting in a chair next to Steve's. It took all of five seconds, but was enough time for him to notice that she walked in time to the music. The severe suit and very high heels accentuated her trim figure and long legs. The mane of dark chestnut hair she'd tossed around when they first met was caught in a slick ponytail.

"Welcome to the Lemrow. I wasn't exactly gracious when we met," she said.

He studied her welcoming, open expression, contrasting it with the angry set features he recalled from Thursday.

"Sorry about Mary L.," Monika said.

Steve looked puzzled, then realized she was referring to Mary L.'s dopey remark about his looks and brains. "I've dealt with her before," he said, implying he understood Mary L.'s ways.

"No need to be discreet, Detective. She loves talking about her brother being in Sing Sing," the director said. Her face darkened and she lowered her voice. "I've been at the Lemrow for all of six months, and we have a suicide. It has us all rattled. Luckily, the museum had just opened this morning when someone discovered the body. Maybe fifty guests were here. It could have been worse. I've just finished talking to everyone in the Music Room."

"The assembly hall next to the reference library?" Steve said.

"Very good, Detective."

"Where did he kill himself?" Steve knew from his phone conversation with Kenny but wanted to hear Monika's answer.

"In the Green Room."

"The Green Room?"

"It's a room off the Water Court, used to take photos, store supplies."

Steve recalled that on Thursday he had seen the director and two men coming out a room that was to the right of the Water Court.

"Why did he kill himself in the museum?"

"Personal reasons? Who knows?" The director concentrated on her Smartphone, an indication that the conversation was over.

But not for Steve. "Who found his body?"

Monika looked up. "You were in homicide, Detective?"

Steve nodded.

"Well, you're not now."

Steve tightened his lips at the snub, but secretly he was pleased he'd gotten a reaction.

"I'm sorry. I'm anxious." Monika leaned closer. "Chen's grumbling about not going through with the exhibit. I have to turn that around at the meeting. If only C. E. were here."

Steve looked over at the photo.

"C. E. is our nickname for Charles E. Stowbridge."

Steve nodded.

The director continued. "He was the curator emeritus of the Renaissance wing. Wellington and C. E. were at Harvard together. It's primarily because of his influence that Wellington's lent us part of his wonderful collection. Also, his niece, who happens to have been C. E.'s goddaughter, is one of our interns."

"There are interns and interns," Steve said, thinking of the meteoric rise of Captain Holbrook, thanks to his dad's influence.

Monika gave him a rewarding smile before continuing. "You met C. E. Remember?"

Steve nodded, recalling an elderly man who had accompanied Monika and a young Chinese on Thursday.

He also remembered that Monika had been suppressing her feelings. Once again he wondered why she was so angry. And why, in spite of her present anxiety, she seemed upbeat. It didn't add up.

"C. E. had a fatal heart attack two days ago. He knew Chen and could handle him. It's important that Chen respects you. Impress him with your expertise, Detective. Your provenance expertise," she added, handing Steve a manila folder. "You've seen this?"

Steve glanced at the file. It was a list of statues in the Chen exhibit, including photos and a brief summary of their history. He didn't know squat about provenance, but he could count. "Only six statues?" he said.

"Only? Detective, lose that remark, okay? Each one is priceless."

"I meant that I'd seen six statues and two unwrapped ones."

"I misunderstood. Of course, those have to be added to the list. Thanks for reminding me." She smiled very prettily, revealing small even teeth and two sharp incisors. "In addition to everything else, the assistant I had inherited left less than a week ago. She left things in a mess. So I'm a little behind in my paper work."

Steve was adding up the deaths of two employees at a seemingly staid institution. The prestigious victim of a second heart attack would attract the media's obituary section, but a suicide on the premises would have them salivating.

"Have the media started circling?" he said.

"You concentrate on provenance and security, okay? I'll take care of the media." Her put down was less harsh than the last time, but it was still a put down.

She caught the annoyed look on his face. "Ever hear of Kuan-yin?"

"The Chinese goddess represented in the exhibit?" Steve said. This assignment was morphing his indifference to art into hatred.

"Kuan-yin is the goddess of compassion. I'm sure she'd forgive you."

"Forgive me for what?'

"That at the moment you hate me and art." The hint of a smile and a dimple on her left cheek defused the teacher tone. Monika uncrossed her legs, stood up and ran her hands down her sides, smoothing her skirt. She leaned over her desk and picked up six black and white photos. Holding them like a card hand, Monika stood behind Steve's chair and held the cards at his eye level. "Here she is – the mother goddess of the Asian world." Originally ironic, her tone softened as she gazed at the images. "Lovely, aren't they?"

"Are these Wellington Chen's – the ones in the exhibit?"

"Always the copper, right detective?" She slid the photos back onto her desk. "You shifted from homicide to provenance?"

He figured, what the hell. She'll poke around and find out the truth. "I was transferred. Screwed up an investigation."

"So we're your punishment." She grinned. "Know anything about art?"

"No."

"What a relief."

He raised his eyebrows, brought up short by her remark.

She smiled, pleased at having confused him.

He surprised himself by laughing.

Steve stood up. "So what about those two wrapped pieces? I need their documentation."

"Of course, I'll get them for you right now." She walked behind her desk and riffled through some papers.

He knew she knew he was watching her and that she was used to it. Museum work was looking up.

"Moneybags, will be at the meeting," Monika said.

"Moneybags?"

"I better lose *that* remark. Harry Ross is always going on about raising revenue." She widened her light blue eyes. "So Harry, Mary L., me, Wellington Chen, and you will be at the meeting."

"And the security guy," Steve said.

"Oh?" Monika said.

Mary L. swept into the room. "I told Kenny to be there. Let's go."

"And now, like Marie Antoinette, I go to my beheading," Monika said.

"You must show Steve her desk," Mary L. said.

"He hates art." Then Monika turned to him. "Does that include furniture?"

"Isn't she hilarious?" Mary L. gazed at Monika like a prized possession. "C. E. said she was shy, hiding behind her books. He and I pushed for her appointment."

In a camp display of humility, the director held up her hand to fend off further remarks

"Not expecting trouble at the meeting?" Mary L. asked.

"One retired curator dying with a Riccio in his hands, one suicide on the premises plus one benefactor having second thoughts and one trustee demanding we lower our costs. Let's not forget the media's unsheathing their claws." Monika reached into the desk drawer, took out a mirror, inspected her makeup, threw the mirror back into the drawer and slammed it shut. "Piece of cake."

"The Staff Day?" Mary L. said.

"Damn," Monika said.

"Cancel it?" Mary L. said.

Steve watched Monika thinking about what to do. After a few seconds, she shook her head.

"Let's not change our routine. We keep the Staff Day," Monika said. "Before you ask, Detective, it's a half day when staff members share amusing activities, get a new slant on the art that surrounds them every day."

Steve looked politely confused.

"I'm confused too, Detective," Monika said. "This is my first Staff Day and if I have anything to say about it, my last."

"Now, now," Mary L. said.

"What's a Riccio?" Steve said.

The two women looked puzzled.

"You said C. E. died with a Riccio in his hands."

"Nothing - A statue." Mary L. glared at Monika. "Why did you bring it up?"

"He would've found out. Wouldn't you, Detective?"

"Tell me now."

Monika glanced at her watch. "Later. God, we're late."

"The papers for the two statues?" Steve said.

"Have mercy, Mr. Detective." Monika said. "I promise I'll give you those papers after this meeting. Okay?" She flashed him a mischievous smile and grabbed *The New York Times*. "Come on. Off to the wars."

"There was that mention on New York One," Mary L. said as they rushed down the corridor. "I haven't seen anything in the papers."

"What mention?" Steve said.

"Geoff's suicide was described as an untimely death."

Steve figured the word, untimely, was apt since Geoff was probably in his twenties. He wondered but didn't ask why Geoff killed himself at the museum.

"And attendance is down, and Harry wants more revenue," Mary L. said.

"I can handle him. Let's go."

Chapter 7

11:30 a.m. Tuesday, September 5

Steve followed Monika and Mary L. as they rushed down the corridor and stopped at a wooden door. Its plaque identified it as the Chestnut Room. Monika nodded to a nearby guard who opened the door.

They entered a room that had the still air of a long ago dinner party and seated themselves around a rectangular mahogany table. Six places were designated by individual mats to protect the table's finish.

A draught from the open door tingled the five-branch chandelier above their heads. The beige walls were hung with nineteenth century landscapes.

"I don't want anything interfering with Chen's bequest." The one person on time for the meeting growled at them. "A guy I know at the Post called me this morning. He sniffed around about the photographer. I got him to back off for now."

Harry Ross, Steve figured.

Monika stood next to Harry and Mary L. seated herself on the other side. Steve sat across from them.

"Anything about C. E.?" Monika said.

"Not a peep – for now," Harry said.

Steve thought the Lemrow board members would be right at home in a Mafia meeting.

Mary L. and Monika knew that Harry's concern about Chen had something to do with a joint venture, but one of the unspoken rules at a museum meeting was never to bring up outside connections.

"Chen's due any minute and you're late." Harry ran his eyes up and down Monika's body.

"Stop, Harry." She pulled out a chair and sat down.

Sleeping together? Steve figured. He realized he had a little crush on the director's sassy ways and those long legs.

"Let's see what you've got." Harry looked across at Steve.

"Harry, this is the world's greatest…" Mary L. began.

"Steve Kulchek. Harry Ross," Monika interrupted.

Steve and Harry studied each other as they shook hands.

"Dick Holbrook recommended you. Great guy, even if he is putting his head in the noose," Harry said.

"How so?" Steve said.

"What do I know? I'm kidding." Harry slid away from the subject. "Back to business – Dick understands this is a unique situation."

Unique, my ass, Steve thought.

"You were in homicide?"

Steve nodded, expecting Harry to pry. Instead, he grunted, "These two guys dying isn't great. C. E.'s heart attack wasn't on the premises. So that's okay. The suicide. Why do it here?" Harry thought aloud. "Maybe it'll increase attendance."

"We have to wait for the police to get back to me." The director placed her cell and a newspaper article next to her. "What's your take on this, Detective? Think we can reopen?" Harry said.

"If it's a suicide, you can open. If it's a crime scene, they'll close you down." Memories of past investigations filled Steve's voice with longing.

"Crime scene - Murder?" Harry's face was ashen.

"Wellington Chen can withdraw the entire collection up to three months after its installation," Monika explained to Steve. "If we're very lucky he'll bequeath it to us. Now, we have this suicide on the premises."

"Screwed," Harry muttered. "Listen. Why not make Wellington a member of our board?"

"It's too obvious. Let's wait on it," Monika said. "And we need the entire board present."

"We could suggest it," Mary L. said.

"Let's respect Wellington's sensibilities," Monika said.

"What's that supposed to mean?" Harry said. "We have to discuss revenue." He raised his voice, "And get costs down."

"But not today." Monika's tone was firm. "Let Wellington drive the meeting."

Steve was impressed at how Monika took charge.

"Speaking as a past board head," Mary L. cleared her throat, "I'd like to get back to Harry's suggestion of asking Wellington to join the board."

"Let's see how it plays," Monika said.

There was a timid knock at the door; Kenny slipped in.

"Sit down, Kenny," Mary L. ordered. Kenny obeyed, never taking his eyes off her. "I want you to stick to Mr. Chen like glue."

"We have to discuss something before Wellington arrives," Monika said. "The police found some compromising photos Geoff took at the museum."

"What?" Harry yelped.

Monika sighed. "Some sexually explicit photos of himself."

"Why wasn't I told about this?" Harry slammed his hand on the table.

"You're being told now." Monika's cell buzzed. "Monika Syka." After listening for a few minutes, she said into her cell, "Keep the bodyguards downstairs, unless Dr. Chen wants them." She clicked off. "The front desk. Wellington Chen is coming up."

"Look pretty, everybody," Mary L. said.

A few minutes later, the door was opened and an imposing Chinese in his mid-sixties walked into the room. His presence proclaimed his vast resources. He could have bought the Lemrow and the rest of Seventieth Street and yet, when he walked into the museum he morphed into his seventeen-year-old self, a Harvard freshman from Hong Kong. Then, he was in awe of the riches the nineteenth century Lemrow had acquired, bought and stolen. Although now worldly wise, Wellington Chen still was dazzled.

Everybody stood up.

Delegating herself official host, Mary L. introduced Wellington Chen to Steve, the only person in the room he hadn't met.

Chen took a seat next to Monika. He looked across at Steve. "Tell me what your job entails."

"I'm here on temporary assignment in the NYPD's Art Squad. It's the Art and Antiques Provenance unit." Steve forced himself to describe his new assignment in a natural tone of voice.

"I've heard of the FBI's but not New York City's," Chen said. His voice was gentle but steely, his accent English, overlaid by American.

"Formed last year," Steve said. "Proof of ownership has become a top priority."

Chen gave a comprehending nod.

"Used to be in homicide," Harry said.

"You were describing what your job entails," Chen said.

Before he continued, Steve thought of Erika Moreau throwing him some crap about being responsible for the security of objects in public places.

"My focus is not only on the provenance of the objects in the museum. It's also to ensure that they're installed properly so that no one can walk out the door with one in his coat pocket." Steve said.

"Provenance is something you'll discuss with Monika," Wellington said. "My friend, C. E., introduced me to her. When it comes to art, I'm in her hands."

Monika bent her glossy head over a glass of water.

Steve continued, "You have the necessary insurance for the objects?"

"That I took care of," Wellington said, every inch the successful businessman.

"Once the exhibit is in place and open to the public, I'm out of here," Steve said.

"What about security then?" Wellington said.

"You have a professional who's updating your facility." Steve nodded at the head of security. "Kenny's a liaison with other museum art security personnel."

The director's cell buzzed. Eyeballs shifted in that direction.

"I see," she said as she listened, her voice low and grave. Then, finally, "That's very reassuring, Captain." She gave the rest of the room a thumbs up, then flipped shut her cell and looked around the table. "It's suicide. We can open."

"I beg your pardon?" Chen said.

"That was Captain Holbrook of the NYPD. We can go ahead with the opening."

Chen looked utterly confused. "I want to know what's going on. My dear friend, C. E., dies Sunday night and this morning someone kills himself here."

"Complete coincidence, Wellington," Harry said. "C. E. had a bad ticker and the photographer was unbalanced."

"How was he unbalanced?" Chen persisted.

"Harry means that he was disturbed," Monika said.

"Why did he kill himself here?"

Harry threw his hands in the air. "Who knows?"

"Seriously, why did this man kill himself at the museum?" Chen turned and looked at each of them. His grave expression forbade any more flippancy. "Is Phoebe working in a dangerous place?"

Steve thought about Chen's leap from the photographer's suicide to his niece's safety. He didn't get it.

Harry and Monika exploded with protestations.

"That's not fair, Wellington," Mary L. said.

Ever courteous, Chen addressed Steve. "We're talking about my niece, Phoebe Chen, who is an intern."

Wellington had a determined but gentle poker face.

"Phoebe has just been granted the Stowbridge fellowship," Monika said.

"Named after C. E.'s family," Mary L. whispered to Steve.

"Does Phoebe know?" Wellington said.

"No, it was decided this morning," Monika said. Harry and Mary L. plastered smiles on their faces.

"It's a great honor," Chen said. "I'll think about letting her stay, but why did this man kill himself here?"

"We don't know why," Mary L. answered, her tone matching his in gravity. "It's very troubling."

"He had a fixation about the museum. I think he imagined he lived here." Monika's little pink tongue raced around her upper teeth and she wrung her hands. A made-for-TV moment, Steve thought. "Wellington, he left some autoerotic photos of himself. Very disturbing."

"My dear Monika, how awful," Wellington said. "Have the media found out?"

"No. And they're not going to," Monika said.

"I chose your museum because of its unblemished reputation." Chen bowed slightly. The others responded to his civility by assuming serious expressions.

"Wellington, I apologize if I seemed unfeeling," Monika said. "It's awful, but I'm relieved he wasn't murdered."

She picked up the *Times* she'd brought with her and spread it out on the table in front of Wellington. Mary L., Harry, Kenny and Steve clustered around it. It was an article about the next day's opening. There was a charming, if grainy, photo of Chen and his niece, Phoebe, as well as images of the statues in the exhibit.

Nice timing, Steve thought. Chen was staring down at the article. "I was delighted to see this first thing this morning. My niece and I are honored. I looked for C. E.'s obituary but couldn't find it."

"There will be an obituary in the *Times* this Sunday. Other museums and various art magazines have been in touch," Monika said. "Of course, we will send you copies, Wellington. Just before you arrived we were discussing C. E.'s memorial. We'll have to decide on the time and place."

"I want an active part in the memorial. Phoebe will too," Wellington said.

"Your generosity means so much to us," Monika said. "Please let us go ahead with the opening." The director's voice was an enchanting mixture of humility, high seriousness and superior sucking up.

Chen turned to her, "It's my pleasure, dear lady."

"Wellington, we would be honored if you would join us on the board," Mary L. said.

A ghost of a frown appeared on Monika's face.

"I'm deeply honored, but don't you think a board member having an exhibit of his own collection will seem like a conflict of interest?"

"Of course not," Mary L. blurted.

"Detective?" Chen looked at Steve.

"You're not planning on selling any of the statues on exhibit are you?" Steve smiled at Chen.

"That's exactly what people would assume," Chen said. He looked at Mary L. "I'll consider your very kind offer and get back to you in a few days."

The subject was closed.

Monika waited a beat. "We know how close you were to C. E. May I suggest that at tomorrow's opening we dedicate the exhibit to his memory?"

"You've read my mind. I will incorporate your kind thought into my opening address."

"We'll continue setting up for tomorrow's opening. Please be in the reference library by five p.m.," Monika said, looking around at the group. "Our guests are due at six."

"My niece tells me that you are having one of your Staff Days," Wellington said.

"It's the day after the exhibit opening," Mary L. said. She looked at Wellington. "Staff members talk about their different specialties. We have other activities relating to the museum's history."

"Is my niece attending?" Chen asked.

"I hope so. It's always great fun."

"May I join her?" Chen asked, looking at Monika.

"What a delightful idea. We thought you were heading back to Hong Kong."

"I have an afternoon flight. May I attend the morning session?"

Steve wondered if this had anything to do with Chen's fear about his niece's safety.

Mary L., Harry and Monika smiled on cue.

Chapter 8

1:00 p.m. Tuesday, September 5

"I want to take another look at the Chen Exhibit," Steve said to Monika.

She checked her watch. "1:00 pm. Let's go."

Monika started down the corridor with Steve, turning left past a tall rectangular oak clock. Its column was a girl being transformed into a tree. Steve stared at it, puzzled why it made him think of Phoebe Chen.

"Daphne, got you? Maybe she's got the right idea." Smiling at Steve's blank expression, the director said. "Your confusion becomes you, Detective. Daphne begged her father to turn her into a tree rather than allow her lover to ravish her. Great art often has silly plots, like opera. God, I'm beginning to sound like C. E."

Monika turned and hurried down the sweeping staircase that led to the museum floor.

Behind them, Chen called, "May I join you?" knowing the answer. Padding beside him was Kenny.

Monika stopped and faced Wellington.

"Of course. I thought you'd want it to be a big surprise," she said.

"I don't like surprises," he said.

Monika continued her rapid descent to the floor below.

Steve realized they were in the mansion's original library, now the Renaissance Wing. They wove around knots of visitors, then sped past Lemrow's imposing cherry wood desk and cabinets of regularly dusted, never read leather bound books.

Near the north door that lead into the Central Gallery, amidst the frontal portraits of male saints and Venetian grandees was an oil painting of a smiling girl. Steve realized it was positioned so that Lemrow could have seen it from his desk.

He stopped and stared at the sweep of red brown hair, recalling his ex-girlfriend and her laughing ways.

"Remind you of someone?" Chen smiled.

Before Steve could answer, Monika said, "Technically, it shouldn't be in the Renaissance Wing. It's eighteenth century, but it was Lemrow's favorite painting," Monika smiled at both Wellington and Steve.

"Keep an eye on my niece, Detective."

Once again, Steve was reminded of Chen's concern about Phoebe's safety.

Reading Steve's mind, Wellington said, "She's the only descendent I have."

"No kids of your own?" Steve said.

"I've never had time for children. What about you, Detective?"

"A daughter."

"A daughter?"

"She's in her first year in college."

"Where?"

"RISD," Steve said, testing Wellington.

Wellington smiled knowingly. "My congratulations. Phoebe would give her eye teeth to have gone to RISD." Noticing Kenny's incomprehension, Wellington said, "The Rhode Island School of Design." His face darkened. "C. E. thought I spoiled Phoebe."

"You travel with bodyguards?" Steve said.

A puzzled expression spread over Wellington's face. "Usually, yes. They're waiting downstairs. Why do you ask?"

Steve figured the truth was the best with Wellington. "You seem preoccupied about your niece."

"My niece is like her late mother, very strong willed." Wellington's raised voice reminded Steve of family fights. "Phoebe absolutely refuses to have any protection, says it scares away people her own age. Please keep an eye on her, Detective."

"I'm out of here in a few days, as soon as I've finished the paper work."

While they talked, Steve was aware that Wellington's eyes were drawn to a painting. He turned to see what interested him. It was a picture of a saint surrounded by animals and birds.

"There's a crane." Wellington gestured at the painting. "We Chinese think it's a harbinger of happiness. One of our emperors said it symbolized a long life of worthy pursuits."

Steve had a feeling Chen wanted to tell him something in private.

"Mr. Chen, I'll make sure she's okay," Kenny piped up. Unaware of personal space, Kenny allowed the tip of his black polished shoes to touch Chen's.

Wellington moved away but kept speaking to Steve. "Two deaths in the museum."

"The one that occurred here was a suicide," Monika interrupted. "The other was C. E.'s second heart attack in his apartment. With respect, Wellington, he was overweight and didn't take his meds. Don't blame us."

"I'm blaming no one. I want Phoebe to be safe. She won't allow me to provide her with a personal guard. She's had one bad experience… a real operator, but she won't tell me who it was."

"Can't you find out?" Steve said.

"I spoke to a friend, a trusted friend," Wellington smiled gravely at Monika, "who advised me to drop it. She pointed out that Phoebe would be furious if she found out I was snooping into her affairs. I persuaded her not to be on Facebook or Twitter."

From Steve's expression, Wellington felt he had to explain.

"There are always people who want to separate us from our money. Privacy and being anonymous are our best protection." Underneath

Wellington's firm tone was a tinge of sadness. He turned to Steve. "You're coming to the opening?"

Before Steve could answer, Monika jumped in, "Of course he is."

They continued their brisk walk through the Central Gallery.

"Here we are." Monika announced as they approached the double oak doors at the west end of the gallery. She signaled to a guard who slid the doors smoothly into the adjacent walls. Since Steve's first visit, the rectangular room had been wallpapered in burnished gold. Subtle lighting underlined the spaces and solids of eight statues mounted on mahogany pedestals. The four Lemrow paintings, each in its own niche, glowed with subtle shading.

They stood at the entrance as if it were hallowed ground. The guard ushered away curious visitors.

Monika looked up at the ceiling and examined the recessed lights. Steve saw from her expression that she was satisfied with the way Wellington's statues were highlighted. The Lemrow Asian paintings were backdrops to the statues.

She led the way into the room. Chen stood in the center, his arms crossed and swept his eyes around the exhibit. Eight versions of Kuan-yin stared back at him.

He turned to Monika. "Thank you."

Steve ran his eyes over the statues and paintings. He admitted to himself that the exhibit was better than the previous time he'd viewed it.

One of the paintings was of a seated Kuan-yin. Near her was a crane. Birds flew overhead.

"Magpies, Detective," Wellington said. "A symbol of happiness."

"Those are new?" Steve pointed to two statues he had not recognized: one of white porcelain and the other of cast-iron.

"In this exhibit nothing is new," the director said.

Wellington smiled at Monika's little joke.

"I meant new to me." Steve forced himself to keep the defensiveness out of his voice. "This is the first time I've seen them. I have to get those papers from you," Steve said to Monika.

"Of course. I'm sorry. I simply forgot."

"Papers?" Wellington said.

"For the exhibit – the two new statues?" Monika made quotation marks with her fingers when she said the word new.

"Thanks to Monika, I bought those two pieces to keep them from being sold to a dealer," Wellington said, a note of gratitude in his voice. "Now they're part of my collection and, perhaps, some day the Lemrow's."

"Thank you, Wellington." Monika's eyes glistened with gratitude.

Steve waited a moment, then dug into his breast pocket and pulled out the exhibit's provenance list. "Mr. Chen, check this over and if it's okay initial each item."

Chen read quickly, looking up once or twice to double check the contents of the room before he scribbled his initials with a sleek pen.

Steve checked the document. Chen had put his initials beside six of the eight statues.

"Monika will take care of the provenance of the other two," Wellington said. He slowly paced around the statues. Mounted on plinths of different heights, the statues were grouped so that all could be seen from every angle.

"They're beautifully exhibited, Monika," Chen said, entranced.

Steve remembered the director saying how choice the pieces were. He admitted to himself that they were okay, but he couldn't understand what all the fuss was about and he didn't care. But he did pick up on something Chen had said.

"Six of the pieces were from your collection. The other two were from a private museum? Like the Lemrow?"

"No, Detective, not that prestigious. Monika can tell you the details. She arranged for me to buy these two pieces. Actually, my niece was also instrumental in my buying them. She loves them." He touched the blue and white porcelain statue then gestured toward the cast iron piece. Chen directed his gaze to another statue and picked it up, ignoring Kenny's look of horror. He sniffed its surface. "Sandalwood, Detective." Wellington held the statue so Steve could smell it. Then, he handed it to Monika who placed it back on its pedestal.

"It was a rare opportunity, unusual for such pieces to come on the market," the director said.

"I don't know what I would have done without C. E. introducing me to Monika. Selecting, judging, hassling." Chen laughed along with the director, obviously sharing a rough negotiating memory. "Now that C. E. is gone, she and Phoebe are my artistic guides."

Steve studied one of the nearby statues.

"What do you think, Detective?" Chen's sharp eyes watched Steve with amusement.

Brought back to the present, Steve said, "They remind me of the Virgin Mary statues in Bayside. Know Long Island?"

"Detective, really…" The director began in a snooty voice.

"When I was at school in Massachusetts I saw those charming statues in Lowell." Chen's face lit up with fond memories. "They reminded me of Kuan-yin."

Steve nodded in appreciation.

Chen stopped in front of the delicate porcelain piece with two figures: a young woman and a little girl holding a bouquet. It was labeled Kuan-yin, Ming dynasty. "I look at this particular statue the way you looked at the pretty young woman." Steve realized Chen was referring to the oil painting of the laughing girl.

Chen reached into his breast pocket, pulled out a hand-tooled wallet, and flipped it open. "Here's my card." He handed Steve the double-sided embossed card, Chinese one side, English the other.

"Here's mine." Steve handed him a flimsy NYPD issued card.

Chen checked his watch. "I'm escorting my niece to a little dinner. Have to look presentable in

Phoebe's eyes." He bowed ever so slightly, first to the director and then to Steve. Dogged by Kenny he left the exhibit.

"Charming, isn't he?" Monika said.

"And smart."

"I want to show you something." Steve thought Monika was referring to the Kuan-yin exhibit. Instead, she instructed the guard to close and lock the doors, then turned her back on the small golden room and headed across the Central Gallery back to the Renaissance Wing.

On a wooden side table, a bronze statue sat by itself. "Riccio. Bronzes aren't to everyone's taste," the director said, implying that Steve was among the great unwashed. She pulled some latex gloves from her pocket and slipped them on before picking up the statue.

"This is what C. E. had in his hands when he died? " Steve stared down at the gravy-like patina that slid over the Riccio angel.

"Detective, he took it without authorization. I have it on good authority. Can't be proven."

"Who's your authority?"

"I can't say. I gave my word. Sorry."

"Why didn't you put on gloves before?"

Monika thought a moment, "You mean when Chen picked up the Kuan-yin statue? Wouldn't have been political, would it? He picked it up with his bare hands. A real no-no, but if I'd put on gloves, it would have been a put down."

Steve said, "Notice Kenny's reaction when Chen picked it up?"

They both laughed, recalling the shocked expression on the security guy's face.

"And another thing," she said in a confiding tone, "we're not mentioning to Chen that C. E. took the Riccio. They were life long friends, Harvard classmates. For the record, C. E. was assessing it for the Lemrow."

"Taking objects without authorization would make any benefactor nervous," Steve said.

"Too true, Detective. I'm glad we speak the same language." Monika looked him in the face. "Pretty impressive."

"What?"

"Your daughter being accepted to the Rhode Island School of Design. A man who hates art has a kid who loves it," the director said more to herself than to Steve. "What's she specializing in?"

"Fine Arts." Steve shrugged, but he couldn't hide the pride in his voice.

Monika smiled gently, drinking in Steve's fatherly feelings.

Steve lowered his voice, "What's the big deal about Kuan-yin?"

"She's a cultural icon to the Asian world, especially to Chinese Buddhists who revere her for her miracles. Your analogy between her and the Virgin Mary was astute."

"You didn't act that way at the time."

"Detective, I come from a working class background. Sometimes, my insecurities get the best of me." Pushing away from the personal, Monika said, "The statues have the twin values of being esteemed spiritually and aesthetically." She added, in an attempt to break the mood, "Kuan-yin adds up to big bucks."

"Before I forget," Steve said, all business, "can I get the provenance forms for the porcelain and cast iron statues?"

"You're like a dog with a bone," Monika snapped. Then she recovered herself. "Of course." She thought a moment. "Can I give you a copy at the opening?"

Chapter 9

8:35 a.m. Wednesday, September 6

Steve stood at the corner of Fifth Avenue and Seventy-second Street inhaling and thinking about the two museum deaths. He took a final deep drag before heading toward the Lemrow. To check out security, he and Kenny were going through the museum's three floors. Although the museum didn't open until 10 a.m. a small crowd was lining up at the entrance doors. It figures, Steve thought, recalling the six a.m. news flash on NY ONE about C. E.'s death being followed by the mysterious death of a photographer on the Lemrow premises.

Steve had looked at the death scene photos thanks to a pal in the coroner's office. Using his own belt, Geoff had strung himself up from a hook in the Green Room ceiling. Studying the shot, Steve figured Geoff hadn't weighed more than one hundred and forty pounds. The porn photos were the all too familiar shots of private sex. Judging from the shots' background, they were taken in the Green Room. *Why would Geoff jeopardize his job?*

After reminding his coroner pal of past favors, Steve examined the photographer's belongings. The usual stuff was there: his wallet, his driver's license, his cigarettes, his duffel bag, several cameras and lenses, but no Canon and no cell. Did the guy throw them into the Hudson, down an incinerator or leave them in his desk at the Lemrow? Tricky with a suicide.

There was no doubt it was suicide, but his contact said some elements were fishy: no suicide note; someone had gone through Geoff's pockets, meaning someone saw him hanging from that hook and searched him.

Steve had a gut feeling something was going to go wrong again. He figured the retired curator had died of natural causes, but the photographer's death bothered him. Hang yourself in the Lemrow? Leave porn photos? The guy would have destroyed them, wouldn't he?

He flicked his Lemrow ID at a red dot on the wall to the right of the swinging doors. As soon as they parted, he walked through and nodded to the guard behind the glass-enclosed control room.

Kenny was watching the bank of video monitors. He clicked the door open so Steve could join him. Steve thought Kenny had aged a few years. His pink skin was tinged gray with fatigue.

Glancing down at Steve's briefcase, Kenny said, "You want to leave that in my office?"

"Fine. I'll need some office space."

"You can share mine."

Steve didn't say anything. They both looked back at the entrance monitor and studied the growing crowd. "All because of the poor guy's suicide?" Kenny said.

"You bet." Steve didn't add to Kenny's worries by suggesting the size of the crowds if the porn shots were leaked.

Steve scanned the videos of the Water Court, the Central Gallery, the Renaissance Wing and the Library. Since the museum didn't open to the public until ten a.m., the galleries were empty except for an occasional cleaner or guard.

"No shots of the Chen Exhibit?" he said.

Kenny clicked on a remote control, activating a blank monitor. It showed the eight statues and four pictures.

"How about the Green Room?"

Kenny gave him a sharp look but didn't say anything. He pressed a button and brought up a large barren room with a sturdy table and a hook hanging from the ceiling. A computer was on the table.

"The guards have been instructed to say it's not open to the public and nothing else," Kenny said.

"What's it used for?"

"Storing merchandise for the shop or for photographing."

"What's the hook for?"

"To hoist heavy stuff, like marble statues onto the table so they can be photographed for catalogues." All the time Kenny was talking, he was sweating. "The most frequented rooms are kept on the monitors, but we check all areas, frequently except the restrooms. Ready for the tour?"

Steve thought of something. "You keep the room tapes for how long?"

Kenny pursed his lips and blew out a stream of air. If he'd been in a bar, it would have been a stream of profanities. "Amateurs," he muttered.

"Go on."

He nodded at the nearby guard, held open the controls room door and waited for Steve to precede him.

As soon as the door was closed, he said, under his breath, "They're rewound."

"So they're not kept?"

"No."

"Whose idea was that?"

"The board's been cutting expenses. I don't know which genius came up with the idea of reusing tapes."

"How long has it been in place?"

"About five months," Kenny shook his head as he led the way down a corridor. "Let's start here." He led Steve into a large room with a large desk and behind it a large chair. On one wall was a bulletin board filled with security regulations. On another wall was the Lemrow's floor plan.

"This is my office." Kenny said with pride. He indicated a shelf. "You can put your stuff here for now. This room will hold another desk easy."

"Thanks," Steve said.

"And down here," Kenny led the way out of his office. He walked a few more steps and turned right into a locker room, "is, obviously, the locker room."

Steve looked over the gray, metal lockers. "Close to your office."

"Exactly. Where you came in, everyone's purses, briefcases, backpacks are checked before they can leave."

Steve thought, maybe the rank and file's stuff was checked, but he didn't figure a minimum wage guy questioned C. E. Stowbridge who had walked out the door with a Renaissance statue.

"Everybody has a locker?" Steve said.

"Some of us have our own offices: the director, the curators and me."

"Any stealing?"

"Pilfering of cafeteria food, but no stealing."

"But you make everyone aware that they're under surveillance," Steve said.

"Exactly."

From Kenny's assured tone, Steve was pretty sure he didn't know about the Riccio theft.

"Stairs or elevator?" Kenny said.

"Stairs." Steve thought aloud about the layout. "You have three floors: the basement which is this floor, directly above us is the first floor – that's the museum and the reference library and, finally, the floor above that with offices, board rooms and the restoration department. The director's office is on the north side of the third floor?"

"Correct. The other offices and rooms are on the south side of the same floor."

Kenny led Steve up the marble stairs to the museum's collection.

This guy is good at security, Steve thought, but how do I get him to talk about the photographer? He figured he'd circle around to it.

"Can we inspect the rooms closest to the Chen exhibit?"

"Why not?" Kenny led the way, flashing his ID automatically at the series of red dots near all the doors. As they entered the Water Court Steve brushed against the delicate branch of a lavender and cream orchid springing from a wall sconce. He was surprised by his pleasure in hearing the now familiar plashing of water and smelling the faint greenhouse aroma.

Steve was getting a sense of the museum's layout. He pointed to a discreet door to their right. "Isn't this the Green Room?"

"Want to see it?" Kenny said.

"Sure." Surprised at how easy it was.

"You're the third person today."

"Yeah? Who were the others?"

"I can understand Cristobel. She was the guy's friend."

"Who else?" Steve said.

"Phoebe Chen. That surprised me. First of all, because she's seldom here this early. Also, I didn't know she knew Geoff."

"You showed them the room?"

"I felt sorry for Cristobel. I unlocked the door and let her peek in. Of course, I showed it to Phoebe. Refuse her something? It's not like it's a murder scene."

"Isn't Phoebe an intern?"

"There are interns and then there's Phoebe who plays at work. We go along with it."

"Because of her uncle," Steve said.

"And because C. E. was her godfather." Kenny lowered his voice. "Not to mention he was mucho instrumental in getting the current director appointed. Yeah, we go along with whatever Phoebe wants."

Steve recognized the resentment of a guy who worked for a living.

"Did the younger staff hang out together?"

Kenny thought a moment then shrugged his shoulders. "Everybody did except Phoebe. Aside from Elliot, her boyfriend, she kept to herself. Kenny stopped.

"Go on," Steve said.

"She was always on her iPhone, even more than the other kids. They were intimidated by her. Too much power to have a beer with." Kenny lowered his voice. "I heard there's tension over Elliot Ross. Girl stuff. I should be so lucky." Kenny flicked his ID at the door, opened it and stood to one side. "Here's the Green Room."

Steve entered and looked around the large, green space. It was definitely a work area. He noticed a door. He also noticed it wasn't coded. "Where does that lead to?"

"It's a little room, no more than a closet." Kenny grabbed the knob and swung it open.

He was right. It was a closet but it had a window overlooking a little garden.

"Mrs. Lemrow liked to garden. This was her patch." Kenny stepped into the room and looked out the window. "Needs weeding."

Steve said, "This is fine."

"For what? You mean as your office?" Kenny's voice was filled with horror. "It's next door to the Green Room."

Steve laughed.

"But there's no desk, no chair, no computer. My office has better light, more room." Kenny beseeched like a kid.

"Come on, Kenny, you can find me a desk and chair. I've got a laptop."

From Steve's tone, Kenny knew the discussion was closed.

"I'll see what I can do." Kenny ran his right hand through his thinning hair.

They backed out into the Green Room. Steve shut the door of his new office.

He looked around at the faded, bilious green of the four walls. "I see why it's called the Green Room."

"It's like a storage, general purpose room," Kenny said.

"Did Geoff spend much time in here?" Steve was thinking of the porn photos.

"What does that mean?" Kenny looked at Steve curiously.

"It means did he shoot in here?"

"Set up stuff over there for catalog photos, exhibit photos." Kenny pointed to a wide worktable, empty except for a Mac. Behind it, suspended from the ceiling, was a seamless paper backdrop like a gigantic toilet roll. Professional strobe lights were aimed at the area.

"Why did he hang himself here?" Steve said more to himself than to Kenny.

Kenny shrugged. "Who knows? Weird."

"The porn photos?"

Steve shook his head, something wasn't adding up.

Kenny interrupted his thoughts. "I know what you're thinking. How could he do that?" he said misinterpreting Steve's expression.

Steve ignored him. His source in the coroner's office had told him that Geoff's memory card was found in the Green Room's Mac. Did he print out the porno shots as a final humiliation? Why not delete them? Why keep them on the Lemrow Mac in the first place?

"Scattered all over the room." Kenny's chatty self-assurance vanished. He was back to sweating mode.

"You've seen them?"

"Yeah." His face grew red.

Steve looked up at the hook in the middle of the ceiling.

"That's where he did it," Kenny said.

"Why kill yourself here? Any ideas?" Steve waited, prompting a man-to-man remark.

"Let's get out of here." Kenny twisted his watchband. He flung open the door, waited for Steve to walk out of the room, and shut the door firmly.

The guy wasn't used to death. He was normal. Steve felt more at home in that barren, haunted space than he did in the rest of the museum. He sighed as he walked into the overly civilized water court. It reminded him of the perfume counters at Saks. Stuck in art and antiques he couldn't keep nudging Kenny about what he thought about Geoff killing himself.

Steve seized his chance to get rid of Kenny. "You're busy? I'll check things out."

"What about the Chen exhibit and the third floor?" Kenny said.

Steve held up his ID. "Can I get into them with this?"

"It's activated for all areas."

"I'll call you if I have any questions," Steve said.

"The library is in the east wing. So are the Renaissance Wing and the Music Room." Kenny gestured to the right before setting off down the corridor.

Steve waited until Kenny had turned the corner at the far end of the Water Court. Instead of heading to the library, he turned left and headed toward the Chen exhibit, blind to the magnificent Bokharas underfoot, oblivious to the Central Gallery's Turners and Goyas.

Steve was surprised to find the exhibit doors open. He heard voices inside the room. Noticing a guard, he showed him his ID, positioned himself in front of a nearby Constable and kept listening.

Inside the room, a girl was saying firmly, "It's over."

Steve expected to hear another voice about the same age. Instead, an older man said, "You don't understand. My son's a guy. Cristobel doesn't mean anything."

"And that's a recommendation?" The angry girl said.

At that moment Steve entered the room. Harry Ross and a beautiful Asian girl stuck out their heads from either side of a Kuan-yin statue giving her the appearance of a three-headed goddess.

Recognizing Steve, Harry grinned sheepishly. "Hi, Detective."

"Detective?" the beautiful girl asked.

"Steve Kulchek," Steve said.

She stepped out from behind the statue. He drank in the graceful walk as she came toward him.

Behind her, Harry was checking his watch. "I'm out of here, guys. You coming, Phoebe?"

"No," she said not bothering to look at him.

As nervous as Kenny, Steve thought, watching Harry scurry out of the room and across the yards of Oriental rug.

"I'm Phoebe Chen." She brought his attention back to her lovely face. "Uncle likes you a lot."

She's like the statues of Kuan-yin. Steve and Phoebe smiled at each other.

"Can I tell you something?" Her serene smile didn't mask the anxiety in her almond shaped eyes.

Without waiting for an answer, she led him to a chestnut bench and sat down. He sat at the far end and waited.

Steve expected her to say something about Geoff.

Phoebe folded her hands, straightened her buffed shoulders and looked him straight in the eye. "I feel so guilty," catching sight of the guard near the door, she lowered her voice. "There's a thief at the Lemrow."

"That's why you were in the Green Room?" He watched her reaction closely.

"How did you know that?" Her placid look hardened.

"Didn't you go there today? Why?" He kept his voice low.

"Don't laugh?" She licked her lips.

Steve nodded gravely.

"C. E. said there was a thief but not in the usual sense."

"What does that mean, not in the usual sense?"

"I haven't a clue. He wanted to talk about it the night he died. Was C. E. referring to Geoff? Is that why Geoff killed himself? Did C. E. confront him?" She shook her head. "To think I put C. E. off to be with Elliot."

Sensing that Steve didn't recognize the name, she said, "Elliot's my boy friend." Her voice shook. "My ex-boy friend."

Steve remembered the conversation he'd overheard between Phoebe and Harry. Wasn't Harry defending this Elliot?

"Elliot is Harry's son?"

"Yes." When she knitted her brow, she reminded Steve of her uncle. "I get it. You heard Harry and me."

Steve nodded and said, "C. E. said there's a thief? He's the dead curator, right?"

"Head curator of the Renaissance wing, actually. And my godfather," said in snooty tones that didn't hide an underlying sadness.

Steve smiled more at his five-minute crush on this girl who was not much older than his daughter than at the lofty description of the dead man.

"You don't believe me? You think I'm exaggerating?" She whispered, misinterpreting Steve's rueful expression. Her eyes glassed over. She jumped up and cast a mournful look down at him, "You're as bad as Uncle Wellington."

"Sit down. I'm not laughing about anything."

"So who told you I was in the Green Room?" She folded herself back onto the bench.

Steve had no intention of offering up Kenny. He shrugged his shoulders.

"Let me guess." She curled her lip. "Kenny?"

"The thief?" Steve prompted her.

"C. E. wanted to talk about it, but then he died." She was looking down at her hands and taking deep breaths. "I hate this exhibit."

Hadn't Wellington claimed that his niece loved it? Steve recalled the pride in Wellington's voice when he said he depended on Phoebe and Monika as his artistic guides.

"Why do you hate it?"

"Detective, have you ever done anything wrong?"

"Many times."

"I mean bad. Have you ever betrayed someone you loved?"

"Where's this leading?"

"I don't know." Her shoulders were hunched and she was staring at the parquet floor.

"C. E. died of a heart attack?" Steve said.

"Maybe."

Steve waited. Phoebe had closed down, but her guilt swept over him. Was she imagining that C. E. had been murdered? He thought of his daughter's dramas.

Suddenly, she lifted her head. "I should've seen him. I knew he wanted to talk about something important. So did I." Phoebe took a deep breath. "His boy friend told me he found C. E. clinging to his phone. Was I the last person he spoke to?"

"Go on."

"Aren't you in provenance?"

"We all compare evidence. Go on."

"What I'm saying is, did he have a heart attack because I canceled our date?" She looked at him. Her expression hardened. "Why is a provenance detective here? We need someone from homicide."

Why did she say that, Steve thought.

"Did I kill C. E.?" she cried.

"Officially, it was a heart attack." Steve also knew from a tech buddy that C. E. had spoken to three people. First, Phoebe, then Yoshi, his boy friend, and then someone on a throw away cell.

"What about Geoff?" Phoebe whispered.

"Suicide."

Phoebe looked over at the statues and turned away. There was a suppressed sob in her voice. Her youthful stoicism moved him.

"You still haven't answered my question." He smiled to soften the remark. "Why were you in the Green Room?"

Phoebe said nothing.

Steve was thinking: a thief and now a suspicious death. He almost licked his lips. He was about to ask her about the porno photos.

"Excuse me." A blond girl stood at the door.

Startled, Steve and Phoebe scrambled to their feet.

"Hi, Cristobel." Phoebe said, regaining her composure.

Cristobel gave a cool nod.

After a few silent seconds, Phoebe looked at Steve. "We'll talk later." She walked out of the room.

"The exhibit isn't open until tomorrow. Did she bring you in here?" The husky voice coming from the slight frame surprised him.

"Steve Kulchek." He stood up and showed her his ID. "I'm checking out the provenance."

"You don't look like someone in art. I'm sorry. I mean you… I'll stop while I'm ahead." She extended her hand. "Cristobel Gregersen. I'm putting on the finishing touches." She held up some labels. She flashed an engaging, awkward smile.

Steve recalled Kenny saying Cristobel had been in the Green Room that morning.

"Okay if I ask you a few questions?" Steve asked.

"About Kuan-yin's provenance? Sure. What I don't know I can research. I helped install most of this exhibit."

"That's nice." Steve expression said he couldn't have cared less.

"It was wonderful. Imagine, a curator came all the way from China to help us." Cristobel ran her eyes down the sandalwood statue of the goddess and the regal child who was holding a single flower. "Lovely, aren't they?"

"Yeah. Listen, I'm interested in the Green Room because of its proximity to this exhibit." He pointed to a floor plan next to a fire extinguisher. The five percent part of him that recalled he was in art theft traced the route between the Green Room and the Chen exhibit.

"I know where it is." Pain covered her face like a mask.

"I'm looking into security, making sure there's no place the statues can be hidden." He figured he couldn't sound stupider.

Cristobel glanced at the statues, the smallest being about a foot tall and then studied him as if he were crazy.

She took a deep breath.

Her head drooped and she turned her back to him. He watched as she turned her head upwards to Kuan-yin's compassionate face. After a few seconds she tried to push a label into a transparent holder at the statue's base. Her trembling hands lost their grip and the label fluttered to the floor.

Steve picked it up and handed it to her. "You okay?"

She kept her back to him. Her shoulders were shaking.

"Here." Steve handed her his handkerchief. His Uncle Con, the retired cop, told him to always have one handy. She took it and blew her nose, still with her back to him.

"My friend killed himself in the Green Room."

"The photographer?"

She swung around. "Geoff said, 'Why hate me so much?' I said, 'I don't hate you.'" Cristobel put her hands over her sobbing face. Steve couldn't make out what she said next.

Over her shoulder, he saw the guard, his face alight with curiosity. Steve walked over and shut the door.

Cristobel's discrete mascara had left light brown tears on her flushed cheeks. "He smoked a lot of pot, and I thought maybe that was it."

The door swung open. A young man barreled into the room, looked around and then tried to cover his confusion by grinning at Cristobel. "Hi, there."

"She left five minutes ago," Cristobel said as she moved to another statue and fitted in a label.

"What are you talking about?" The young man widened his eyes in an unconvincing display of innocence.

"Please, Elliot...I'm sorry, Detective ..."

"Kulchek," Steve filled in.

"This is Elliot Ross."

Elliot's youthful eyes lit up at the word, detective. "Dad, said you used to be in homicide."

Steve nodded.

"Now, you're into art?" Elliot's distain matched Steve's own. He glanced at Cristobel then studied her face. "What's on your face?"

She raised her left hand to her cheek. "I don't know."

"Not crying again?"

"Go to hell, Elliot."

Elliot glanced nervously at Steve. "She's upset because a really mixed up guy who never should've worked here died."

"Killed himself," Cristobel cried.

The guard was gawking at the door.

"See how far it gets you, sticking up for a loser like Geoff." Elliot backed out of the room.

"That, Detective, is why I hate nepotism. He works here because of his father." Cristobel glared at Elliot's retreating form.

"What's his job?" Steve said.

"Assistant Controller." Cristobel rolled her eyes. "Emphasis on the assistant. Phoebe has a phony job too, in between trips to Bergdorf's, because of her rich uncle. And working stiffs like me who love art but come from nothing are screwed royally."

Her bitter tone reminded Steve of Kenny sounding off in the Green Room.

"You went into the Green Room after Geoff's death?" Steve said.

Cristobel caught her breath, confused by the change of topic. She bowed her head. "Yeah."

"Why?"

She opened her mouth, then shut it. Finally, she said, "I wanted to be close to him. It sounds weird." She shook her head, agreeing with herself. "I thought maybe I'd get in touch with why he did it. I don't know."

"What do you do here?"

"I'm a research assistant. Looks good on the resumé and pays for my doctorate," she said, as she moved to a dark wooden statue, sorted through the remaining labels and fitted one into a slot on the base.

"Like working here?"

Instead of answering the question, she said, "I almost quit."

Steve nodded, encouraging her to continue.

"I told my supervisor this morning, but Hilda - that's her name - said you'll do no such thing." Cristobel mimicked the older woman. "I'm getting the Fellowship, at least according to Hilda. It'll be announced tonight."

She looked straight at him. "I'm tired of losing."

He noticed how exhausted and how young she was. The brown tears had dried on her face like cartoon freckles.

The Fellowship. Something stirred in Steve's memory.

"It's a big deal?"

"Very big deal. Only one Stowbridge Fellowship is awarded each year."

"Stowbridge? C. E. Stowbridge?"

"Very good, Detective," she said mocking him gently as she glanced at her watch. "I better get moving."

"Did C. E. know the photographer?"

Cristobel hesitated. "C. E. retired about the time Geoff was hired, but of course C. E. was here a lot."

She stopped talking, obviously thinking about something.

"Yes?" Steve said.

"It's nothing." Like lightning, her sad expression changed to an amused glance. "Are you coming to ze grand opening, monsieur?"

"I am," Steve said. "See you this evening."

"Yeees." She clenched her tiny hands in fists and gave an imaginary knock out punch. "Behave, Cristobel. You're among the gentry," she scolded herself, then turned and left the room. A second later, she stuck her head around the door. "I'm not about to give you your handkerchief in this condition. I'll wash it first." She gave him an impish grin and then disappeared.

Poor kid, Steve thought as he headed out of the exhibit. The guard was standing in a military stance and staring straight ahead.

"Lots of excitement for one morning," Steve said.

The guard gave an abrupt nod.

"Anyone assigned to the Green Room yesterday?"

"Me."

From the way he said it, Steve figured he'd gotten a lot of mileage out of it.

"Anybody go in the room?"

"You the detective?"

"Correct. Steve Kulchek." He extended his right hand.

"Jean Pierre," the other man said as they shook hands. "A lot of people – police, the director, Cristobel, Phoebe."

"Phoebe say why?"

The guard shook his head.

"Know where she is?"

"Try the library."

Chapter 10

11:15 a.m. Wednesday, September 6

Steve opened one of the oak paneled doors and was once again transported to the Bayside Children's Library he had practically lived in as a kid.

He remembered reading that the Lemrow Library had been the creation of a daughter who had never married. Her beloved pets were immortalized in the two marble busts of dogs' heads which flanked a table at the front of the Lemrow reading room.

Last Thursday when he had seen the library for the first time, the rows of rectangular tables were being used by museum patrons. At the moment workmen were placing the tables against the bookcases that ran around the room.

Standing in a far corner and ignoring the bustle, Phoebe and a man in a velvet jacket were studying various photos spread on one of the long tables. As Steve looked across at him, the man automatically sucked in his stomach and straightened his shoulders. In a moss green velvet jacket and Hermes scarf, he was a throwback to another era. All he needed was a cigarette holder. In the dim library, Steve wondered why he was wearing dark glasses.

Then he removed his glasses. Steve saw the soft-boiled egg eyes, a sign of heavy drinking. Phoebe looked up and favored Steve with an enchanting smile. "Max Stowbridge, this is Detective Kulchek."

Steve and Max Stowbridge shook hands. Recognizing the last name, Steve said, "You were related to C. E. Stowbridge?"

"I'm his twin and the last member of the Stowbridge clan," Max said.

"You can help us decide," Phoebe said.

"Decide what?" Steve said as he glanced down at a dozen photos. He recognized a younger, reed thin Wellington Chen. The other man in the photos, slightly pudgy at twenty, increased in weight as he progressed in years.

"That's C. E.," Phoebe picked up a recent photo and smiled at it.

Steve looked at Max Stowbridge – it was all there, the same sparse, crinkly hair, the rounded torso and long skinny legs.

Phoebe said, "I thought it would be a great idea to have photos of C. E. and Uncle at the Opening tonight."

"I found this," Max murmured. He reached into a manila folder and pulled out another photo.

With a theatrical flair, he turned the photo over. It showed C. E. reaching out his gloved hand to take the small Renaissance statue by Riccio.

"He's cropped the photo," Phoebe said.

"Indeed he has. C. E. didn't like competition," purred Max. On the right side of C. E. were the tips of four, gloved fingers handing him the statue and on the left side, part of the shoulder of a man's jacket.

Steve watched Phoebe tracing the shoulder of the unknown man's jacket. Then, as if she were remembering something, she outlined with her index finger the four gloved fingers.

Steve wondered why C. E. had kept a photo of himself with a statue he was supposed to have stolen.

Steve asked Max, "Where did you find the photo?"

"In my apartment."

"Your apartment, Max?" Phoebe said.

"The apartment was C. E.'s," he said defensively, looking at Steve. "He left it to me."

"What about Yoshi?" Phoebe said.

"Impertinent girl. It's none of your business, but we – C. E., Yoshi and I – had discussed over the years what would happen to me if C. E. kicked the bucket first. We decided that I'd get the apartment so my name was put on the lease."

"And Yoshi?" Phoebe persisted.

"Phoebe, mind your own business."

"Max, I was C. E.'s goddaughter."

"He's left you a trinket or two and Yoshi will get a little something."

Phoebe had a cat-like expression on her beautiful face. Steve figured she was more interested in the photo than what C. E. had left her.

Max placed the cropped photo next to a picture of Wellington and C. E. in their Harvard days.

For no reason, Steve asked, "You went to Harvard?"

Max grimaced. "Briefly."

Steve smiled at his honesty.

"Maxi hangs out here. All that's missing is booze, right Maxi?" Phoebe said.

"Clever girl," Max said. "Working yourself to the bone?"

But Phoebe hadn't heard the last remark. She had picked up the altered photo and was studying it. She ran her eye around the library's paneling, then back to the photo. "Where was this taken?"

"No idea, darling," Max said. "Shall we use it?"

"Of course." She looked toward a dais with a small table in front of it. "Let's keep the montage a surprise. I'll present it at the last moment."

"What are you up to, Phoebe?" Max asked.

Steve was wondering the same thing. He was also wondering when he could ask her about why she went to the Green Room.

"She'll never tell me," Max said. "I'm off. Coming to the Opening tonight, Detective?"

Steve nodded.

Max pecked Phoebe on both cheeks then headed toward the exit.

"Wandering around?" Phoebe said to Steve. She continued to play with the photos, switching them around. Now, the one in the center was the cropped picture of C. E. and the Riccio.

"I was looking for you," Steve said.

"Why?"

"Why did you go to the Green Room?"

"What does that have to do with provenance?" Phoebe said.

Jesus, she reminded him of Dick Holbrook. Five minutes ago, Steve had checked his messages. He had one from Holbrook: What's contacting the coroner's office got to do with provenance?

"Your uncle asked me to keep an eye on you." Steve knew that was a mistake the minute it was out of his mouth.

"Keep an eye on me?" Phoebe said in a mocking tone. "And report back to Uncle Wellington? I'm not a child."

"Your uncle was concerned about the curator's death and then the photographer's. He would've made a good detective."

"You should tell him. He'd like that." She went back to arranging snapshots around the Riccio photo.

"You feel guilty about C. E.?"

"Very good, Detective," she said without taking her eyes off the photos.

"What about the photographer?"

Phoebe looked up, considering what Steve had said. She was recalling something.

"What are you thinking about?" He kept his voice low.

"I never noticed him," she said, not answering the question. "He was a nerd."

"Go on."

"Something I saw. It made sense but it didn't."

"Go on," he said.

"Hello."

Steve and Phoebe shifted in the direction of the voice.

"I didn't mean to startle you," the director said. She walked toward them beaming a sunny smile while she scanned the room. "The usual chaos, I see."

Phoebe was busy stacking the photos.

"What have we here?" Monika put out her hand to see the pictures.

"A surprise." Phoebe pushed the photos into her satchel.

"Sounds ominous," Monika said.

"Have a business card, Detective?" Phoebe said.

"Sure." Steve handed her one.

Monika raised her eyebrows but said nothing.

"See you in a few short hours." Phoebe waved to them both and walked rapidly out the door.

"Such drama." Monika put the back of her hand to her forehead like a silent movie star. "Let me tell you the set up. We'll be in here for the first hour. Wellington will say a few words about C. E.'s contributions, culminating in the Chen exhibit. Then I'll present the Stowbridge Fellowship."

"To Cristobel," Steve said.

"God, no." The director thought a moment. "How do you know Cristobel?"

"Ran into her in the Chen exhibit."

She nodded, dismissing it. "The Stowbridge Fellowship is going to Phoebe, of course. You were at the meeting. Don't you remember? This is where you come in. Wellington has asked that you accompany him to the Chen exhibit."

As a guard, as a fucking security guard, Steve thought.

"Sulking? Calm down, Detective. He actually likes talking to you."

Stung, but impressed at her perception, Steve said, "So after the presentation, we go to the exhibit's opening?"

"Exactly. Everyone will be on their best behavior, I hope. By the way, keep an eye on Max Stowbridge. You'll recognize him. He thinks he's Oscar Wilde. He manages to get drunk on our white wine."

"He's C. E.'s twin brother?"

"How did you learn that?" She buried her question in a little laugh.

"He told me."

"When?"

"About five minutes ago."

"He was here – in the library?" She nodded her head, answering her own question. "He takes full advantage of being C. E.'s brother. Hangs around the Lemrow like a second home. Some things have to change."

Chapter 11

6:15 p.m. Wednesday, September 6

Three hours later, Steve walked into the transformed library. He studied the small groups of museum patrons in tailored cocktail clothes.

The director walked toward him with the confidence of a runway model. *Karl Lagerfeld? Chanel?* Steve smiled with appreciation at the diagonal slit in the midnight blue blouse. Before veering off to join a group in banker outfits, the director gave him an approving smile.

Mary L. joined him and ran her practiced eye up and down his frame like a horse trader. "Detective, welcome."

"Tell me who's here."

"Well," Mary L. swung around. "Friends of the museum." She made quotation marks with her red tipped fingers. Steve got the message. She was referring to generous donors. "You've met Wellington and Harry." Mary L. lowered her voice.

"That handsome young man is his son and Phoebe Chen's fiancé. I'll introduce you."

"I've met them."

"Fast mover," Mary L. said.

At the far end of the temporary bar, Harry Ross and his son, Elliot, were hanging on Wellington's words. Standing next to her uncle, Phoebe stood, twisting a pearl necklace around her long neck. She kept darting glances toward the dais. When she saw Steve, she favored him with a tiny smile.

He took a sip of white wine, usually hating it, but it belonged here and, for the first time, he felt he did. Steve followed Phoebe's appraising glance. She was looking at a tall, slender young woman who was smiling and turning around, obviously looking for someone. Her red-brown hair fluttered around her shoulders as she moved.

Carmen. My Carmen. Steve was flooded with memories of their first date. When he told her she reminded him of his childhood collie because of the color of her hair, she'd laughed a sexy, lilting sound, full of joy.

Steve put down his wine glass and walked toward her. He had a flashback of them hiking in Guatemala near her home, Jutiapa.

"Steve?" She frowned. "What are you doing here?"

"He's working." Captain Dick Holbrook said, as he came up to them.

Like I'm a Seeing Eye dog, Steve thought. Don't pet.

Steve's bile rose. In addition to destroying other cops' careers, Holbrook managed that anti-drug fund that helped rich kids get into rehab and Holbrook the Good get invited to fancy openings like this one.

Before he could say anything, Mary L. grabbed his arm, nodded to Holbrook and Carmen, and pulled Steve toward an easel as if she were breaking up a brawl. "Harry must have invited them. I didn't know they were coming," Mary L. whispered. Her voice was louder than if she'd shouted.

Steve reclaimed his arm and forced himself to concentrate on the easel which was placed on the table under the dais.

When she wasn't complaining about his smoking, one of Carmen's complaints was that he put his life into compartments. *You bet I do, Baby*.

He studied the montage of C. E. and recognized the photos Phoebe had been examining that afternoon. In the center of one photo, C. E. stood with his right hand stretched out being handed the Riccio statue by an unseen person. Clockwise, around this photo, were placed pictures in chronological order. From two infant twins, C.E. and Max, through prep school, Harvard and Wellington Chen, more Harvard and more Wellington, and, finally, several snapshots of C. E. and a Japanese man.

Maximillian Stowbridge and Steve nodded to each other. Max, resplendent in a burgundy dinner jacket, was taking a wine glass from the caterer's bartender and popping a tiny canapé into his mouth.

"Who's that?" Steve glanced at the group of photos.

"You mean the Japanese? That's Yoshi. He was C. E.'s partner."

"Did they live together?"

"For eons, Detective, and no, Yoshi didn't resent me inheriting the apartment. He'll get C. E.'s money when probate is finished." A note of resentment tinged the last remark.

Mary L. raised her glass of wine to Steve as he approached her.

Nearby, Cristobel was standing with the director and a middle aged woman Steve couldn't identify.

"Who's she?" Steve said to Mary L.

"The young blonde?"

"The other one."

"Hilda. She's the senior librarian and Cristobel's mentor. Which reminds me, I have to speak to her. Be back in a minute."

Steve kept his back to the entrance to avoid seeing Carmen and Holbrook. He concentrated on Cristobel's happy, hopeful expression. She stood to one side as Mary L. gabbled into Hilda's ear. Steve figured Cristobel was anticipating the announcement of her winning the Stowbridge Scholarship. Poor kid.

Max snagged another white wine then walked toward Steve, "The Stowbridges of Scranton... Now I'm the only one left. Only the director and me."

"The director and you?"

"She's from Scranton too. C. E. got her this job. Didn't she tell you? No, she wouldn't. Monika was a twin."

"Monika?"

"Excuse me," Max said in an exaggerated fashion. "Mo*ni*ka, accent on the penultimate syllable. That's the second to last syllable, Detective." He smiled, pleased at his little taunt. "Much more exotic, don't you think?"

Steve smiled back, amused the director had changed her name.

"Mousy," Max said.

Mousy? Steve eyed Monika. In that black dress that followed every contour of her body and the nude-colored platform heels in snakeskin, Steve would never have described her as mousy. His robbery days kicked in. He was wondering how the director could afford $1000 shoes.

"Once upon a time she was mousy," Max said, interpreting Steve's thought. "I preferred Kitty, her bad twin." Max took a deep drink, a sly look in his eyes. "Now Monika and I are left, two halves. C. E. was talking about Scranton a lot. After his heart attack, he insisted on going back. Wanted to check out something. The last week of his life he was a bore about it. I say let sleeping dogs lie; don't you, Detective?"

Instead of answering him, Steve said, "What happened to the director's twin?"

"Died in a car crash years ago. The whole family was wiped out except for Monika."

Steve stole a look around the room. Nearby, Harry was talking to Carmen and Holbrook. He turned to Steve. "Detective, you know everyone, don't you?"

The three of them nodded uncomfortably just as a slender Japanese man entered the room. Dressed in designer black jeans and a turtleneck, he moved gracefully toward the group.

"Yoshi?" Carmen cried. She kissed him on both cheeks and held out her hands to clasp his. He lifted her left hand, brushed it with a kiss then brought it closer to his eyes to examine a ring.

"Yoshi, my man," Holbrook said, as if he pitched for the Yankees.

"I'm so glad you're here." Phoebe cried out as she stepped forward to greet him. He took her hand and bowed slightly.

"Not for long, dear Phoebe." Yoshi's face was a stoical mask.

"What?"

"My mother's ill. I have a flight to Tokyo later this evening."

The director joined them.

Yoshi bowed. "I must thank you for…"

"You must do nothing of the sort." Monika cut him off.

"Yoshi's going to Tokyo," Phoebe said to Steve before turning to Yoshi. "But you're coming back, aren't you, Yoshi?"

"For what?" His voice was low. His face was sunk in deep sorrow. "I can work in Tokyo." Yoshi was referring to the textile and jewelry firm he had founded.

"What about C. E.'s memorial?"

"Of course, I'll return for that."

"We'll miss you, Yoshi. Please stay in touch." Monika glanced at her watch. "I'm afraid I have to start the program."

"How can I contact you?" Phoebe ignored Monika and held on to Yoshi's hand. "We have to talk."

"I'll give you all that," the director said. "We have to get started." She stepped in between Yoshi and Phoebe, directed a sweet, gentle smile at Yoshi and whispered, "Bye."

Phoebe stepped around the director, grabbed Yoshi's hand and led him to the pastiche. "What do you think?" she said watching him intently.

Yoshi's eyes watered as he studied the photos. He managed a smile. "Lovely, Phoebe."

Phoebe stamped her foot. "Look, really, look, Yoshi."

Yoshi studied her frantic expression. "I did. It's lovely."

Then he broke down. Yoshi put his trembling hands over his face. He moaned, "He died with the phone in his hands. He was clutching it."

"He died after I phoned him?" Phoebe whispered. "It's my fault."

Steve remembered the emergency services report had stated that Yoshi found C. E.

"C. E. was scrunched up in his big ugly chair clutching the phone," Yoshi cried. "He still had his gloves on."

Gloves? Steve thought and recalled the director slipping on a pair before touching the Riccio.

"So he wasn't holding the Riccio when he died?" Steve said.

"No, Detective," Phoebe said, speaking to the village idiot. "He was holding the phone."

Yoshi sobbed, "The Riccio was between his knees. Like he was clinging to everything, anything."

"Yoshi!" Max grabbed two glasses off a passing tray and advanced toward the slender man. "Drink up."

"I can't." Yoshi held up his right hand to ward off the wine.

"Yoshi is running away," Phoebe said.

"Why?" Max's head swung from Phoebe to Yoshi.

"Do you really have to ask that?" With great dignity, Yoshi bowed and edged toward the door.

"You can always stay in the apartment," Max called after him.

Steve dug out his NYPD card, caught up with Yoshi, and handed it to him. Yoshi bowed politely.

"I'm a detective," Steve said. "Checking out provenance."

"Provenance?" Yoshi's sad face was layered with bewilderment. "What do you want with me?"

"Tell me about C. E."

"What does that have to do with provenance?"

Instead of answering the question, Steve said, "Do you have a card?"

"No," Yoshi said and backed out the door.

"Detective?" Monika held out an envelope. "As promised."

Steve realized it was the provenance documentation of the two statues that he'd asked her for.

"May we now begin?" Monika said. Above the bowls of autumnal chrysanthemums flanking the photo pastiche, she stood at the dais. If she'd had a gavel she would have banged it.

"Since Wellington Chen obtained his undergraduate and graduate degrees from Harvard, he has distinguished himself as one of Asia's leading businessmen. Fortune Magazine characterized him as "a unique combination of eastern wisdom and western inventiveness. If Asia is the tiger, Chen is the ring master." She raised her eyebrows at the journalese. "We characterize him as a generous patron and friend of the Lemrow. Doctor Chen?" The director backed away from the podium and stood demurely to one side.

Wellington walked to the podium and graced the small, select audience with a little bow before he began.

Steve half listened as he thought about Yoshi. Approaching him like a homicide detective had been a bust. His eyes drifted around the room. Max was devoting himself to drinking, Harry Ross was hanging on Wellington's every word, Elliot was standing like a marine looking politely bored.

Phoebe's head was bent, her dark hair framing her face. No Carmen and no Holbrook.

Wellington bestowed a bittersweet smile on the group. "Before we proceed to the exhibit, let us honor the memory of Charles Edward Stowbridge. C. E. and I met at Harvard. It was he who opened my eyes to the wonders of Western art. C. E. was the one who introduced me to the Lemrow at the tender age of seventeen. It's fitting that he should have ended his illustrious career here – in the place he loved most in all the world." Wellington stopped speaking, gulped and then continued. "We –with the incomparable Director Monika Syka at the helm – are planning a memorial for C. E. You will be notified as plans develop. I will now beg your forgiveness, for droning on too long, and thank you for allowing me to display my collection at the Lemrow. I suggest we see the exhibit."

"But first, Wellington, the Stowbridge Fellowship," the director said.

The heavyset woman next to Cristobel squeezed her arm.

"Of course." Another charming bow then Wellington smiled at the gentle applause as he glided into the small audience and sat next to Phoebe.

"The recipient's love of scholarship, extraordinary research skills, and a maturity of writing are some of the attributes that helped the Stowbridge Fellowhip Committee select this year's appointee," the director said.

Cristobel's face was suffused with a lovely flush. She and Hilda exchanged an anxious glance.

"With great pleasure, I present the Stowbridge Fellowship to Phoebe Chen."

Most of the people present fell over themselves with genteel applause. Wellington gave his niece a ceremonial bow.

But Steve was watching Cristobel's face drain of color and Hilda putting a protective arm around her waist.

It did no good. Tears welled in Cristobel's eyes.

"Phoebe, always Phoebe," she whispered.

Aghast, Hilda let her arm drop from Cristobel's waist.

Wellington offered his arm to Phoebe and they led a procession out of the library, over the Central Gallery's thick Bokharas and into the Chen Exhibit.

Chapter 12

11 a.m. Thursday, September 7

"Quite a spread." Monika held up a section of Thursday's *The Wall Street Journal*, and read aloud, "In spite of recent troubles, the Goddess of Compassion reigned at the Lemrow last night."

The director and staff were gathered in the north end of the Water Court. Aside from the gentle rustle of the newspaper, the rhythmic splashing from the Triton fountain and the director's low voice, the museum was still. On Staff Days the Lemrow was closed to the public until one p. m.

Monika passed the Chen exhibit clipping to Wellington, seated at a marble bench next to Mary L. and Harry.

An assistant handed a copy of the article to Theodora, dressed today in layers of velvet and topped by another of her original hats. Hilda looked over Theodora's shoulder at the story about the Chen exhibit.

"For our distinguished guest," Monika smiled at Wellington, "let me explain our next Staff Day activity. The goal is to imitate with inspiration one of the floral arrangements in a Lemrow work of art. Then there will be a vote to select the most successful."

"Please put your creations here." Monika gestured to a long table placed near the fountain.

Cristobel was standing apart from the group. Steve stood next to her. "Last night I didn't get a chance to tell you how sorry I was."

"The fellowship?" she replied dully, her arms folded tightly across her chest. "Don't bother. It's always the Phoebes of this world. I'm resigning. That reminds me. I have to speak to Elliot."

"Elliot?"

"Oh, that." Blushing, she recalled her outburst against Elliot in the Chen exhibit. "He's not so bad. Especially when he's lending me…never mind."

Steve kept quiet and kept listening.

Like most of the other employees, Cristobel was dressed down. Way down, as if she were performing in an indie rock group.

"It's not just the fellowship. What about Geoff?" Cristobel said. She folded her arms tightly against her sequined denim jacket. "No one cares. Phoebe even had the nerve to suggest that he stole something."

"Stole something?"

"I overheard her talking to you about a thief at the museum."

"This was in the Chen exhibit, yesterday morning?" Steve recalled how Phoebe had felt she'd let down C. E.

"Why blame poor Geoff?" Cristobel raised her voice. "He's not here to defend himself."

The director shot her a glance to keep quiet.

Cristobel continued in a whisper. "How could Phoebe think Geoff stole something?"

The person in the last row handed Cristobel the Chen exhibit cutting. "Lovely," she sneered, glancing at it. Then she really looked at it before she handed it to Steve. "I worked on that. I loved it."

He read *The Journal* article before placing it on a table.

Wellington caught his eye, stood up and led him into an alcove. "I'm worried about Phoebe. She's acting strangely. Says she doesn't want the fellowship."

"Still feeling guilty about C. E.?" Steve said.

"She told me you think I'd make a good detective. I wish I could solve what's going on."

Once again Steve recalled Phoebe's guilt over canceling her dinner date with C. E.

"She told me C. E.'s remark about fraudulent activity at the museum," Wellington said.

Steve thought the guy's got millions of dollars worth of art practically in the next room and his niece is telling him there's a thief in the museum. As an art detective he should have been nervous, but his homicide antennae told him they weren't dealing with someone as obvious as a burglar.

"Phoebe keeps bringing it up. It worries me."

"Did she say anything about Geoff?"

Behind Steve came a voice, "My two favorite detectives."

Wellington's expression changed. He forced a smile as Phoebe joined them.

Alone among the younger employees, Phoebe wasn't in denim. She wore a metallic cotton dress, a single gold bracelet and tiny ballet slippers.

She held up the framed montage of photos of C. E. and raised her voice. "I brought it back."

"Back?" Steve said.

"Last night I took it home. I wasn't leaving it here."

Wellington had a deeply troubled expression on his face.

Is she screwed up, Steve was wondering or does she know something the rest of us don't.

"It should be where we can all see it," Phoebe said, a little too loudly. She pointed to the center picture, the one in which gloved fingers were handing C. E. the Riccio. "Follow me, please."

Phoebe led them out of the garden court, down the corridor and into the Green Room.

Steve and Wellington followed her into the room, empty except for a Mac on a table sheathed in a dust cloth and a hook swinging from the ceiling.

"What's that?" Wellington was staring at the door to Steve's temporary office.

"It's a small room. I'm using it." Steve opened the door. Wellington and Phoebe stared at the small desk, folding chair and closed laptop.

"You fit in there?" Wellington said.

"Barely." Steve closed the door.

Phoebe led them back to the Green Room table. "Observe closely." She placed the frame on the table, then ran her hand along the room's molding that circled the four walls. She pointed to the same detail in the photo.

"So it was photographed in here," Wellington said.

"Who took it?" Steve asked.

"We'll go back to the group and find out." Phoebe picked up the frame and clutched it to her breast. Her hands were shaking.

"Phoebe, dear, calm down," Wellington said.

"C. E. didn't tell you he wanted to talk. I let him down and he died."

"What's wrong?" The director and Harry stood at the door. "Anything we can do?"

"Nothing." Phoebe pulled herself together.

"Who took this photo?" Steve asked, indicating the pastiche.

"May I?" Monika came closer and took the frame out of Phoebe's reluctant hands. She and Harry studied the photos and then both shook their heads.

"I hadn't noticed that particular photo before." Monika pointed at C. E. holding the Riccio. She looked around the barren room and sighed.

"I'm planning on renovating this space and making it a real photo studio."

"Phoebe, where's a smile? Aren't you the fellowship winner?" Harry said.

"I don't want the fellowship," she said through gritted teeth.

"Come on," Monika said, humoring a spoiled child. "You've earned it."

"Earned it? You mean paid for it?" As Phoebe said this, she lifted the photo out of Monika's hands.

"Phoebe!" Wellington Chen frowned at his niece. "I apologize for Phoebe's rude remark. She's not herself."

"Uncle," she cried, tapping the photo of C. E. being handed the Riccio by a gloved hand. "Did Geoff take that photo? Is that why he killed himself in here?"

Shocked silence fell over the group.

"I was in the Green Room last Thursday. Geoff was shooting in here," Phoebe said.

"I have a small favor to ask," Monika said. "May I borrow that wonderful montage? I'd love to include it in the members' newsletter."

"Of course, you may," Wellington said, still embarrassed by Phoebe's behavior. He took the frame out of his niece's hands and gave it to Monika.

"Thank you so much, Wellington and Phoebe. I'll take good care of it."

"It's not mine, Uncle." Phoebe looked at Wellington. "It belongs to Max."

"Phoebe," Wellington said in a stern voice. "Max will be honored to have his brother remembered in this way."

"Shall we join the others?" Monika gave a warm, forgiving smile. "Don't worry, Wellington, you don't have to join in. I can arrange a tour of the museum."

"Please, do not go to any more trouble," Wellington said, still rattled. He checked his watch. "I have to leave soon. I'm catching a helicopter to Kennedy. I hope you understand."

"Let's have lunch together first, Uncle."

"Perhaps you shouldn't leave your Staff Day," Wellington said.

"We can make an exception," Monika said.

"Of course you can," Phoebe said with mock humility.

Wellington glared at her as Harry led them back to the floral arrangements. Tubs of roses, daffodils, lilies, tulips and other flowers lined the Garden Court's north wall. Calla lilies and orchids were set apart in tall vases. Florists' tools and various containers were distributed on sturdy, rectangular tables. The tables were strewn with flowers, leaves, shears, wire, buckets of water and containers.

People were going back and forth to the galleries to double-check their floral arrangements and to take photos of them.

"Come on, Uncle, let's dazzle them with orchids," Phoebe said in a mood swing.

Wellington threw a rueful glance at his niece. He turned to Steve. "I grow them. Very relaxing."

"We'll copy the orchid bouquet the little girl is holding," Phoebe said. "Detective, you remember the porcelain statue of Kuan-yin and the little girl?"

Steve nodded.

Wellington smiled, appreciating his niece's reference to the exhibit.

The next fifteen minutes were spent in ignoring the gardener's repeated instructions and edging out other flower enthusiasts for the best container.

"What are you doing here?" the director said to Max Stowbridge resplendent in a chocolate corduroy suit and black watch plaid tie.

"Picking up some of C. E.'s things." Max raised his cell and snapped her photo.

"Put that thing away," she said.

"Monika, surely you don't mind?" He ignored her and clicked away.

"Max," Wellington Chen approached, his hand out. "I'm so glad you're here. I'm sorry I didn't get a chance to talk to you last night."

But Max didn't extend his hand. He was busy shooting someone.

Steve followed where Max was aiming his camera – toward the Entrance Hall. All he saw was a female guard closing a closet door.

Near the Green Room, Cristobel was whispering to Elliot as she stuck some roses into a vase. After glancing to right and left, Elliot handed

Cristobel something. Defiantly, she held it up and jingled it before slipping it into her purse.

Steve saw that it was a set of car keys. At the same moment, he noticed that the director turned around when she heard the keys clink. She stared at them with a still expression.

Standing near Steve, Phoebe said, "Elliot doesn't waste time."

Steve gave her an encouraging look.

"I told Elliot it was over. This time I meant it. He was distraught." Phoebe's deft fingers were busily arranging stems of creamy white orchids in a narrow necked vase. Steve followed her as she went to the table near the fountain and placed the orchids. "Correction. His father was distraught."

As if hearing her, Elliot glanced over at Phoebe.

Mischievously, she raised her iPhone, adjusted it this way and that, and said, loudly, "A lovely picture of the lovely couple."

After clicking a few shots of Cristobel and Elliot, she kept shooting around the room before tossing her cell into her tiny purse.

Nearby, Hilda was taking a photo of Theodora arranging grasses on a rocky and sandy flat.

"The Bellini, Theodora?" Phoebe said.

"Yes." Theodora blushed, embarrassed and thankful for a word from Phoebe.

Theodora turned her attention to Phoebe's orchids. "That's the little girl's bouquet?"

As Phoebe nodded, Monika said in a placating tone, "How charming."

Phoebe smiled at the director. "May I?" Without waiting for an answer, she slipped the pastiche of photos of C. E. out of Monika's grasp and then asked Theodora and Hilda, "Who shot this?" She pointed to the photo of C. E. and the Riccio.

Theodora and Hilda studied the photo. Hilda said, "That's the Riccio." She looked up at Phoebe. "Why's he handling it?"

Phoebe shrugged. "Who shot it?" she repeated.

Hilda shook her head. "Geoff," Theodora mumbled.

"Geoff," Cristobel called across the hall.

"Geoff?" Phoebe looked first at Theodora and then at Cristobel.

"He was shooting the bronzes a few days before…" Cristobel stopped, too cowed by her surroundings to say he killed himself.

Phoebe looked across at her. "Thanks," Phoebe said, a momentary truce in her voice.

Wellington approached his niece. "I have to leave."

"Uncle, Geoff took it."

Wellington looked confused.

"Geoff was the photographer who took this photo." She pointed at it. "It's cropped."

"I see," Wellington said. His mind had switched to Hong Kong. "Monika, it's been a wonderful opening. And thank you so much for allowing me to attend the Staff Day."

She smiled very sweetly. "It's been our pleasure and honor, Wellington."

"We'll be in touch about C. E.'s memorial?" Wellington said.

"Of course," Monika said.

"Max," Phoebe said to the approaching man. "The director is borrowing the photo to put in the newsletter."

Max studied the director. "Is she?"

Without saying a word, Wellington took the pastiche out of Phoebe's grasp and handed it to the director.

"We have a meeting at three, Phoebe." Monika's tone balanced professionalism and liberality to perfection. "It's about the Stowbridge Fellowship. Give me a call if you're held up, okay?"

"Phoebe wouldn't dream of missing the meeting. Would you, Phoebe?" Wellington said.

"No, Uncle."

Coming toward them were two muscular, expressionless men in nondescript business suits. They could only be bodyguards.

Phoebe linked arms with her uncle. One guard preceded them. One walked behind.

Chapter 13

1:30 p.m. Thursday, September 7

Wellington and Phoebe were seated at the back of a Japanese restaurant near the 34th Street helicopter port. Phoebe had dragged her uncle into it, promising that he could order cooked food. For all his sophistication, Wellington blanched at the idea of eating raw fish. His two bodyguards sat at the front of the restaurant.

After they were served, Wellington raised his cup of tea and gave Phoebe a slow, understanding smile. "To the recipient of the Stowbridge scholarship. I'm very proud of you."

Phoebe looked up from her iPhone and halfheartedly raised her cup. Wellington clinked his against hers.

"Don't, Uncle. It's bad luck unless they contain alcohol." She slipped a piece of tuna sushi into her mouth.

"What's wrong, Phoebe?" Wellington studied his niece's discontented face. "You've been awarded a prestigious scholarship, you're engaged to be married." He sighed and sipped his tea. "Is it C. E.'s death? You heard Monika."

"I sure did," Phoebe muttered as she fiddled with her iPhone.

"Why do you dislike her so much?" Wellington stared across at her lovely face, her eyes glued to the iPhone screen.

With secret pride, he remembered that when they entered the busy restaurant men and women, too, looked up from their plates and gawked at her.

"Monika's so phony. Always sucking up to you."

Wellington winced at his niece's language. "It's her job to be diplomatic. Anyway, as she pointed out, C. E. was overweight and did not exercise or watch his diet. I too miss him, but death is part of life."

"Uncle, you sound like a fortune cookie."

"Not a Chinese invention." Wellington smiled. Phoebe looked up and smiled back. "This isn't bad." Wellington speared some noodles with his chopsticks and put them into his mouth.

"Rare praise indeed," Phoebe said, smiling a second time at her uncle. "I feel guilty. C. E. wanted me to have dinner with him and I canceled to be with Elliot."

"What did he want to talk about?" Wellington gazed at her shrewdly.

"Something odd at the Lemrow. He hinted about it but didn't come out with it."

"I chose the Lemrow because it seemed like a haven of stability and safety." Wellington wiped his mouth with his napkin. "I'm beginning to feel very foolish and I'm worried about you. Why are you so edgy, so unhappy?"

"Have you ever done anything bad, Uncle?" Phoebe sucked on an edamame pod.

"I've had business deals go wrong. You remember the one a few years ago?"

"Yes, I remember."

When Phoebe didn't say anything else, Wellington continued, "And I've been married three times. Do you want to marry Elliot?" Wellington glared at the iPhone in Phoebe's hand. "Please put that thing away."

She shoved it into her little purse.

"I don't think so."

"Are you still in love with that other person?"

"Off limits, Uncle."

"At least that's something you and Monika agree about."

Phoebe sat up straight. "What do you mean?"

"Well, I had to talk to someone. I asked her if I should learn his identity."

"Track him down, you mean. What did she say?"

"Told me - very politely, of course - that it was none of my business and that you were an adult. So, you see, she is on your side."

Phoebe lowered her head. Wellington tried to see her face. All he saw was one tear drop onto the bag she was clutching.

"My dear child…"

"I'm not a child." Like a doe about to be slaughtered, she bowed her head.

"Why are you crying?"

Phoebe raised her head and gazed at Wellington. "I love you, Uncle."

No profanity could have shocked him more. "Are you all right?"

Phoebe laughed. "You're a long way from embracing the American lifestyle. People are forever saying they love one another." She lowered her voice. "In my case, it's true." She reached into her bag and pulled out her iPhone. "Last time, honest. I have to text my ex-fiancé," tapping away as she said this. Phoebe pushed the iPhone back into her purse.

"What about that photo of C. E. holding a statue?" Wellington said. "Why did you make such a business of that?"

"Max gave it to me."

"Stop right there. Max is not like C. E. He is a leech and a liar. Be polite but avoid him." Wellington glanced at his watch and signaled to the waiter. As soon as he settled the check, he stood up. "I have to get going and you have a meeting at the Lemrow in exactly forty-five minutes."

Phoebe stood up quickly. Her purse fell to the floor. Wellington bent down and picked it up. At the same moment, one of the security men caught Phoebe's eye and pointed at his watch.

"Thanks, Uncle," Phoebe said, taking her purse.

In front of the restaurant, one of the men hailed a taxi, the other held the taxi's door and

Wellington gave Phoebe a hug before she got into the car.

The taxi went across on 34th Street and took a left uptown on Park. In the back seat, Phoebe shivered and hugged herself. I'll tell him. Uncle will understand. For the first time in weeks, she felt her tormented soul calming down like a hurricane that's spent its force. She reached into her purse, rooted around, and looked on the floor. At that moment the cab slid through a yellow light and stopped at 72nd Street and Fifth. She examined the cab's floor again and ran her hands down the seat; she jumped out and handed the cabbie some money.

Phoebe jaywalked across the street, still looking into her purse. She looked up and saw Elliot on the sidewalk. They smiled at each other.

A blue Lexus inched around the 72nd Street corner and turned south. It accelerated to the legal speed of thirty miles an hour. Then, it speeded up. Phoebe turned her head toward the noise. The Lexus aimed right for her. Phoebe started to run. She stumbled and fell forward, smashing her head against the Lexus' side view mirror.

Chapter 14

3:45 p.m. Thursday, September 7

Stasia, a Lemrow security guard, was longing for her break. She checked her watch, 3:45 p.m., and hoped her replacement would be on time. She was dying for a cigarette. Staff Days were very long and work, work, work. Arranging chairs and tables for some dumb activity then rearranging them. Finally, she was doing what a security guard was supposed to do.

A tourist asked her where the Cassatts were, and she said in a snooty tone she'd learned from the other guards, "We don't have any Cassatts. Try the Met."

Here was the other guard at last.

"Get back on time, okay, Stasia?" she said.

Stasia didn't bother to answer. She wanted to spend as many of the thirty minutes as she could smoking. She flicked her badge at the electronic light and rushed through the door, flicked her badge again, went through another door and headed down the interior stairs to the locker room. Behind her she heard steps, but didn't bother to turn around.

"We don't have any Cassatts. Try the Met," Max Stowbridge said, imitating her middle European accent. "What a snob."

She giggled. Then froze. The director was standing in the middle of the locker room. When she saw Stasia staring at her she started up the stairs from the locker room. Monika nodded as she passed them and continued her climb.

"Maxi." Stasia whispered, not moving as if in close proximity to royalty.

"Let's go, girl." He raced past her and touched her locker. "I won. You have to give me a ciggie."

Stasia shrugged her shoulders, used to her pal, Max, showing up for her breaks in order to cadge cigarettes and mimic the Lemrow staff including herself.

"You get a job," she said in mock severity to Max as she opened her locker. Different photos of Pope John Paul II and Lech Walesa were pasted on the inside of the door. Stasia reached inside. Then she flung open the door and looked inside. "Saint Mary, it's gone."

"What's gone?"

"My coat," she wailed.

"Saint Mary, my eye. Nobody in his right mind would steal that rag."

"Now I remember," Stasia put her large right hand over her heart and wailed, "I left it in the hall closet. Now I can't smoke. Maxi, give me a cigarette, please."

Max patted down his jacket. "All gone. Sorry."

Stasia moaned, near to tears.

"Stop wailing. Go and get them."

Just then Theodora came in. "Oh, hello," she said, her tone suggesting something highly improper.

Max picked up on this and threw his arm around Stasia's beefy shoulders. "Just a quickie."

Theodora, blushing, withdrew behind her own locker's door. "What's this?" She pulled out an old raincoat.

"It's mine. Thank you. You didn't steal it, did you?" Stasia said like an idiot.

"Of course not," Theodora replied, all ruffled feathers. She dropped the coat into Stasia's outstretched hands.

Max roared with delight as Theodora quickly left the room.

"I need a cigarette," Stasia said, leading the way out one door then another and up the external stairs to the patch of concrete on which they could smoke until October 11. She blew a long stream of smoke out her nose.

Glancing at the notice banning smoking, Max made a raspberry before he draped his long form against it.

"Did you notice the tension at the Staff Day?" Max asked as he inhaled one of Stasia's cigarettes.

"I notice nothing. I was late."

"I know, dear lady. I caught you with my sweet little cell." He patted his pocket. "By the way, what did you do with your coat? One minute you had it on, the next minute it was gone and now it lands in holy Theodora's locker."

"I stuff it in the front hall closet and plan to get it later, but I forget."

"How did it land in Theodora's locker?"

"A miracle?" Stasia was still worrying about being late. "Taking my picture in my coat? My God, Max. You and your funny ways will get me fired."

"Calm down. They have a lot more to worry about than one guard who is late." He couldn't resist adding, "habitually."

Stasia was staring down at something she'd fished out of her pocket.

"A cell?" Max said. "Since when have you joined the modern world?"

"It's not mine," Stasia whispered, afraid to raise her voice in case the building exterior was bugged.

"Let me see. It's a throwaway." Max took the cell and pushed a few buttons. "How did it get into your pocket?"

"I don't know. Maybe Theodora put it there."

"I doubt that. Why?"

"She'll say I stole it," she moaned. "They'll believe her and I'll be fired."

"Don't be silly. Want me to keep it for you?"

"Would you? Oh, thank you, dear Max."

"Give dear Max another cigarette and shut up about the tiresome cell." He slipped it into his jacket pocket. A crumpled piece of paper fell out.

Stasia picked it up and read aloud the one word on the paper. "Twins?"

Max snatched it out of her hand and shoved it into his pocket. "Mind your own business, Stasia." He took a deep drag and poured smoke into her face. "I'll tell you about this morning's staff day. Have you ever noticed how Monika and Phoebe hate each other?"

"I notice nothing. I work. I smoke. You owe me for Tuesday." Stasia referred to her after hours, part time work as a cleaner in what was C. E.'s apartment and now was Max's.

"What was she doing in the locker room?" Max said to himself, ignoring Stasia's remark.

"She?"

"The director, dear girl."

"It's her museum."

"She works here. She doesn't own it. I have no idea what she was up to, but I will have." He looked up from his cigarette. "What have we here?"

Elliot had stopped inside the door.

"Peek-a-boo. I see you," Max called to him.

Scowling, Elliot slunk past them.

Chapter 15

3:50 p.m. Thursday, September 7

Steve was listening, he hoped for the last time, to Kenny discussing all the Lemrow security details.

Steve's cell rang. He checked the caller: Dominique Leguizamo – known to all as Dom. She was once his partner, now one of the homicide squad's chiefs. He was swept with a Kenny-like chagrin. Their last case together had been a complete failure.

"You know a Phoebe Chen?"

"Yeah." Steve also knew Dom wouldn't be taking a telephone poll.

"She's dying. Maybe she's dead." Dom put her hand over the cell, automatic with people outside the loop like Steve. He heard her mumble something; then she was back on the line. "Still alive. Hit and run. She had your card and she said your name."

"Christ. Anything else?"

"We can't figure it out. Get over to Lenox Hill Emergency."

Steve shoved his cell into his pocket. "Gotta go."

Within minutes, Steve was in the emergency room. Although he didn't recognize the two patrolmen standing at the entrance, they were expecting him and directed him to Phoebe's cubicle.

Lieutenant Dominique Leguizamo was talking to a doctor who was half in, half out the drawn curtains. The doctor disappeared behind the curtains.

"She's rich, her family's rich?" Dom said, when she saw Steve. "How do you know her?"

"Her uncle is a Hong Kong businessman. He's lending the Lemrow some statues." Steve thought of Chen getting on a plane that moment. "Notify him?"

"No."

"He's leaving from Kennedy. Get him."

Dom issued orders to a sergeant. Then she said to Steve, "Go on."

"Phoebe works at the museum. She was going with him to the airport. What happened?"

"Hit and run, 15:05, 72nd Street and Fifth. A civilian took these." She showed him some shots of a silvery blue Lexus as well as a shot of a small ring of people surrounding the emergency van rear. On a stretcher, Phoebe was being lifted into the van.

The doctor stuck his head out of the curtains. "He can see her for a few minutes."

Steve entered the small cubicle and looked down at Phoebe whose head was bandaged. Her slender hand lay on top of the white top sheet.

Her eyes opened and she attempted a smile. Steve noticed a thin rim of blood.

"Detective Kulchek," she mouthed.

"Phoebe."

She opened her mouth wider and raised her hand.

He stared at her, willing her to speak.

"C. E." She forced a thin whisper. Her head fell sideways on the pillow.

"Leave, Detective," a nurse said behind him.

He backed out of the cubicle into Dom, who repeated, "See E? What's she talking about?"

"C. E. are the initials of Charles Edward Stowbridge, a retired curator at the Lemrow. He died a few days ago. Heart attack."

"Steve?" someone roared. Harry Ross had stepped out of the ER's waiting room. A patrolman escorted him back into the room. This was followed by a sharp rapping on the waiting room window. The detectives turned and stared into Harry Ross's bewildered and angry face.

"Who's he?" Dom said.

"Harry Ross, head of the Lemrow's board. How did he find out?"

Dom turned her back on Harry. "Spare me the important ones."

Steve watched Harry spread his arms across the glass like a giant octopus. Behind him, Monika walked into the waiting room, hugging herself. In her jogging pants and t-shirt with her glasses sliding down her nose, she looked like a miserable thirteen year old.

"Know her?" Dom tilted her head toward the director who sat down on the edge of a battered plastic chair.

"Monika Syka, the Lemrow director. You call her?" Steve said.

"No."

"Who notified them?" Steve motioned toward Harry who was bent over Monika.

The nurse poked her head out of the curtain. "Who's in charge here?"

"I am," Steve and Dom said together.

"Well?" the nurse said.

"I am," Dom said.

The nurse lowered her voice. "She died two minutes ago."

"Shit," Steve said. "Her uncle didn't get here in time."

Dom got on her cell. "King, listen. I want you to work this." For old times sake, she threw Steve a dirty look.

He headed for the exit.

"Get back here," she said.

Steve forced himself to turn around.

"You talk to her uncle. He'll be here soon. He's at Seventieth and Lex," Dom hissed before talking into her cell.

Harry was banging on the waiting room window.

Dom frowned at him. "Stop that clown."

A patrolman went into the soundproof waiting room. Steve watched him telling Harry to calm down or leave. Behind him, Monika sat with her head in her hands.

A few minutes later, Wellington Chen, flanked by his security men, walked into the emergency room. The minute he saw Steve, he rushed up to him. "Where is she?"

"In there." Steve motioned toward the cubicle. "Wellington, wait." Steve looked into his face. "She died a few minutes ago."

Wellington staggered. One of his handlers put his hand under his elbow.

"Died? My Phoebe?"

He pulled out a handkerchief and wiped his face.

"Wellington," Harry mouthed behind the soundproofed glass.

After a quick glance at the waiting room, Wellington looked back at Steve. "How? What happened?"

"A hit and run."

Wellington stared at the cubicle. "Stay here," he said, addressing his security without looking at them. He stood in front of the cubicle, straightened his shoulders and then disappeared behind the curtains. Seconds later, they heard him sobbing.

Steve thought, he told me to keep an eye on her. I failed. Dom stared at him. He assumed she was reading his thoughts.

Dom tilted her head toward an alcove. He followed her. "Hit and run?" she said with the old intimacy from before he'd screwed up the homicide case.

"Phoebe was baiting someone," Steve said.

"Who? Why?"

"She was obsessed with C. E."

"C. E.?" Dom said. She answered her own question. "The retired Lemrow curator?"

"He was Phoebe's godfather and Wellington's oldest friend." Steve jerked his head in the direction of Phoebe's cubicle. "C. E. told Phoebe there was something illegal going on at the Lemrow. He wanted to talk to Phoebe about it, but he died before he could. Heart attack."

"When was this?"

"Four days ago, last Sunday."

"This Phoebe talked to you? Why do I bother to ask." Dom curled her lip.

"She talked to everybody. Maybe that's why she's dead."

"Aren't you in provenance?" Dom needled him.

The curtains opened. Wellington stood in the parting. His sad, tough gaze froze the group before him. He studied it, searching for someone, going from the security men, to the patrolmen, past Harry and the director until he found Steve and Dom.

"Steve?" Wellington said before turning and pulling closed the curtains. He walked over to the two detectives.

"Wellington Chen, this is Lieutenant Dom Leguizamo," Steve said.

"I head up the investigation, Mr. Chen." Dom stuck out her hand.

Chen shook her hand and studied her face. "What happened?"

"Hit and run, 3:05 p.m., 72nd Street and Fifth. What was she doing there?" Dom asked.

"Returning to the Lemrow. She'd accompanied me to the helicopter port." Guessing their next question, he said. "The one on Thirty-fourth Street."

"Know those people in the waiting room?" Dom asked without turning around.

Chen looked over her shoulder. "Harry Ross? Monika Syka? Yes, of course, I know them." Wellington moved toward the ER waiting room. "Monika and I go way back. I'll speak to her."

"In a minute." Dom stopped him.

"You and Phoebe had lunch, right?" Steve said.

Wellington nodded. "She went on about C. E. Can there be any connection? I have to speak to Monika."

Dom said something to a patrolman. Two minutes later he escorted Monika to them. As she walked toward them, Steve thought she was in a trance – Prozac? Would he have recognized the classy, sexy, wry director if he'd seen this blank face in the street?

"Monika," Wellington said in an old man's voice. He stepped toward her.

"Is Phoebe conscious?" Monika said. She put one foot in front of the other, lost her balance and fell forward. Steve thought fast and grabbed her before she fell onto Wellington.

Monika cradled her head against his right shoulder and looked up at him. "Thanks, Detective."

He held her in his arms until an ER doctor led her to an available gurney and helped her sit on it. The doctor listened to her heart through his stethoscope, and then pulled open her left eye's upper lid. "It's shock. Give her a minute." He looked across at Dom while he held her right wrist, taking her pulse.

Dom moved toward the gurney. Steve and Wellington stayed where they were. Both aware that they were blocking the hospital staff and their patients, they made it worse by jumping back and forth instead of standing still.

Dom said to the doctor, "Can I speak to her now?" He nodded. "Ms. Syka, I'm Lieutenant Leguizamo. How you doin'?"

"Is Phoebe... How is Phoebe?" Monika whispered.

"She passed away," Dom said.

Monika burst into tears. She patted down the gurney as if feeling for a tissue. Steve and Wellington joined Dom.

"Monika," Wellington handed her his handkerchief.

She stared at him. "I was there, at the scene."

"You saw..." his voice quavered. "Really? Why?"

"Jogging."

"Did..." Wellington stopped speaking, gulped, then continued, "my niece say anything?"

Monika swung her head back and forth.

"Ms. Syka, you saw Phoebe?" Dom said.

Monika nodded her head in agreement.

"Did you see the vehicle that hit her?" Dom said.

Monika whispered something. Dom, Wellington and Steve leaned closer.

Monika patted the bedding around her. "Where is it?"

Frantically, she pushed herself up.

"Stay down," the doctor said.

Monika fell back.

"Is this what you want, Miss?" The patrolman had slipped into the waiting room and returned with a purse.

"Yes. Yes. Give it to me." Monika grabbed it from him and clutched it to her breast. She looked up and panted, "I'm so sorry, Wellington."

"Just tell us what you saw," he said gently.

"A crowd was gathered in front of the Lemrow." Monika hesitated as if recalling the scene. "I was returning from jogging. That's when I saw the crowd and then I saw Phoebe."

"Did she recognize you?"

"I don't think so."

"Was she conscious?"

"I don't think so."

Wellington turned to Steve. "Is this a random hit and run?"

"I don't know."

"Whatever it is, I want you working on it."

"I didn't do a good job protecting her."

Out of the corner of his eye, he caught Dom glaring at him.

"Neither did I." Wellington looked at Monika. "I'm sorry about doing this to you, Monika."

"I feel responsible. Phoebe was so young." Color was returning to her cheeks.

Steve was watching Monika, who was hunched over her purse. "Missing something?"

She looked up at him and smiled. The director's gloss was overlaying the frightened girl of a few minutes ago. "My keys. I'm always leaving them somewhere."

"Find them?'"

"Yes."

"Good," he said, not believing she was looking for them.

A young patrolman came into the ER and looked around.

"What have you got?" Dom addressed the cop.

"We found the vehicle."

Before going on, Dom turned to Wellington, "Wait in the waiting room. We have to talk to you. Is there a relative or a friend we can call for you?"

"Monika, will you wait with me?" Wellington said.

"Of course, dear Wellington." She slid off the gurney, held onto it to steady herself, then took his hand and led him into the waiting room.

Wellington walked mechanically, too upset to say anything.

"Where did you find the vehicle?" Dom said to the patrolman.

"Tavern on the Green's parking lot."

"What's the DMV got?"

"Belongs to Elliot Ross."

"Elliot Ross? Who's he?" Dom looked at Steve.

"His son," Steve swung around and looked at the waiting room." It was empty. He eyed the policeman on duty. "Where's Harry? In the can?"

The cop shook his head. "He was texting then he left."

"He left?" Dom's voice rose. "When?"

"A few minutes ago."

Dom took out her cell. "I want Elliot Ross and Harry Ross in my office."

Ten minutes later Steve, Dom and Wellington huddled on the scratched plastic chairs in the soundproofed waiting room. A patrolman sat apart, recording their conversation. Outside, Wellington's handlers stood with their backs to the waiting room, shielding their boss from public view.

"We have to talk to you now. Time is everything," Dom said. "Tell us whatever you're thinking, feeling."

"I hope it was a random hit and run," Wellington said.

Dom nodded.

"I can't bear the thought of my Phoebe having any enemies. Who would kill her?"

The raw pain in his voice prompted Steve to say, "Want something?"

Wellington looked confused. "I want my Phoebe."

"Tranquillizers?"

"No, nothing."

Steve leaned over to the water cooler, shot a squirt into a cone shaped cup and handed it to Wellington who drank it obediently.

"We're pretty sure it wasn't a random hit and run. We found the car and we're checking it out."

"How can I help?"

"Listen, Wellington, you told me she was involved with some guy. Was that in the States or Hong Kong?"

"No idea." Wellington reached into his pocket. Then pulled his hand out, empty.

Dom thought he was looking for his handkerchief. She grabbed some tissues from a nearby container and handed them to him. He used them to mop his brow and blow his nose.

The two detectives realized he was thawing, coming out of deep shock and going into indescribable pain.

"Who benefits from her death?" Dom said.

Wellington gulped, but the businessman's voice emerged, "Elliot Ross and Phoebe..." His voice broke. He took a deep breath. "They had a joint bank account so he gets that, I assume."

"What about the condo?"

"I bought that for Phoebe."

"Were they going through with the wedding?"

"Ever since C. E.'s death Phoebe hasn't been herself. She was cooling toward Elliot."

"What do you think of him?"

They watched him closely.

"He seemed okay. I thought his father was more interested in the marriage than Phoebe and Elliot." He surprised them by laughing. "Detectives, I've been married three times. I'm a failure at marriage."

"What about Harry Ross?"

"He's a businessman. He thought an alliance would strengthen our business connections."

"Would it?"

Wellington thought a moment. "He's in debt. If they'd married, I'd have thrown him a bone."

"Did Phoebe have a will?" Steve said.

"Yes. I insisted that she meet with our Hong Kong lawyers about nine months ago. I brought the will up today, but she closed down." Wellington took a deep breath, trying to hold in all the suffering. "All she talked about was C. E. She went on and on." Then, he sobbed, "We had lunch today and now this."

"You understand, Mr. Chen, we're looking for motive," Dom said.

"Of course. Phoebe meant more to Elliot alive than dead."

"If she went through with the wedding," Steve said.

Wellington was ventilating. Dom and Steve sat in silence for a few moments.

"Thank you." Wellington patted his wet brow with a wad of tissues.

"Listen, we have to ask you a favor. A big one," Steve said. "Don't remove the exhibit, okay?"

"Exhibit?" He thought a moment. "Oh, that. Why?"

"It might help us find the perp."

"Keep the killer in the net," Dom added.

"I don't understand what you're talking about, but the exhibit doesn't mean anything to me now."

"Let it remain intact until we solve this," Steve said.

"Mr. Chen, you understand that this interview is strictly confidential?" Dom added.

Steve thought Dom sounded like a jerk, telling Chen to keep his mouth shut.

"Here." Steve scribbled something on a piece of paper. "That's my private number. Call me any time. And remember we're counting on you to find that guy Phoebe was seeing."

Ten minutes later, Steve stepped outside the ER and called his daughter. "You okay?"'

"Fine, Pop. How are you?"

"Okay, darling."

"You okay, Pop? You're not hurt or anything?" For the first time in recent memory, she didn't give him a hard time about his smoking.

"Of course not. Can't I call you up to see how you are?"

"Now you sound more like yourself. I'm glad."

"Glad?" Steve said.

"Not glad. Relieved. At least, Art and whatever it's called isn't dangerous."

More and more Jessie was sounding like her mother, Steve's ex-wife. He didn't say danger was the whole point. At least you knew you were alive as long as you weren't dead.

Chapter 16

7:20 p.m. Thursday, September 7

Steve stood in Dom's corner office, one of the
showpieces of the new precinct. While he had been
going down hill, his ex-partner had been climbing
the professional ladder with a sherpa's skill. Latest
evidence was the corner office and her nameplate
on the door, Lieutenant Dominique Leguizamo.

The office was neat like Dom. Papers were
stacked in the in and out wired trays, artifacts from
the old building. The shades were evenly drawn
across the three windows. Dom's computer was
exactly at a right angle to her desk, which was
facing the squad room. A digital clock placed at eye
level from the Dell laptop clicked 19:20. On a
bulletin board that covered the entire right wall a
city map and various reports were pinned with
precision.

Dom would have made a great surgeon, Steve
figured, if she remembered the anesthesia, but

compared to Dick Holbrook she was a warm, cuddly Pomeranian.

At the moment Holbrook was pounding on Dom's desk and turning red in the face. He kept hitching his trousers he hadn't had altered after his recent weight loss. Steve would have laughed if he weren't terrified of being permanently assigned to Art Provenance.

"He was at that museum, thanks to you," Dom said. "Listen, I know you're right, Dick, but when he keeps his fly zipped, he's a good investigator. People talk to him."

What am I, a potted plant? Steve thought, but he kept his mouth shut.

"It's on you," Holbrook wagged a finger at Dom. "He fucks up and it's your career as well as his. Got it?"

"Got it."

His right hand clutching his belt and his left hand's index finger still in Dom's face, he lowered his voice, "Only this case."

"Get your finger out of my face."

"You're crazy," Holbrook backed out of the office.

"Close the door," Dom said.

After a final glare, Holbrook slammed it shut.

Dom took a deep breath and gave Steve a beady look. "He's right."

"I'm honored," Steve said, half meaning it.

"I'm not," Dom said. "Wellington Chen got his way."

Steve smiled to goad her.

"Tell me about this Lemrow Museum," Dom said. "No. Tell me about Monika Syka."

"She's the director."

"Keep it zipped, Steve."

Steve hated Dom when she guessed his thoughts. He also hated her for not minding her own business. Imagine, a man telling a female subordinate to keep her pants on. Internal Affairs would have a field day.

"I saw you looking at her. I mean it. Last chance."

"Now you're a nun?" That was a dig at Dom's preference for the younger female recruits.

"Now I'm a lieutenant." She leaned forward and said in a different tone, "Calculated?" The old partner, Dom, was speaking.

Steve raised his eyebrows, at first not getting her meaning. Then, he said, "You mean Monika Syka's dizzy spell in the ER?"

"Nice catch."

"Maybe." He thought it over. "She was appointed head of the Lemrow six months ago."

"Looks young. How old is she?"

"Forty-one. The guy who died, Charles E. Stowbridge, pushed for her appointment."

"He died of a heart attack Sunday night?"

Steve nodded. "According to the director, he stole a statue."

"Yeah?"

"They're pretending he was appraising it."

"So?"

"So maybe he had a fatal heart attack because he was fat and stressed out from stealing," Steve said. "The statue was found on him."

"Who found him?"

"His boy friend, Yoshi."

"Yoshi? Why don't these guys have normal names?"

She made a church steeple with her long, strong fingers. "What's his story?"

"This guy, Yoshi, called in to ES at nineteen hours and thirty-three minutes," Steve said, quoting from the Emergency Services report. Among themselves the squad used military time.

"They lived together?" Dom said.

"For twenty-five years."

"Listen to the tape?"

"Yeah. Hysterical."

"What's your take on Yoshi?"

"I met him once – at the Opening."

"Opening?" Dom made the word sound dirty.

"The Chen exhibit opening. Yoshi was knocked out by C. E.'s death. Jeez, they were together twenty-five years."

Dom raised her eyebrows. "Who inherits?"

"C. E.'s twin brother, Max, gets the apartment. Yoshi gets the money. It's still in probate. She's a twin," Steve said.

"What?"

"Monika Syka is a twin. Max told me that they all come from Scranton. That's where C. E. Stowbridge first met Monika. Two sets of twins. Two of them dead."

Dom digested this. "How much did C. E. leave?"

"About two mil. Max was resigned but pissed about inheriting only the apartment."

"Amazing what provenance includes these days."

"Ain't it? Yoshi's in Tokyo. His mother's dying. I don't think he's coming back except for C. E.'s memorial."

"We have one guy dead from a heart attack, one suicide on the premises and one hit and run - maybe a vehicular homicide," Dom said. "All three are associated with the Lemrow."

"Hey…" Steve extended his right hand as a good-looking young black man walked into the room.

King gave Steve a glacial glance, remembering the balls up Steve had made on the murder-felony case they worked together. Steve had trained him. He caught his eye. King looked straight through him.

King's disdain seared Steve. Because of Steve's lack of judgment, his apprentice -- their joke term -- scorned him.

Then, King thawed.

"Glad you're back." A grin cut across the guy's face as he shook Steve's hand.

"Don't get too excited, King. You're taking the media crap." Dom said. "Where's Harry Ross and his son?"

"Coming up now," King said.

Dom's cell phone buzzed. "Leguizamo." She listened. "No shit." Then hung up. "Well, well, well. A world record. That was the M. E."

Steve and King looked at Dom as if she were stoned.

"The vic isn't dead four hours and we have a report."

Steve and King slapped high fives.

Dom gave a rare smile. "Jesus, this Wellington makes things happen. Phoebe was pregnant. Six weeks." She sat in thought. "Okay. King, keep them out there until I signal you. Set up for a tech to be waiting with a swab. Then, King, Check out Cristobel Gregersen."

"Do I tell her about Phoebe being pregnant?"

Dom thought a moment. "Not yet."

As he left, King gave Steve a thumbs up.

"Fill me in on Harry and his son." She looked at Steve.

"Harry's on the Lemrow's board. Had a business deal with Wellington Chen. He pushed for his son to marry Phoebe Chen."

"Would he kill her?"

"Harry? Why?" Steve shrugged his shoulders. "Phoebe's worth more to him alive."

"The son? What's his name?" She looked down at her desk. "I see. It's Elliot."

"Elliot was Phoebe's fiancé, but I heard her and Harry quarreling about it," Steve said. "Harry wanted it more than the kids."

Dom looked out at the cesspool, the nick name for the criminal investigation room in which most of the detectives had groups of desks.

Steve watched Harry pacing back and forth, glaring at anyone who made eye contact.

"Nervous little guy, isn't he?" Dom said. "We're all set?" She meant audio and video stuff was set up and working.

In the adjacent room facing Dom's office, standing with his arms folded and looking very anxious was a taller, younger version of Harry, obviously Elliot Ross. A third man with a brief case and a professional look stood next to Elliot.

Dom motioned to King who escorted the three men into the room, handed Dom a folder and then left. Steve perched on a high stool in a corner of the room. Knowing someone was sitting behind them made people nice and nervous.

"Lieutenant Dom Leguizamo." She stood up and extended her hand across her desk. Steve had noticed how she always said her title to disabuse any warm and furry notions, like first name stuff.

"I'm Harry Ross. This is my son, Elliot. And our lawyer, Saul Ackerman."

After the hand shaking was done, the men looked over at Steve. Steve nodded, feeling right at home making witnesses edgy. He noticed that Elliot's thick hair was combed and he'd shaved. He'd probably been coached by the lawyer to look respectable. True to his age group, he had his backpack slung over one shoulder and he was wearing his Nikes without socks.

Then, the men looked back at Dom.

"Grab a chair, gentlemen," the gracious one instructed.

Obediently each man unfolded a chair from a stack against the wall and faced Dom.

Harry half turned in his chair. "What are you doing here, Steve?"

"Detective Kulchek is helping us with the investigation." Dom opened the folder King had handed her. "Elliot Ross, are you the owner of a blue Lexus, New York state license plate MOMZER?"

Elliot looked at their lawyer who nodded his assent.

"Yeah."

Dom picked up a copy of Elliot's license and examined it.

"Elliot, your car was photographed at a hit and run scene. Tell me about that."

Elliot was going from pale to paler.

"Tell her everything," Harry said like a stage mother.

"There's nothing to tell, Dad."

"My client wasn't driving his Lexus at Seventy-second Street and Fifth Avenue at 3:05 p.m." Saul Ackerman said.

"Who was?" Dom said.

"Tell her." This time Saul said it through gritted teeth.

After a long and deep sigh, Elliot said, "I lent the keys to Cristobel Gregersen."

"Elliot, where were you?"

"Having lunch with me," Harry said.

"Where were you, Elliot?"

Dom's ignoring his old man did wonders for Elliot. He sat up straight and his color returned. "Me and dad grabbed some stuff from a burger shack."

"Where?"

"In the Park, 68th Street near that statue of what's-her-name."

"Alice in Wonderland," the lawyer said.

"Anybody recognize you?"

Elliot looked at his father and then at the lawyer.

Dom was expecting an explosive affirmative from Harry. Instead, his eyes edged sideways toward the lawyer. "My client was there, Detective." The lawyer placed his brief case on his knee, opened it, pulled out a folder, rifled through some papers and then handed Dom a copy of a credit card receipt.

Very obviously, Dom glanced back at Steve. The three men followed suit.

"So Cristobel Gregersen had your keys? Why?" Dom brought their faces around to her.

"She had an appointment," Elliot said.

"What appointment?" Dom said.

"I don't want to say."

"You better. This is a murder investigation."

"She had an appointment at Sarah Lawrence in Bronxville. It's a college."

"And?"

"A job interview. She was fed up at the Lemrow, but she didn't want anybody to know."

"Mr. Ross." Dom directed a gimlet eye at Harry, "why were you in Lenox Hill Hospital's ER's waiting room?"

Harry ran his right hand down his tie. His expression registered the shock of the preceding hours. "Monika Syka called me. She was hysterical. I told her I'd meet her in the ER."

"You left the ER waiting room in a hurry," Dom continued. "Why?"

"My son texted me. I had to get to him."

"Elliot, where were you when you texted your dad?"

Elliot looked at the lawyer who nodded. "Seventy-second Street and Fifth Avenue."

"What time was this?"

"About 3:15."

"At about two p.m. you and your dad had lunch and you walked out of the park. What did you do then?" She looked at Elliot.

"I waited on the curb for Phoebe."

"Did you see her being hit?"

Elliot waved his head up and down. "She jaywalked across the street. Then my Lexus came out of 73rd Street."

The room was silent.

Elliot put his big, puppy hands over his face. He sobbed. Harry put his right hand on his son's back.

"Did she see the car?" It was the first time Steve spoke. The three men turned and looked at him.

"Come on, Elliot," Dom said.

Elliot took his hands away from his face. He rubbed his nose on the back of his right hand, took a deep breath and thought a moment. "Yeah."

Dom and Steve waited, sensing Elliot was holding back.

"Describe what you saw," Steve said.

Harry started to speak.

Elliot looked up.

"Shut up, Dad. Phoebe was walking across the street. She was looking down at her purse like she was searching for something. The Lexus accelerated. She must have heard it because she looked up. I thought it was swerving to miss her, but the driver aimed at her. Phoebe was clipped."

Steve recalled there hadn't been any skid marks indicating the driver hadn't slammed on the brakes.

"Clipped?" Dom said.

"Yeah."

Once again, Dom sensed Elliot was holding back.

"Who clipped her?" Dom said.

"No idea. I saw it from behind."

"Which side clipped her?"

"The passenger's side."

"Go on."

"The driver accelerated."

Dom looked at Elliot but she didn't say anything. Finally, she said, "You're standing at Seventy-second Street?"

Elliot nodded.

Dom looked at Harry. "Where were you?"

"I was walking in the park. Near the pond."

"Busy man like you, walking in the park?"

"I had a lot to think about."

"How did you find out about Phoebe being hit?" Dom said to Harry.

"I told you. Monika called me. I went straight to the Lenox Hill ER."

"You were in the waiting room alone?"

"At first. Then Monika came in." Harry turned in Steve's direction. "Right, Steve?"

"Right, Harry."

"What clipped Phoebe?" Dom said to Elliot.

"The passenger's side of my Lexus. She stumbled into the mirror."

"The side mirror smacked Phoebe in the head. It was knocked off," Dom said. "The mirror killed Phoebe. We haven't found it – yet."

"The Lexus' side mirror comes off on impact?" Steve said and answered his own question, "Because the driver was going fast."

The three men swiveled in their chairs and stared at Steve.

Steve remembered that Elliot had had an accident because he'd been on drugs.

"Go on," Steve said.

Careful Steve, Dom texted him.

Elliot glanced at his lawyer but kept his mouth shut.

"I can text the DMV right now," Steve said.

"My client had smoked an illegal substance. He was in rehab for six weeks. Clean as a whistle since then."

Steve was thinking that Harry and Holbrook knew each other. Ignoring Dom's glare, he said,

"So that's how you and your dad met Captain Holbrook?"

"He's the head of that task force," Harry said. From his tone it was obvious he didn't know where the interview was going.

"The drug one?" Steve said. Our Harry meets Holbrook after sonny is caught with some pot or something else and makes a donation to Holbrook's cause.

"Anti-drug one," the lawyer corrected. "What does this have to do with Phoebe's death?"

"Let me get this straight." Dom's fingers resumed their steeple formation. "You lent your keys to Cristobel and she ran over Phoebe."

"No," Elliot shouted. He sat, paralyzed. Then he shouted, "Cristobel texted me. She lost the keys."

Dom's long right hand stretched across the desk. "Let me see the cell."

Her other hand was rooting around in her top drawer for something. She pulled out what looked like a plastic bag. "Put the cell in here."

"Why?" Elliot said. He clutched his backpack.

"It's evidence. Forensics will take a look at it. You'll get it back. I'll even give you a receipt."

"Do it," the lawyer said to Elliot.

Elliot hesitated.

"Do it," the lawyer repeated.

"There's stuff. Personal stuff," Elliot said.

"We've seen and heard everything. Prefer prison?" Dom said.

Steve had a flashback to the photographer's photos. Did he kill himself because they were found? He thought how easily embarrassed young people are – like his daughter.

Elliot pulled the cell out of a small pocket on the backpack and dropped it into the bag.

Dom addressed Harry. "I want yours, too."

"Why?"

"Coordinate times."

Harry and the lawyer exchanged looks. Then he slid his cell across the table.

"Let me get this straight," Dom said. "Between two-thirty and three you and your dad were eating lunch at the 68th St. Shack. Who had your car?"

Silence.

"Cristobel Gregersen?"

Elliot shook his head back and forth.

"Tell me about Phoebe."

Elliot's chin sunk on his chest.

"She was only my son's fiancée," Harry snarled.

Ignoring Harry, Dom said, "Elliot, why didn't you go with Phoebe in the ambulance?"

"The cops were questioning me. Nobody could leave."

"After they let you go, why didn't you go to the ER?"

"Dad called me. He told me…" Elliot gulped, "that she'd passed on."

Dom waited.

"I didn't want to see her dead."

"Elliot, tell me about her."

Once again Elliot's eyes slid in the direction of the lawyer who nodded his head.

Elliot cleared his throat. "I'm not used to talking about her. She was strong." His tone suggested this wasn't a virtue.

"Intimidating?" Dom asked.

"Had a temper. Used to getting her own way. That doesn't mean I ran over her."

He leaned forward and put his head in his hands. The room was quiet except for his embarrassed sobs.

"Did you want to marry her?" Dom said in a soft, steely tone.

"Yeah. I guess." He didn't look up.

"Prenup?"

"I don't see what this has to do…" Harry said.

"Elliot, look at me," Dom said.

He looked up. The lawyer handed him a white handkerchief. "Prenup?"

"Yeah," he said, blowing his nose.

"Your idea or hers?"

"We both thought of it."

Harry smiled at his son's brilliant answer.

"Who has more money, you or Phoebe?"

"Detective, I don't see the relevance of this line of questioning," Saul Ackerman said.

"Never heard of money as a motive? There is one other thing. Elliot, we'll need a sample of your DNA."

"What?" Harry screamed as if bitten.

"Calm down, Mr. Ross. Standard procedure."

"Detective, my client …" the lawyer began.

"Phoebe Chen was pregnant," Dom said. "Just have to check it out. Take a few minutes."

The three men didn't look at each other.

"Can I talk to my client?" the lawyer said.

"Of course." Dom and Steve stepped out of the room. Then turned around and watched the three men. Dom noticed that the lawyer didn't have much to say to Elliot. Instead, he and Harry were in a huddle.

"You're all set, right?" Dom said to the tech guy who was going to take Elliot's DNA as the lawyer opened the door.

"Well?" Dom said.

"All right," the lawyer said.

Later, Steve called Con, his uncle, from his Stuyvesant Town apartment. "Still in touch with your old buddies?"

"Why?"

"Check out Holbrook Junior, his connection with that anti-drug task force and his connection with Harry Ross."

"Why can't you do it?" Con said.

"I can't go near any other case."

Chapter 17

10:15 p.m. Thursday, September 7

A half hour later, Dom stood in front of a large bulletin board at the north end of the cesspool. The only decoration was the stenciled words on a nearby wall: WHO ARE THEY? WHERE ARE THEY? HAVE THEY BEEN ARRESTED?

Her team of Steve, Rosaria and King, as well as the Reliables, detectives pulled off other cases, were sitting on chairs and desks or leaning against a nearby wall. Not one of them was slouching. They were full of energy, all of them night owls ready for the hunt.

On the left side of the bulletin board were photos of Phoebe, CE, and Geoff. Next to them was a blow up of Central Park and Fifth Avenue between Sixty-fifth Street and Eighty-sixth Street. The map was dotted with different colored thumbtacks. On the right side of the map were photos of Elliot, Cristobel, Harry, Monika Syka, Elliot's Lexus, and a rear view mirror.

"Listen up," Dom yelled over the office chatter. "Phoebe Chen gets top priority. Forget vacation, sick leave, weekends." She tapped Phoebe's picture. "Steve Kulchek will fill us in."

She was interrupted by hoots. Someone shouted, "Mr. Antiques Roadshow." Steve bowed gravely.

Snickering Dick Holbrook came out of his office followed by his lackey, Shaun Roberts, and stood at the back of the room. Both men were formally dressed. Holbrook had on a well-cut suit that emphasized his weight loss. In his lapel was a sprig of drooping honeysuckle.

Shaun Roberts pointed at Holbrook. "Some guys never learn."

Holbrook made a playful punch at Shaun.

"He tied the knot five hours ago," Shaun said, "but his wife gave him permission to come to this meeting."

The Reliables guffawed and applauded. Some clown shouted, "She knows cops."

Holbrook folded his hands over his tailored jacket and smirked at Steve.

So Carmen had married him. Steve kept his face passive. The last thing he wanted was these sharks tearing at him in front of Holbrook. He recalled Harry saying Holbrook was putting his head in the noose and Yoshi examining a ring on Carmen's finger. So Harry Ross had known Carmen and Holbrook were engaged. How many other people knew, he wondered. His cheeks were a dull red under his one-day stubble.

"Congratulations, Holbrook," Dom said. "The rest of you shut up and listen."

"Phoebe Chen," Steve pointed to her photo, "was hit by a Lexus SC10 at 15:05 today at Seventy-second Street and Fifth." Steve touched a thumbtack that indicated Seventy-second Street and Fifth. "She was six weeks pregnant."

"We'll let you know about the DNA results ASAP," he said, reading the squad's mind.

Steve moved to the left side of the bulletin board covered with crime scene photos of the hit and run.

"The Lexus." He pointed to a shot of the car's passenger's side. The tinted windows hid the interior. The rearview mirror was missing. "That's what hit Phoebe Chen."

Moving his index finger on a line of red thumbtacks, he followed the Lexus route from Seventy-fifth Street to Sixty-sixth Street and the Sixty-fifth Street Transverse Road and then to the Tavern on the Green parking lot.

He waited, letting the Reliables digest the route and the different photos of the car. There was a shot of its license number, taken as the Lexus accelerated toward Sixty-sixth Street and one of its passenger's side.

"Who took the Lexus' shots, Steve?" a young Reliable said.

"A civilian," Joe, the senior Reliable, answered. He had been in charge of the door-to-door interviews of the neighborhood immediately following the hit and run.

Steve, along with the rest of the team, studied the shots. "She was shooting from the Seventy-second Street north west curb."

He tapped on the official NYPD crime scene shot of Phoebe lying on the blacktop. Her full skirt was spread around her like a golden petal. A numerical evidence marker dwarfed a tiny slipper that had been knocked off her right foot. Another marker was next to a pair of Ray-Bans.

Then he pointed to a grainy shot of somebody's Nikes standing on the edge of the sidewalk, above two objects near the curb. "Taken by the same civilian. It's the rear view mirror and Phoebe's purse. Both are missing."

"I can't believe a Lexus mirror would fall off like that," Joe said.

"Holbrook, you drive a Lexus, right?" Steve raised his voice to make sure everyone heard. "You think a rear view mirror comes off like that?"

Caught off guard, Holbrook produced a strained laugh.

"Elliot had an accident three months ago. Smashed the passenger's side into a tree," Dom said.

Everyone stared at the photo of two scuffed running shoes on the curb and directly beneath them a tiny purse and a smashed rear view mirror.

"Elliot admitted he was waiting for Phoebe at 15:05 at Seventy-second Street and Fifth," Dom said.

"So where are the purse and mirror?" a detective said.

"Gone. Maybe he panicked," Steve said.

"There are thousands of Nikes all over Manhattan," Dom said. She raised her right foot to show her own Nikes. The other detectives looked down at their feet.

Steve pointed at the photo. There was a Chinese character tattooed over the right ankle. "Elliot has one over his right ankle," he said. "During the interview, I noticed it."

He moved to the next photo: spectators and cops gathered around the EMS ambulance. A crowd was standing in a semicircle on one side of the familiar yellow tape. "Daily News shot. This is Monika Syka, the Lemrow's director." He tapped the shot and then pointed to Monika's photo on the other bulletin board.

"What's that, Steve?" A young detective indicated something next to the director.

"Her duffel bag. King?"

King flipped open his notebook. "I questioned her about that. She'd been jogging around the reservoir."

"With a duffel bag?" the detective asked.

"She claims she had water, a comb, stuff in there in case she needed them. She hid it behind a tree. Said everybody did it. Anyway, there was nothing valuable." They all stared at the grainy group photo. Something hanging out of the duffel bag was circled.

"What's that?"

"The sleeve of her jacket."

"See it?"

King nodded. "She showed me a jacket."

"No more shots of the car?"

"That's it." Steve tapped.

Dom took over. "You guys report to me: Rosaria, King and Steve."

"These two," she pointed to the photo of C. E. "This guy was a retired curator at the Lemrow who died of a heart attack on September third. He told Phoebe that there was some illegal activity at the Lemrow. He wanted to talk about it, but she canceled their dinner date. He died that night."

Dom poked at Geoff's photo. "This guy killed himself at the Lemrow a day later."

Dom pointed to Cristobel's photo. "Elliot Ross lent her his car keys. They both claim someone took the keys and she didn't drive the Lexus. She was Elliot's girlfriend before Phoebe. She works at the museum and was bitter about Phoebe getting a fellowship and her boyfriend. Devastated by the death of her friend, Geoff, the photographer."

"What happened with the warrant for Cristobel's apartment?" Dom said to Rosaria, a heavy-set woman who pushed herself away from the wall and put her hands on her hips. Rosaria was the detective who broke bad news to Dom, the one the old timers griped to and the one, if they didn't know any better, the ambitious Reliables sucked up to.

"Cristobel shares an apartment with Mary Ratt…."

"Mary Ratt? What kind of name is that?" a young Reliable said.

"Until a month ago she was the Lemrow director's personal assistant. They live at 313 Third

Avenue, 4D. We found nothing, no Lexus keys.
Then we checked out the Lemrow," Rosaria said.
"Steve tipped us about the lockers. We found the
Lexus's keys in Cristobel's locker."

There was a ripple of appreciation.

"Moving on," Dom said.

"The tech guys found some glass fragments
in Elliot's locker."

Another ripple of appreciation.

"So we got a warrant for the Rosses' co-op.
And what a co-op," Rosaria rolled her eyes.
"Market value is five million."

This was greeted by some whistles.

"It's in a building on 79th Street and Fifth
owned by Trident and the major share holder in
Trident is Harry Ross."

More whistles.

"Don't get too excited. It's close to
bankruptcy."

The Reliables made smart ass sounds.

"So Harry and Elliot Ross live in a Trident
co-op," a Reliable said. "Where's Phoebe?"

"Phoebe's was down the hall. Penthouse."

"Who inherits?" someone asked.

"We checked out Phoebe's will and the
prenup. Everything goes back to the Hong Kong
trust," Rosaria said. "Elliot gets the stuff in the co-
op and what's in their joint bank account. A very
juicy second prize."

The other detectives were listening like
second graders to a great fairy tale.

"Nice," one of them said with a deep sigh. "So how does the Trident bankruptcy affect our boy, Elliot?"

"Harry's in deep financial shit," Rosaria said. "Monika Syka lives at the Trident, too. She has a co-op owned by Trident. It's a perk of the job. Very cozy," Rosaria said. "They're the only occupants of the penthouse, popping in and out of each others co-ops, borrowing sugar all day."

"Enough. Move on," Dom said, breaking the spell.

"Boss, that's what she said," Rosaria replied.

"Who?"

"Monika – well she didn't say anything about sugar, but she did say they were in and out of each other's places. And, no, we didn't find the purse or rear view mirror at Harry's and Elliot's."

There was a collective groan.

"But look at this." Rosaria reached across her desk, opened a drawer, pulled out a plastic bag and held it up. Like beagles, the detectives' heads instinctively turned at the encased running shoes and then swiveled in unison to the photo of the purse, rear view mirror and running shoes on the bulletin board.

"No shit. Elliot's?" Joe, the older detective, called out.

"Correct," Rosaria said.

"So he didn't kill her."

"Who's to say he isn't an accomplice? Maybe Dad's behind the wheel," King said.

"And the dumb kid picks up the rear view mirror to protect him?"

"And his own ass. It's his car."

"Stick to the purse. Find it," Dom said. "We want Phoebe's cell."

"Elliot and Phoebe were fighting, but there's nothing legal saying they were over," Steve said.

"Okay, so the kid, Elliot, didn't whack her – we've got that shot of him in his Nikes standing at the curb, but his father could've, right?" Joe said.

Everybody nodded in agreement.

"From fourteen and thirty to fifteen hours, Elliot and Harry were eating at the 68th Street hamburger shack," Steve said.

"Elliot then walked to the 72nd Street curb. He waited on the west side of the street. Phoebe got out of a taxi at the intersection of Seventy-third Street and Fifth and crossed the street to join him," Dom said. She placed her right hand on the map.

Her middle finger pointed to where Phoebe got out of the cab and her index finger pointed to where Elliot was standing. As Steve had demonstrated previously, Dom went through the Lexus' route.

None of the team said anything, letting the information sink in.

After a few seconds, Steve said, "Listen up. At the Lemrow Staff Day…"

"Oooooh, a Staff Day," Some smart ass said.

"They made flower arrangements." Steve, realizing he sounded like a wimp, laughed. "They took photos."

The detectives bayed, booed, hooted.

"Stevie, do me an arrangement."

"I'll arrange you in a minute. You," he pointed at the loud mouthed Reliable, "Check out financial stuff, credit cards of the Lemrow employees." He pointed to Joe, the oldest Reliable. "Check out the staff's cells for different photos." A thought struck him. "At the Staff Day Max Stowbridge…"

"C. E.'s brother?" a Reliable piped up.

"Yeah, his twin brother. Max Stowbridge was taking shots. I remember he took several of a woman entering the museum and several of Monika Syka. Check out his cell, Joe."

Rosaria raised her voice. "C. E.'s computer only had research stuff on it. He never used his cell. Geoff's cell and Canon are missing."

That got the detectives' attention. "Missing?"

"Yep." She went on. "Porn stuff was downloaded on his work computer and on his home computer. Phoebe's computer stuff is being checked out now. Find her cell," Dom repeated.

"Rosaria, get Cristobel's story. King, bring in Elliot. You," she pointed to a young Reliable, "check out Monika Syka's ex-assistant, Mary Ratt."

Dom extended the thumb on her right hand. "Number one, find Phoebe's cell." She extended her index finger. "Number two, find that purse." She extended her middle finger. "Number three, find the mirror."

Chapter 18

11:00 p.m. Thursday, September 7

Forty-five minutes later, Cristobel sat on the edge of a chair in an interview room. The harsh, overhead light blanched her fair, lightly freckled skin.

She ran her hand over the table before setting her purse on it and looked around the barren room. Although part of the new precinct, the interview rooms aged quickly and resembled one another regardless of borough.

"Like "Law and Order"?" Cristobel said.

"I charge for answering any questions about TV shows." Rosaria pulled out a chair and sat across from her.

Cristobel's grin lightened her tired and nervous expression.

"Tell me about Phoebe," Rosaria said.

"She had everything: looks, money, power. I think she even had brains."

"How did you feel about her?"

"She was from another planet." Cristobel lowered her voice and said in a dreamy tone. "Imagine, never having to worry about anything. I hated her."

"Why?"

"Because it wasn't fair. She was handed everything I worked for."

"Including your boyfriend?"

"Him, too, but the Stowbridge Fellowship was the final straw."

"Did you kill her?"

Cristobel's mouth flew open. "No, of course not."

"Tell me about Elliot's car keys."

"When I heard that Phoebe had been run over, I thought I'd be questioned."

"So answer. It's late."

"When I didn't get the Stowbridge Fellowship, I decided to go for a job interview at Sarah Lawrence and asked Elliot if I could borrow his car."

"Why ask him if he dumped you?"

Cristobel shook her head. "I don't know why."

"When did you ask him to borrow the keys?"

"Wednesday night. The minute Phoebe was awarded the fellowship, I wanted out of there."

"How did Elliot react?"

"How did he react?" Cristobel repeated. "Elliot was spoiled like Phoebe, but unlike Phoebe he wasn't much of thinker. If he could help you without too much effort, he was usually willing."

"Lending you his Lexus is generous."

"I was his girlfriend, well, his ex-girlfriend. He knew I drove well."

"Were you in the Lexus when he broke the rearview mirror?"

"You know about that? Dumb question. No, but I heard all about it –while I was playing chauffeur when his license was suspended for about two minutes."

"Let's get back to when he lent you the car keys."

"That was yesterday at Staff Day."

Rosaria remembered Steve saying that Cristobel had held up the keys and jangled them.

"Then what happened?"

"I don't know. One minute they were in my purse and the next minute they were gone."

"That purse?"

Cristobel looked down at the cute little embroidered thing on the table. 'Yeah."

"Can I see it?"

Cristobel hesitated a moment before she handed it to Rosaria.

"Okay if I look inside?"

"Sure."

Rosaria took a pen out of her side pocket and poked around the inside of the tiny, bulging purse. It didn't have a zipper top.

"Ever lose anything else?" She shoved the purse across to Cristobel.

"I don't lose things, usually."

"When did you notice the keys were missing?"

"About one p.m. My appointment was for 2:30."

"Where was this?"

"On Seventieth Street and Fifth. I checked in my purse. Thought I'd dropped them and walked back the same way I'd come. I didn't find them so I called Elliot."

"How did he react?"

"He was pissed off. Can't say I blame him."

"How did you react?"

"It was like a sign. I was relieved. I don't want to leave the Lemrow. So I called Sarah Lawrence and said I couldn't make the appointment."

"Who took the keys, Cristobel?"

"I don't know."

"Where was the last place you saw them?"

Cristobel thought a moment. "At the Lemrow Staff Day."

"Who could've taken them?"

Cristobel shook her head.

"Elliot lends you the keys, you put them into your purse. Correct?"

"Correct."

"You notice the keys are missing around one p.m. You call Elliot and tell him. He's pissed off. You call Sarah Lawrence and cancel the appointment."

Cristobel nodded.

"What did you do from one p.m. to three p.m.?"

"I grabbed some lunch in the cafeteria and went back to work in the reference library."

"Who did you see in the cafeteria?"

"Hilda, other people from our department."

"I want their names."

"Detective, I'm scared. You're treating me like a suspect."

"Cristobel, when and if I treat you like a suspect you'll have a lawyer present. Get this straight. You are the last person we know of to have the keys to the Lexus, *the murder weapon*. The Lexus's keys were found in your locker." Rosaria let that sink in. "I want you to think hard about who got their hands on those keys."

"I have no idea how they got into my locker. No one except Elliot knew I was borrowing them."

"Didn't you hold them up at Staff Day?"

"What are you talking about?" Cristobel said, confused.

"Someone saw you shake them after Elliot handed them to you."

Cristobel blanched. "My God. Do you have spies following me? So I jingled them. What's the big deal?"

"The big deal is that someone saw that you had the keys."

"Why not question your informer? He or she is probably the one who put them in my locker."

Since Steve was the informer, Rosaria said nothing.

"Can I say something?" Cristobel said.

Rosaria nodded.

"Why wasn't anything done about Geoff?" Cristobel's voice trembled.

"Geoff?"

"The photographer who died -- killed himself -- on Tuesday at the Lemrow. I'm being interviewed at midnight the day Phoebe died, but what about Geoff? No one cares."

"Phoebe was killed. That's murder and this is the homicide squad. Geoff committed suicide. It's different." Rosaria softened her tone. "You were close to him?"

"Very. Not sexually. Like brother and sister."

Rosaria studied the kid across the table. With her curly blond hair and freckled face smeared with eye make up Cristobel resembled a Disney version of Huck Finn. She's no kid, Rosaria said to herself.

"How old are you?"

"I'll be twenty six next week."

"So was Phoebe."

Cristobel flinched.

"What's it like living with Mary Ratt?"

"The Mouse? Crowded."

Rosaria recalled the stuffed closets when they were searching the apartment for the Lexus's keys. "Vintage clothes?"

"She's nuts about them."

"Why did Mary Ratt quit her job at the Lemrow?"

"Claims she got a fellowship. That's another reason why I wanted to leave. I can't afford the rent on my own."

"What do you mean, claims?"

"She went to a community college and works as a secretary. She's getting a fellowship?"

Rosaria, who had switched from a community college to John Jay, thought how Cristobel had absorbed the snobbishness she hated in Phoebe.

"Do you like Mary Ratt?"

"Not especially. Theodora took a snapshot of Elliot and Phoebe kissing and couldn't resist showing the Mouse. She thought it was her duty to tell me that Elliot was cheating on me."

Rosaria thought about the Lemrow old timers doing their own thing: taking indiscreet snapshots, gossiping, handing out unsolicited advice.

"How long were you and Elliot together?"

"About a year."

"A long time. What broke it up?"

"Phoebe waved her bank account in front of his little eyes."

Rosaria heard the sadness under the bitter tone.

"That's all for now," she said. "Wait. What are you doing about the apartment?"

"The Mouse is having second thoughts about the supposed fellowship."

At 12:10 a.m., King flashed his badge at the Trident doorman and said, "Elliot Ross." After he and a patrol officer arrived at the penthouse floor, King buzzed the Rosses' entrance.

When there was no answer, he called Elliot. "Hi, Elliot. Detective King. I want to speak to you."

"Why?" Elliot sounded very young and very tense.

"Where are you?" King said.

"Home."

"Let me in. I'm at your door."

"I'm at Monika's."

King looked across the hall at the two other co-ops on the floor. Phoebe's had yellow police tape across it.

The other door opened.

"Detective King, isn't it late for an interview?" Monika smiled.

"Is Elliot Ross in your apartment?"

She swung open the door. "Please, come in."

King walked into the subtly lit room with its bare windows black except for prickles of light from the mix of apartment houses and skyscrapers across Central Park. The patrol officer stood by the door.

Elliot and Harry were standing near the coffee table.

King glanced at Elliot's shoes, long enough to unnerve the younger man.

"Detective." Harry managed a weak smile. "Returning our property?"

"I'm here to ask your son a few questions." King placed his briefcase on the coffee table and clicked open the latch.

"Please sit down, Detective. Let me get you a drink," Monika said.

"Tell me about this." King ignored Monika and held up the photo of the Nikes, the purse and the rear view mirror.

Elliot dry retched.

Ignoring this, King said, "Where are the purse and the mirror?"

"You've invaded our home, taken our property, taken our cells, interrogated us…" Harry said.

"We can do this at the precinct," King said.

Harry ran his hands through his hair. "Go on," he grunted.

"Elliot, the purse and the mirror?" King held up the photo and jabbed his index finger at the two objects.

Elliot, his face covered with sweat, glanced at Monika.

"What do you know about this?" King addressed her.

"I've been encouraging Elliot to tell you anything he knows."

King caught a flash of bewilderment on Elliot's face before he resumed a guarded look.

"You know and we know these are your Nikes." King pointed to the photo.

"Who took that?" It was the first thing Elliot had said.

"A civilian. Rough, huh? You tell me what happened to the purse and the mirror or we go down to the station."

Monika nodded. Harry glared but his shoulders sagged.

Elliot blurted, "I picked up the mirror."

"The purse?" King said.

"No way."

"Where's the mirror?"

"We dumped it."

"That was my idea, Detective," Harry said.

"Where?"

"A receptacle," Harry said.

"When? What time?"

"No idea," Harry said.

"You can do better than that."

"Around six-thirty?" Elliot said.

King checked his watch. "Let's go."

"Where? I want my lawyer," Harry said.

"He can meet you at the station," King said. "We're checking every trash receptacle between here and the Lemrow."

At 1:45 a. m. King clicked on the department's recorder and video, stated the time and date, then said, "Detective King interviewing Elliot Ross. Attorney Saul Ackerman is present."

In a nearby waiting room Harry was pacing back and forth.

Dom and Steve were observing the interview through a one-way mirror, occasionally feeding suggestions to King.

"Elliot, did you pick up the rear view mirror in this photo?" King said.

Elliot, his lawyer and King studied the photo of the Nikes, purse and rear view mirror projected onto the wall.

Elliot nodded.

"Speak up," King said.

"Yeah. It's mine."

"Tell me what you did from three p.m. yesterday, September Seventh."

"Again?" Elliot gulped. He kept sneaking looks at the photo on the wall. "Me and dad ate lunch."

"What did you discuss?" This was a new question.

Elliot came out of auto-pilot and stared at King. "What does that have to do with anything?"

"Answer the question."

Elliot's face registered that he thought they were also questioning his father. King played on this. "We'll compare what you and your dad say."

"Phoebe wanted to end our engagement. She'd told me earlier in the afternoon. We – I – didn't want her to. Dad gave me advice. I texted her that we had to talk. She texted me back saying she'd fit me in." A bittersweet expression flooded Elliot's face before he continued. "She'd fit me in before a meeting and meet me at Fifth and Seventh-second Street about three."

King knew this from Elliot's I-phone.

"Where was Phoebe's meeting?"

'The Lemrow."

"Go on."

"I walked out to the curb and waited for her."

"Where?"

"West side curb, Seventy-second Street," Elliot took a deep breath. "A taxi swung out of Seventy-third Street and stopped at Seventy-second. Phoebe got out, started walking across the street. Then my Lexus came out of Seventy-third Street. You know all this," Elliot shrieked. "How many times do I have to say it?"

His lawyer put his hand on Elliot's arm.

"At what time?" King said.

"I don't know." Elliot took a deep breath. "About three?"

"Describe the scene."

"It swerved and hit Phoebe. She was sideswiped by the mirror. My car was hitting my girlfriend."

"Then what?" King said right away to keep Elliot moving along.

"Then what, what?" Elliot cried. The lawyer put his hand on Elliot's shoulder.

"What happened to Phoebe?"

"She didn't see the Lexus coming toward her. She was jay walking across to me. She was hit by my car and went down."

"What about the car?"

"I've already said this, man." Elliot was rocking on his uncomfortable chair.

"Say it again."

"The driver swerved to hit her. Then accelerated down Fifth and turned west on Sixty-sixth Street."

"Tell me about the purse." King swung his pointer toward the wall and highlighted the image of the tiny canary purse lying by the smashed rear view mirror.

"I told you," Elliot cried. "I don't know anything about it."

"Tell me about the mirror."

"I told you. I panicked." Elliot ran his hands through his hair.

"What did you do with the mirror?"

"I shoved it into my backpack."

"Go on."

"The cops were talking to me. I told them I was her fiancé."

"But you didn't go to Lenox Hill."

"No, I didn't."

"Why?"

"I didn't want to see her...." he gulped, "like that."

"Maybe you wanted to hide the mirror. Isn't that what you did, Elliot? Your girlfriend's dead and you're hiding your mirror."

Elliot was panting. "I couldn't put it back. I didn't know what to do. So I texted Dad."

"Go on."

"He met me in front of the Lemrow. I told him I put it in my locker. So he told me to get it. And on the way home we dumped it."

"What time?"

"I don't know. About 6:25."

"Then what happened?"

Elliot looked at King. "You called Dad and told him we had to be in Detective Leguizamo's office in five minutes."

King nodded and said, "Where did you dump it?"

"Fifth Avenue and Seventy-fourth Street," Elliot muttered.

"Be more specific."

"Northeast corner -- in front of the apartment house there's a trash receptacle."

"Then what did you do?"

"We went to the precinct. Detective Leguizamo interrogated us."

King thought, kid, you don't know what interrogation is.

"Go on."

"We went home."

"Walking? Riding?"

"Took a cab."

"Go on."

"We got home."

"Did you go to your apartment?"

"We ran into Monika in the lobby and went up to her coop for a drink. Then you came."

"Go on."

"What's to go on? You made Dad and me take you to where we dumped the mirror."

"We had a squad go through the receptacle and guess what they didn't find."

"The mirror?"

"No, they found the mirror. They didn't find the purse. Elliot, ever hear of evidence tampering?"

Saul Ackerman, the lawyer, showed signs of life. He frowned.

"Because we can charge you with that," King said. "You removed the mirror from a crime scene."

"I didn't know that. I thought it was a hit and run."

"That's not a crime scene? Didn't you say the Lexus swerved -- your Lexus -- and hit Phoebe on purpose?"

Chapter 19

2:10 a.m. Friday, September 8

Steve's cell rang. He checked the caller, left the cesspool and went out into the hall before he answered it.

"Are you still planning on interviewing me? It's late," Monika said. "Can we do it in the morning?"

"No."

"Can you interview me here? I'm dead." She paused, then scolded herself. "Well done, Monika. Scratch that dead remark."

Steve thought about interviewing Monika at home, about seeing Monika's condo, about – let's face it – Monika. Twenty minutes later Steve approached the Trident, the East 79th Street building where Phoebe, Harry, Elliot, and Monika Syka had lived on the same floor. Eight blocks from the Lemrow, it would take them about ten minutes to get to or from the museum.

Steve thought about the Elliot Ross interview he had just witnessed. The kid admitted to grabbing the rearview mirror from his locker and that he and dad threw it into a receptacle, Harry gets a call from King to come to the precinct for Dom's interview, after the interview the Rosses head home, bump into Monika and go to her apartment. What about the purse? Elliot admits to taking the mirror but will not admit to taking the purse. It didn't add up.

Steve figured that Elliot's backpack was checked by an officer when he entered the precinct. If the purse had been in it, it would have rung bells.

Steve walked up to a portly doorman who was flicking a rag at a highly polished Mercury Mariner. In the fall night the guy's dark uniform blended with the car's lustrous paint job. He was humming an old Sinatra tune.

"Nice car," Steve said.

The guy jumped. He covered his nervousness with a big smile. Steve was used to cop jitters in the innocent and guilty alike.

"You can go up. Penthouse." The doorman's man-to-man tone showed that he knew Steve was a cop.

"Thanks, Hector." Steve took a final drag as he glanced at the guy's ID badge.

He entered the lobby, looked up at the monitor cameras and moved as far away as possible from the doorman's flapping ears. He speed dialed Rosaria. "Got the videos, sweetheart?"

"Where you at? Elliot's?"

"Yup." Steve watched the doorman checking the cars parked in front of the building.

"Way ahead of you, Stevie. We'll have a show and tell when you get back." Before Steve had screwed up the homicide case, he and Rosaria had a running gag. They flirted openly and outrageously, mostly to annoy Dom. Steve was relieved they were back on their old footing.

"Looking forward to seeing them," he said in a dirty tone and clicked off.

Waiting for the elevator, he looked around at the only objects in the lobby, a weird sculpture and several artistic chairs. Space, he figured, was the ultimate luxury.

The elevator arrived, but Steve didn't get in. Instead, he texted Rosaria again. "How long will it take you to get over here?"

"Ten, fifteen minutes."

"Do it, okay?" He signed off.

Out of the corner of his eye, he saw the doorman was edging toward the intercom system at the front of the lobby.

Steve got into the elevator, pressed the open button, and put his right hand against the door to keep it open. Outside, he heard the doorman's mumble. Then he caught, "Now you take care of me."   Steve waited. He watched Hector's back come into view, squaring his shoulders like a man's gotta do what a man's gotta do.

Was the doorman talking to Harry, Elliot, Monika or someone else at the Trident? Steve wondered as the elevator vaulted to the thirtieth floor.

He rang Monika's bell and the door opened immediately.

"Hi." She stood before him in shorts, not discreet unflattering Bermudas, but short shorts and a halter top. Espadrilles laced up her long legs and her dark hair was piled up on her head. She reminded him of a 1940s pin up in his Uncle Con's garage.

"Sorry, about the late night interview," he said.

"Usually, I come alive after midnight." She had a way of making provocative remarks sound demure and vice versa.

The image of a roll in the hay with a good looking, hot woman stirred Steve until he recalled the results of his last roll in the hay while on duty. His instincts had been right. He owed Rosaria.

"Are you okay?" He looked down at Monika.

"Hardly okay. How's poor Elliot?"

"He'll be all right." Steve placed his recorder on a nearby coffee table.

Monika stared at it and laughed. "It's like a cop show. Aren't you going to whisper the date and our names into it?"

"All taken care of."

"My God, what Harry and Elliot have been through. I hope you're not too rough on them."

Steve didn't answer. He pulled his eyes away from her and looked around. To his left were square glass windows, black boxes in the late night. Beyond them was a terrace. To his right were custom built blond bookcases and an array of framed photos. His eye caught one of Monika standing next to a good-looking Chinese. Her outfit in the photo was a well-tailored suit that said work, her seductive smile said play. He was aware that she was following his every move.

"Where was that taken?"

Monika studied the photo. "Northern China. Some conference."

"That's Sami?"

Monika looked surprised for a moment. "That's right. You met him. Of course, it was the day you met C. E."

"What does he do at the Lemrow?"

"He's a visiting curator."

"What does a visiting curator do?"

"Sami helped install the Chen exhibit."

"Give me more details." Steve thought of the two wrapped crates.

"Let me think." She did a very pretty job of thinking. First she ran her small pampered hands around some loose curls and tucked them into her hair. Her breasts rose with the gesture.

"Sami walked out of a room with you and C. E. The Green Room, right?"

He recalled how pissed off she'd seemed. She was the closest to flustered he'd ever seen, but now with Phoebe's murder, C. E.'s fatal heart attack, and Geoff's suicide, she was answering questions as if she were at a cocktail party and energetic enough to flirt.

"You know Sami well?"

"Not especially. I've run into him at different conferences. I got to know him better when we were arranging the exhibit."

"Who hired him?"

The doorbell rang.

Startled, Monika swung around. She went to the door and put her eye to the spy hole. A second later she swung open the door and in walked Rosaria.

"I'm surprised the doorman didn't announce you, Detective."

"I told him not to."

From the Bose audio system, melancholy music flowed through the pale, cold room.

Steve stared out at the blackness of the night as he sat down on a sandstone colored couch. His eyes swung over framed etchings and scholarly books. Most were written by the director and translated into different languages.

Rosaria folded her beefy arms and perched on the corner of a mahogany desk.

"Who hired Sami?" Steve repeated.

"For the exhibit?" Monika said. "Wellington did. He knew him from Hong Kong."

"I guess you found your keys," Steve said.

"What?" she said, at first puzzled. "You mean in the ER? I found them. I have to apologize. I lost it in the ER."

"It was rough." He thought back to Monika almost fainting, then crying, then searching frantically for her house keys. In contrast, Wellington Chen's stoicism underlined his grief more than any amount of wailing would have done.

"You and C. E. both came from Scranton?" he said.

"You've done your homework." Monika stretched before continuing. "Can't we continue this tomorrow?"

"Almost done," Rosaria said. "Scranton?"

"If C. E. hadn't pushed for my appointment, I doubt I would have been hired."

"What was his partner's name?"

"Yoshi. Such a dear and so talented. Has his own textile and jewelry firm."

"Phoebe said he wasn't coming back," Steve said.

"Too painful, I guess."

"What about his business?" Rosaria said.

"Come on, Detective, he can run it from Tokyo."

"What was he thanking you for at the reception?" Steve said.

"Did he? Maybe I was kind to him after C. E. died. It's been known to happen."

The director watched Rosaria's tired, observant eyes estimate the cost of the custom built bookcases, the mahogany tables, and the Eames chairs.

"This place comes with the job. It's a perk," Monika said, reading her mind.

"How does it feel to be down the hall from Phoebe's?" Rosaria said.

"Terrible. That's why I'm playing the Ravel."

Rosaria raised her eyebrows.

"Ravel's 'Pavan for a Dead Princess'?" Monika's tone implied that everyone knew the music. "It's my way of honoring Phoebe."

"Yoshi leaves New York and Max is in C. E.'s apartment now. What's he like?" Steve said.

"Max is a boozy leech." Monika leaned against a bookcase. "He's never done much, thinks of himself as an authority on Etruscan glass. For C. E.'s sake, I allowed him to hang out at the Lemrow."

"To sum up: he's a drunk and his brother's a thief?" Steve said.

"C. E. was besotted by Riccio. I hope -- I think -- it was a one time mistake."

"So who gave you the idea?"

"The idea?"

"That he stole the Riccio."

"I promised not to say. I was told in confidence."

"We can go on with this downtown."

Rosaria rocked her rump against the desk.

"Phoebe. Satisfied?" Monika said.

"When and what did she say exactly?" Steve said.

"It was two days after C. E.'s death." Monika took a deep breath. "I was jogging earlier than usual."

"What time was this?" Rosaria said.

"8:30? 9:00? All of a sudden she was running along beside me."

"Where was this?"

"Central Park – around the reservoir."

"Phoebe jogged?" Steve said.

"Jogged, biked, hiked – you name it."
Monika attempted to lessen the bitterness in her
voice, but both detectives caught it.

Steve checked the recorder.

"She said that C. E. wanted her to replace
the statue and she'd refused."

"When did this occur?" Rosaria said.

"Sunday night."

"The night he died?"

Monika put her head in her hands. She
looked up. "It's all so horrible. A decent, wonderful
scholar steals a Renaissance statue and has a fatal
heart attack over it. The media can't get hold of
this."

"What did Phoebe say exactly?" Rosaria
said.

"She phoned C. E. and he begged her to
smuggle the statue back into the museum."

"Nobody at the museum had noticed it was
missing?" Steve said.

"C. E. had posted a sign where the statue
was usually situated, saying it had been removed for
evaluation."

"What did Phoebe do?"

"She told him she'd think about it.
Naturally, she was shocked. "

"Were you close to Phoebe?" Rosaria said.

"She had no one else she could tell. She
couldn't tell Wellington. Her uncle and C. E. were
lifelong friends and Wellington had lent us his
statues largely because of C. E.'s influence."

All three sat in silence for a few seconds.
The detectives were digesting this new information.

"You had no idea C. E. took the statue?"

"No, Detective." Monika assumed a lofty, administrative tone. "It's instant dismissal if we take an object out of the museum and we're all checked every time we enter and leave."

Steve recalled that Kenny had made the same remark. He was as unconvinced by Monika as he was by Kenny. Since when does a guard give more than a cursory glance to an important curator's briefcase?

He was also thinking of the photo of someone handing C. E. the Riccio.

"Remember the photo?"

"The photo?" Monika said.

"Someone's handing C. E. the statue. Max found it in the apartment."

"Listen, Detective, that could have been taken at any time. Maybe a curator handed it to him to determine something." She jumped up and ran her hands down her sides drawing attention to her great legs.

"Like what? Determine what?" Steve said, enjoying the view.

"Determine the age, for example."

"Don't you know that when it's donated or when you buy it?" Steve didn't hide his ignorance.

"Research isn't static. When we find new evidence, we reexamine the art. In this case, the Riccio statue. We don't know when the photo was taken, do we?"

"Correct. Anyway, why would he have his photo taken if he was stealing it?" Steve didn't mention the point that bothered him – that the photo had been cropped.

"You claim that C. E. confessed to Phoebe that he stole the Riccio," Steve said. "I don't get why he had told her there was a thief at the Lemrow if he was the one doing the stealing."

Steve watched her thinking over her answer.

Finally, she answered. "Maybe to deflect suspicion?"

"Did he say anything to you?" Rosaria said.

"He claimed something odd was going on. I didn't do anything." She waited for their reaction. Both detectives kept poker faces.

"What could I do? Wellington had agreed to lend us part of his priceless collection largely because of our unblemished reputation. Harry was already ballistic about his hedge fund sinking. In my first six months do I need a major exhibit being canceled and a major contributor reneging on a Lemrow pledge? No thank you."

"Tell me what C. E. said to you."

"That there was a thief at the museum. A few days later he had his first heart attack."

"That's why he retired?" Rosaria said.

"It made it impossible for him to continue. He was lost." Monika directed her remarks to Steve. "The museum was his life. Maybe he started imagining there was a thief. Maybe he took the Riccio to keep it safe."

A thought struck him. "Wasn't C. E. worried about a thief before the first heart attack?"

She thought back to what she'd said. "Good point. Now that you mention it, I can't remember if he said it to me before the first attack or between the first and second."

The music had switched to jazz. The volume was low, the way he and Carmen had liked it.

He didn't want to think about what she was doing right now.

"Detective?" Monika said, bringing him back to the present.

"Did C. E. have any enemies?" Steve said.

"Enemies? That's a strong word. He had rivals, competitors. C. E. was tough."

"So what's your answer?"

"I don't think so."

"Phoebe?" Rosaria said.

"His enemy? She was his goddaughter, you know."

"She's the one who brought up the thief in the museum. Was she letting him know she saw him take the statue?" Steve said.

Monika stuck out her chin. Steve noticed the slightest indentation. "I'd never thought of that."

"You didn't like Phoebe?"

"Envy."

Steve caught his breath at her honesty.

"I come from a very working class background. She had all the advantages."

Rosaria looked around the room. There were plenty of professional photos. She didn't spot any personal ones.

"How did she feel about you?" Rosaria said.

"Envy."

"You want to explain that?" Rosaria said.

"I wanted her class, her background. She wanted my ambition."

"She figured out the photo had been taken in the Green Room."

"So she did." Monika gave them a sweet, sad smile.

"What's the importance of the Green Room?" Steve said more to himself than to her. He was thinking about seeing this hot woman walking out of it in a suppressed rage, about a gorgeous young girl obsessed with it and now murdered, and a photographer who hanged himself in it.

"You didn't give a shit about the art, but …you're different now." Monika eyed Steve.

Rosaria raised her eyebrows, caught off guard.

Steve liked the way Monika's little red mouth was pursed when she said shit. A dirty talking, sexy curator. Who knew.

"I guess provenance won't be keeping you awake nights," she said in a very mischievous tone.

"It couldn't keep me awake during the day. Tell me about the Green Room."

"It's a space where we shoot photos, sometimes store stuff. It's a big closet."

"I thought it was wasted space. Why not have it on the ground floor?"

"It's used for shooting our collection. We don't move statues, paintings, other objects any more than necessary. In fact, the Green Room had that hook put into the middle of the ceiling to lift sculpture. You're right. It is wasted space." She put up her right hand as if she were taking an oath. "I resolve to turn that dump into a photo studio worthy of the Lemrow."

"Did C. E. know the photographer?" Steve said.

Monika stretched her lithe body and crumpled onto a couch. "I thought you said we were almost done."

"Soon. Did C. E. know the photographer?" Steve repeated himself.

"You mean Geoff?"

"The one who supposedly killed himself."

"Supposedly? You mean there's some doubt? I hope you're not suggesting murder, Detective." Monika drew in her breath. She looked out the windows at the blackness of the night.

"Tell me about Geoff," Steve said.

"Geoff was hired about the time C. E. retired. They might have met."

"We never found his Canon or cell."

"That's odd."

"This past Tuesday you went to the Green Room right after that librarian," Steve paused, then flipped through his notepad looking for her name, "Hilda, discovered Geoff's body."

"Of course. I had to check out what happened."

"Why not lock the door and wait for the cops?"

"Because I'm not a cop. I never even thought of not taking charge."

"Was Hilda in there with you?"

"Are you kidding? She was a sobbing mess. I got her out of there."

"So you were alone in the Green Room."

"Yeees," she sounded exasperated. "Unless you count the guard outside."

"The door was open?"

"I think so."

"What did you do in there?"

"I reached up to Geoff's hand and took his pulse. I know it was stupid, but at least I put on gloves. This is beginning to sound like an interrogation."

"You saw the photos?" Rosaria said.

"Of course. How could I avoid them?" She puffed out her checks. "Homoeroticism? Sex gone horribly wrong?" She sounded as if she knew what she was talking about.

"How did the photos get there?"

"How should I know? He had them on the Lemrow computer." Monika managed a dry laugh. "He left them behind, a final act of masochism. Can we change the subject?"

"Weird isn't it that we can't find his cell or his Canon? His computers at the Lemrow and at home were intact, but the other stuff is gone."

Monika shook her head. "It's too painful to think about."

Steve nodded in agreement. He figured it was time to get out of there.

At the door he stopped and said, looking at Monika, "Phoebe was pregnant."

Monika stared at him.

Chapter 20

4:15 a.m. Friday, September 8

As soon as Steve and Rosaria got off the elevator on the precinct's third floor, they saw Harry pacing outside Elliot's interview room and avoided him by ducking down a corridor, then circling back to the room that overlooked the interview. Once in the soundproofed room, they nodded to King. Dom had taken over from King and was interviewing Elliot while Saul Ackerman sat at Elliot's side.

"The lawyer keeps saying that his client picked up a piece of his personal property and that he didn't know it was a crime scene." King filled them in. He looked exhausted and sounded tired, but Steve knew he was fine. "Ackerman also says his client has no knowledge of what happened to Phoebe's purse or iPod."

Steve and Rosaria ducked out of the room and entered the closet the precinct deigned to call the AV Room.

Rosaria yawned and glanced at the wall clock. It said 4:30. She adjusted the video of the surveillance tapes and flashed a photo on the opposite wall. Along the top of the frame was the date and the time: 9/7 17:26. "Harry and Elliot Ross are walking into the Trident. Maybe the purse is in the backpack. Here comes Monika."

"Straight from the ER. Looks perky," Steve interrupted her. As he watched the video, he recalled how distraught and helpless Monika had been in the ER. "Now Harry, Elliot and Monika are walking in together. Hector, the doorman, is holding the door."

"So Harry leaves the ER after he got a call from his son."

"The guys found glass particles in Elliot's Lemrow locker."

"He takes the mirror out of his locker. Any shots?" Steve meant surveillance shots.

"No monitors near the lockers. We asked Kenny, the security guy. Some shit about privacy."

They flipped through shots of Rosaria and her crew arriving at the Trident, the interior of the elevator, the stairwell, the foyer.

"Aside from the Nikes, we found nada in the Rosses' apartment," Rosaria said. "Maybe Elliot handed over the purse to the doorman in the lobby? Plenty of blind spots."

"That reminds me. When I was standing in the elevator at the Trident, the doorman, Hector, phones someone," he said. 'Now you take care of me,' he says. Check out Hector's car trunk," Steve said to Rosaria.

"A stretch, Steve. They barely had time to dump it and get back for Dom's interview."

"Check it out anyway."

He looked at his notebook and told Rosaria Hector's car plate number.

"So the doorman's talking to someone at the Trident?"

"I think so. Hector was going over to the intercom. Let me tell you about Monika's reaction…"

"Now it's Monika?"

Steve ignored her. "I told Monika that Phoebe was pregnant. She was surprised."

"Surprised?" Rosaria batted her eyelashes. "Or really surprised?"

Steve managed an exhausted laugh.

"Dom told Harry and Elliot and the lawyer during their interview. So - Harry didn't tell her?" Rosaria said.

"Weird. Right? You're sleeping with someone. You're close, but you don't tell her?"

"You know they're sleeping together?"

"Trust me."

"Is Harry playing the grandpa card?" Rosaria said.

"Hoping Wellington will think he has a claim on the family fortunes? Maybe," Steve said, answering his own question.

Steve's cell phone rang. He went out into the hall and bumped into Dom heading into the AV room.

It was Monika on the cell.

"Can you come back here? There's something you should see."

"Give me five minutes."

He stepped back into the AV room.

Dom studied him. "You have a look on your face."

He ignored her while he rummaged in his desk for a miniature camera and checked that his gloves were in his pocket. "I'm out of here."

Ten minutes later Steve gave his name to the Trident's night doorman.

Monika opened her door, still in her 1940's pin-up outfit, very sexy and very vulnerable. He remembered her fit in his arms in the ER.

"What's up?"

"This way," she said out of breath, leading him to a utility closet near the bathroom. She opened the cupboard door and stood back.

He peered in and saw a Lemrow shopping bag. Automatically, he reached into his jacket's inside pocket, pulled out the tiny camera and shot the shopping bag. Then, he yanked out some rubber gloves, pulled them on and lifted the bag out of the cupboard.

He opened it and looked down at a tiny, yellow purse. He took another shot. He opened the purse and saw one wallet, a comb and a circular mirror. Once again, he shot the evidence.

"You could be a curator," she said, watching him tuck the purse back into the Lemrow shopping bag.

He allowed himself to look her full in her heart-shaped face, to travel down her features from the widow's peak, to the light blue eyes, the one dimple, the straight nose and the pretty, little teeth in the tentative smile.

She gulped. "Please, Steve, believe me. I had no idea what this is."

"Come on. You can't recognize a purse?"

"I mean I had no idea it was here."

"How did it get here?"

"I don't know." She ran her little hands through her dark hair. Once again, her breasts had a nice lift. Then, she fell forward.

"Damn. I'm always tripping on that board." She grabbed his arm.

"Again?" he said, catching her.

"Again?" she asked, sweetly confused.

"Ah shucks. I thought you were falling into my arms again like in the ER."

She looked up into his face and laughed.

He leaned down and kissed her.

Monika led him toward the bedroom.

He started to follow. Then stopped and held up his right hand like a traffic cop. "I can't do this."

She gave him a long sexy smile, but he stayed rooted to the spot.

"I'm not myself." Monika tucked in her blouse. "I'm still reeling from Phoebe being pregnant. How much worse can it get?"

"I have to take care of the evidence."

"Oh." She gave him a knowing smile.

"Which means," he already had his cell out and was speed dialing a number, "Forensics will be here in five minutes." He allowed himself to run his eyes over her body, but leaned back from the light scent of her perfume.

"Maybe I should change."

"Good idea."

Within a half hour the crew were photographing the storage closet and checking the door for fingerprints. The Lemrow shopping bag, the purse and its contents had been photographed from every conceivable angle and were now encased in individual evidence bags.

Dom and King arrived with a search warrant. In contrast to Dom's biker babe outfit, Monika was in director mode: a basic, very well cut dark skirt and silk blouse.

King did his usual photo taking on his cell.

When Monika was informed that her apartment would be searched she was a model cooperative executive. During a patting down, instead of exhibiting embarrassment or anger, she reassured the young patrolwoman.

After examining the purse and its contents, Dom called Rosaria and instructed her to tell Elliot that they'd found the purse and to read him his Miranda rights. He was being placed under arrest and would be spending the rest of the night in jail.

As soon as she got off her cell, she said, eyeing Steve's lower lip, "You got a rash?"

King's face lit up, but he had the good sense to keep his mouth shut.

Without saying a word, Steve fished out his handkerchief and wiped his lip. "Cherry vanilla," he said with a straight face.

"I hope for your sake it is."

Conscious of the put down in front of Monika and King, Steve pulled himself together, all business. "I'm out of here."

"One minute, okay, Ms. Syka?" Dom said. She followed Steve into the corridor.

Steve gave Dom a warning look to mind her own business.

"Think she didn't know it was there?" Dom said.

"What's her game?" Steve said.

Dom gave him a look. She said, "You and King tackle Max tomorrow. Make it brief. I want you two in on this." She slanted her head in the direction of the living room.

"There's a video I want to see before I go to Max's," Steve said.

"What's that?" Dom's scowl gave her the look of a demented hawk.

"Elliot and his dad coming to the precinct for their first interview. Who was on the front desk? Who checked his backpack?"

"You think the purse and Phoebe's iPhone were in it?" Dom said. "We'll check it now."

Fortified by cups of black coffee, Steve and Dom stood in the precinct's AV Room watching a video taken twenty-four hours earlier at 7:20 p.m. Elliot, Harry and their lawyer, Saul Ackerman were entering the station. "That's Henny," Dom said, identifying the security guy who was running a detector over the three men's bodies. Standing behind a table was another officer. He was poking around in Harry's brief case. At the same time, Elliot leaned over to tie his shoe. His backpack slid off his right shoulder. He pushed it up. It slid down again. He yanked it off and handed it to his father who had his back to his son. "Hey, dad," Elliot said, but at that point, the lawyer picked up the backpack and slung it over his own shoulder while the officer examined his briefcase.

"Okay," the officer said, waving the three of them on and reaching out for the next person's bag.

"Who's he?" Dom said, pointing at the officer in the video.

"Some new guy," Steve said. "The way the lawyer is standing you wouldn't notice he was carrying a backpack. There was a line so the guy was concentrating on the next person."

Dom scowled at the screen. "He isn't even looking at the lawyer. So Elliot had the purse and the iPhone in his backpack during that interview?"

She tapped something into her Blackberry. Steve figured it was scheduling a reaming of the officer.

Chapter 21

9:30 a.m. Friday, September 8

After four hours of sleep, Steve rolled out of bed and into his unmarked Ford. He had to make a phone call before he met King. He called Wellington Chen who picked up on the first ring.

"Hello, Steve."

"Phoebe was pregnant."

"Was she?" His voice was drained of emotion and hope.

"We got back the results of Elliot's DNA. Not his."

A long pause. As a father and a detective, Steve was wondering who the man was. He figured as an uncle and businessman, Wellington was doing the same.

"When can I have her?" Wellington said.

Steve gave him the pertinent information about claiming the body.

"Are you planning a funeral?"

"Nothing. Nothing now." Wellington changed the subject. "I've been checking around, trying to find out the name of that man who hurt her. Monika thought I should keep out of it. Maybe, if I hadn't …" He muffled a sob.

"Is this guy the father?" Steve said.

"I'm wondering the same thing. I can't talk about it now, Steve."

Steve thought about finding Phoebe's purse. "What kind of cell did she have?"

"An iPhone. She was never off it."

"Keep searching for that guy."

"Listen, Steve, I'm not leaving New York without Phoebe."

Steve was so moved he choked up. "I don't know what to say."

"I have to speak to someone," Wellington said, getting off the line.

At ten a.m. Steve and King headed out of the precinct and drove the twelve blocks to C. E.'s apartment. Steve felt completely at home with King. He'd trained the younger man and was delighted when he made detective. He was aware that King had matured. He was now a seasoned pro. King didn't defer to Steve and Steve didn't expect it.

They didn't call ahead, figuring the element of surprise would loosen Max's tongue. After three rings, Max opened the door a crack and peeked out. When he saw who it was, he threw open the door and greeted them like long lost friends. Even at home, he was in costume: a smoking jacket over well cut jeans. Steve had figured Max would be in the first glow of morning drinking. He wasn't disappointed.

"Detectives, what's your flavor?" Max flicked open a heavy lighter. He lit a cigarette and tilted his head to exhale the smoke over the detectives' heads. Steve almost swooned, but he wasn't going to smoke with this character.

"A coke?" Steve said.

King nodded in agreement.

The detectives heard Max opening and shutting a refrigerator door, a cabinet door opening, a drawer being pulled out. From the kitchen Max shouted, "Sure you won't join me in a beer, Detectives?"

Steve grinned at King before answering, "Coke is fine." King echoed him. At the same time King focused his cell on the dark curtains. Clockwise he circled the room, photographing it. Steve remembered that King claimed the visual clues helped him reconstruct the scene.

Steve had settled in the Lazy Boy and thought about C. E.'s last minutes. He looked around at the curtains that hid all natural light. He ran his eyes over the cute salt and pepper shakers and over the cropped photo of C. E. being handed the Riccio. A thought occurred to him.

"Did the director return that cropped photo of your brother?" He raised his voice so Max could hear him in the kitchen.

King opened a door and shot the bedroom complete with unmade bed, a bureau with the drawers pulled out, and clothing scattered all over the room. Max's attention to detail did not extend beyond his body. King closed the door and shoved the cell into his pocket a second before their host entered the living room.

No cans or bottles for Max. Instead, he emerged from the kitchen carrying with one hand, like a professional waiter, a silver tray on which perched two crystal glasses filled with an amber liquid. His own drink was in his hand. "I'm honored you'll drink with me. According to all the cop shows, you're not allowed to."

Steve didn't bother to answer. Instead, he repeated his question. "Did the director return the cropped photo?"

"You're kidding, Detective. I'll be lucky if I get that back in six months time. Museums run very slowly."

"So what's this?" Steve said, indicating the photo.

"I made a copy. Anything altered always interests me." Max gave Steve a knowing glance as he handed him his Coke. "Don't worry. I didn't poison it."

While King was nosing around the living room, Steve's eyes roamed over various other photos.

"Who's that?" He pointed to a photo he'd seen at the director's. Steve recognized the Chinese curator he'd seen at the Lemrow. Max studied the photo a moment. "That was taken in happier days. Ask the director about him. Gentlemen, I salute you. Cheers."

Neither detective paid any attention to him. "Who is he?" Steve said.

"A curator. They come and go. I think he's back in Hong Kong. Please sit down," Max said to King who was openly examining some objects on a bureau. "You're making me nervous."

"This isn't a social call." Steve got out of the Lazy Boy and walked over to the salt and pepper shakers. Stuck behind them was the cropped photo of C. E. being handed the Riccio by a gloved hand. Steve picked it up and returned to the Lazy Boy. "This photo was a big deal to Phoebe. Why?"

Max shrugged. "Who knows? Phoebe was adorable and spoiled. She was never wrong. God, in my next life I'm going to be a beautiful Chinese girl with a rich sexy uncle," he said, evading the question.

"Did your brother steal the Riccio?" King said.

"Oddly, no."

"What does that mean?"

"Well, Officer King…"

"Detective."

"Detective King, in the art world theft is not unknown."

"You're saying the art world is corrupt?"

Max shrugged his shoulders.

"Are you a part of it?" King said.

"An innocent observer on the periphery."

"How do you earn your living?"

"The old fashioned way, I inherited it. A family trust, fraternal hand outs," Max mentioned the last without a shred of embarrassment. "In my small way, I'm an authority on Etruscan glass."

"What about your brother?" Steve said.

"Squeaky clean. Boringly dedicated to art. He protected it. He would never have stolen it."

"What's odd about that?" Steve said with a straight face.

"Sometimes people cross over the line. From being around great art, they get notions."

"What are you talking about?" King said.

"Maybe he was protecting the statue? Who knows?"

King threw Max an irritated glance.

Steve thought of colleagues who had taken the law into their own hands. Hadn't he, occasionally.

"C. E. was sitting here?" Steve said in the Lazy Boy. He reached over to the side table to see if he could reach the phone. "He died with the phone in his hands and the Riccio between his knees."

"He's having a heart attack," King said.

"His second. He knew what was happening," Steve said. He was staring at a blank notepad. He picked it up and examined it. There were faint indentations from a previous message. "What was written here?"

"No idea," Max didn't bother to hide his boredom.

"His boyfriend found him."

"True. Yoshi lived here and is now in Toyko," Max said.

"Where's his cell?"

"His cell? My brother prided himself on being a Luddite." Max laughed. "Phoebe bought him one, but he never used it."

"What's this? A disposable?" King picked a cell off the mantelpiece.

"Mine. Put it down, please." Max yanked it out of King's hand and slipped it into his jeans pocket.

Max looked at his watch.

"I have an appointment."

Both detectives noticed that Max's debonair act vanished the minute King picked up the cell.

"You hang out at the Lemrow," Steve said, spoke in a laid back tone to drive Max nuts.

"My second home." Max opened the door of a hall closet and pulled out a jacket.

"On Staff Day you took lots of photos. Why?"

"One of your henchmen has already checked my little cell." He held his hands over his head. "I confess," he said dramatically. "I took some snapshots of one of the security guards who is also my cleaner. Just a joke between her and me. End of story. I'm out of here."

Steve settled back in the Lazy Boy. "Tell us about the Lemrow." Steve said in a leisurely tone.

"Well, Detectives, I'd love to," Max whipped off his smoking jacket and yanked on the jacket, "but, as I have said, I have an important appointment."

"We understand," Steve said. "We're borrowing this." He held up the cropped photo.

Chapter 22

12 Noon, Friday, September 8

"He ran circles around us," King said.

Steve shrugged, a yes and no expression on his face. "What about his reaction when I grabbed the photo? When he was questioned about his Staff Day photos?"

Filing a complaint about Steve taking the photo would be the action of an honest citizen, but Steve figured Max wouldn't be calling the precinct.

"I want that disposable cell," King said as they walked into the station house.

Rosaria stopped them in the corridor. "Dom's interviewing Elliot Ross in One. We're bringing in Monika."

Steve raised his eyebrows and glanced at King who didn't seem surprised. Steve realized he had been left out of this decision.

"Dom's keeping it tight. She's focusing on the purse," Rosaria said.

Steve covered his anger at being excluded. He handed Rosaria the cropped photo. "Phoebe drove everyone nuts about this. Take a look before you hand it to a tech. Get me a copy to show Dom."

King opened the door to the sound proofed room that overlooked the Interview Room. An intern acknowledged the three detectives before turning back to the window. They looked over Dom's shoulder across the scarred wooden table at a weary Elliot sitting on an uncomfortable chair. Saul Ackerman sat next to him.

"How'd you sleep, Elliot?" Dom said.

Fuck you, Elliot's expression said. He had spent four hours in jail, before being released shortly before the interview. Aside from the clean t-shirt brought to him by his lawyer, he looked worn out. His chin was stubbled and his dark hair rumpled.

"It's not a good idea for little boys to lie to the police," Dom said.

Inside the soundproofed booth, King said, "Where's Harry?"

Rosaria jerked her head to the right, indicating he was outside the interview room.

Elliot's eyes kept darting to the wall opposite the window. There was a video shot of Harry and Elliot walking into the Trident.

The date and time of the shot ran across the bottom of the screen.

"Tell me about this," Dom said. She watched Elliot studying the video.

"It's me and dad going into the Trident."

"That date mean anything?" She indicated the data running across the bottom of the frame.

"Of course. It's yesterday, the day Phoebe …died."

"Killed in a hit and run," Dom amended. "What's the time on the crawl?" She meant the bottom of the screen.

"22:15."

"What's that in our language?"

Elliot thought a moment. "10:15 p.m."

"Very good, Elliot."

Elliot managed a weak smile.

"You went to Horace Mann?"

Elliot nodded, surprised Dom had ever heard of Horace Mann.

"It shows."

The three detectives and the intern burst out laughing.

"What's in the backpack?" Dom focused a beam of light on the video shot, highlighting the backpack.

Elliot glanced at his lawyer who remained impassive.

"I said, what's in the backpack?"

"The purse," Elliot muttered.

The next shot showed Elliot's running shoes. Near the curb were the smashed rearview mirror and the tiny canary purse.

"Is this Phoebe's?" Dom picked out the purse with a small, intense light.

"Yeah," Elliot said.

"Was Phoebe carrying it when she was hit?"

"She opened it like she was looking for something. She didn't see the Lexus."

"What was she looking for?"

"I don't know."

The next shot showed a Lemrow shopping bag in Monika's closet. Dom clicked on the switch. The next image was the yellow clutch purse.

This was followed by a shot that showed the purse's contents: one wallet, a comb and a tiny mirror.

"You interested in helping us find out who killed Phoebe?"

Elliot didn't say anything.

"Answer me." Dom's jaws were clenched.

Elliot nodded. He was breathing hard.

"But you keep wasting our time. First, we comb through garbage for the rear view mirror and now we find this. Why didn't you hand them over to the police? You picked them up at a crime scene – your girlfriend's just been hit -"

"The purse flew out of Phoebe's hand. So I picked it up." He threw Dom a dirty look. "You're right. She was my girlfriend. I was protecting her purse."

"What was in it?"

"What was in it?" Elliot repeated.

Dom nodded.

"How should I know?" He exploded.

"Did you open Phoebe's purse? No more lies, Elliot."

"Why would I do that?"

"Answer the question."

"No."

"You didn't open the purse?" Dom said skeptically. "Why did you take it?"

"I told you. She was my girlfriend. I was protecting her property."

Dom figured Elliot's lawyer had rehearsed him on that reply.

"What about the rear view mirror?"

"It came off my car. It hit her." He was sweating. "It rolled over to the curb, right near me."

"Go on."

"It's mine. It's part of my car."

"What did you do with the purse and the mirror?"

"You know what I did. I put them in my locker at the Lemrow."

"You hid them in your locker. Look at me, Elliot."

His head came up reluctantly.

"You have wasted police time. You have tampered with evidence. You could go to jail big time."

"Can I go to the bathroom?"

"Did you open Phoebe's purse?"

"No."

"Did you take Phoebe's iPhone?"

"No!"

Dom checked her watch then said, "Interview interrupted. Witness going to the can."

The intern left the soundproofed room, entered the interview room and led Elliot and his lawyer into the corridor.

The minute the door closed, Dom stood up and approached the window. She shielded her eyes to cut down the glare then turned on the intercom. "What about Max?"

"He has a disposable cell I want." King described how Max grabbed it out of his hand.

"No grounds for a warrant," Dom said.

"I bet he has two cells, his own and the disposable. I'll call Joe," he mentioned the Reliable who was checking out Max's cell.

As Steve placed his copy of the cropped photo in front of Dom, he explained how he'd taken it from Max. "Tell Elliot to describe the route he took to the Locker Room. There are two stairs, one outside, one inside."

"Was Phoebe's cell in his back pack when I interviewed him and his father?" Dom shook her head. "Now, it's tainted. If we ever find it." She was talking more to herself than to King and Steve.

"You showing Elliot how they were frisked when they entered the station?" Steve said.

Dom stuck out her lower lip.

Steve knew she was deeply embarrassed that this kid had gotten into the precinct without his backpack being checked. "So Elliott had Phoebe's purse in his backpack all the time you were interviewing him?" Getting even with Dom for calling in Monika without notifying him.

"It was luck. He didn't plan it." Dom gave Steve a dirty look.

Steve recalled the video and nodded in agreement.

"I'm not bringing it up, for now," Dom said.

The light over the interview room door blinked and Dom went back to her seat. The door opened and the officer stood back so Elliot and the lawyer could walk back to their chairs.

"Interview with Elliot Ross continued," Dom said, out of habit, for the video. "Tell me the route you took to the Lemrow's Locker Room. "

"I went in the main entrance."

"What time was this?"

"Four: fifteen? Four: thirty?"

"Sign in?"

"No."

"Are you supposed to?"

"Yeah, but nobody does. I mean like the staff and security have to really, but …"

"So from the main entrance you went where?"

"I went down the stairs to the Locker Room."

Steve was picturing the internal stairwell.

"Anyone see you?"

" I don't think so. "

"Where were the mirror and the purse?"

"In my backpack."

"Go on."

"I put them in the locker, like I said before." Elliot was getting cranky.

"So you were in the Locker Room between 4:00 and 4:15 p.m.?"

"I have a witness."

"Who?"

"The director."

"The director?" Dom purred. "What was the director doing?"

"I don't know."

"Does she have a locker?"

"The director? I don't think so. She has a whole fucking suite."

In the soundproofed room, the detectives laughed.

"What did the director do?"

"Do? She was standing there, like she'd lost something."

"She say anything?"

"No. She looked funny. She was sweating."

In the other room, Steve and King exchanged glances.

"Go on," Dom prodded Elliot.

"So I put the stuff in the locker."

"The director saw you do this?"

"No, I opened the locker door first to shield my body then I put them in."

"Go on."

"By the time I closed my locker door she was out of there."

Dom scanned her cell. Steve had texted: 2 stairs.

"The director took which stairs?"

"I don't know."

"You took which stairs?"

Elliot stared at Dom, surprised she knew the layout. "Uhh, I think, yeah, the ones that led outside."

"Go on."

"I got out of there."

"Anybody else there?"

"I heard voices on the stairs coming in from outside."

"What time was this?"

"How should I know? 4:30?"

"Did you see anybody else in the Locker Room?"

"No, not exactly."

"Not exactly? Explain that."

"There was a security guard and Max Stowbridge standing outside smoking," he said with disgust. "I guess she was on her break. I walked past them."

Steve and King exchanged glances at the mention of the security guard and Max. The detectives moved closer to the window.

"What did you do then?"

"I told you. I texted Dad." Elliot was getting crankier. He needed his bottle.

"Want a coke?"

"Yeah." Hope in his voice for the first time.

"Later. What's the guard's name?"

Beyond the glass wall, Rosaria had a pad out, ready to scribble it down.

"How should I know? She's security. She has a funny accent."

"So what happened when you met your dad near 72nd Street and Fifth?"

"He told me to get the mirror out of my locker and put it in a Lemrow shopping bag."

"What did he say about the purse?"

"He didn't know about it. Listen, Detective Leguizamo, my dad wanted me to tell you right away about the mirror."

"Where did you get the Lemrow shopping bag?"

"Dad had one. He's always buying stuff. Gets a discount."

Another laugh from the detectives.

"Your dad walks around with a Lemrow shopping bag?"

"He had it in his briefcase."

"Go on."

"So I went back to the Locker Room…"

"This is your second trip to the Locker Room?"

"Yeah."

"What time was this?"

"Around 5:15?"

"I met Dad in the Park. He gave me the shopping bag," said in a long-suffering tone, "like I said already."

Elliot stopped, expecting her to say where in the park. Instead, Dom kept her eyes on him and her mouth shut, so he continued, "I went back to my locker and dumped the mirror and the purse in the shopping bag. And put them into my backpack."

"This time which stairs did you take to the Locker Room?"

"Same as before, the inside ones."

"And which ones when you left?"

"The external stairs."

"The second time did you see anybody else in the Locker Room?"

"No."

"Go on."

"We started walking home. Then we got the call to report to you at the precinct. Dad wanted me to give you the mirror. I wanted to dump it. So we did."

"What time was this?"

"I don't know."

Dom checked her notes. The call was made at 6:20 p.m.

"Where did you dump the mirror?"

"Seventy-fourth and Fifth."

"Why didn't you dump the purse?"

"I didn't want Dad to see it."

"What was in the purse?"

"I don't know. I didn't open it," he shouted.

"So I interviewed you and your dad."

Steve could tell from the look on Dom's face that she was thinking of Phoebe's purse and maybe her iPhone sitting in the backpack during the interview.

"That other detective sat at the back," Elliot said.

"Yeah. You didn't mention the purse or the mirror."

"No."

"After the interview, what did you and your dad do?"

"Grabbed a cab and went home."

"Now Elliot, you answer the next question and we'll have a coke. What did you do with the Lemrow shopping bag at the Trident?"

Elliot leaned back in his chair and folded his arms.

"I like ice in mine. Do you?" Dom said. Elliot reminded her of the only time she'd tried to open a clam. Once you found the slit it wasn't so hard.

She said, "I prefer the Classic, none of this no cal shit."

Her little clam opened his large mouth filled with very white, very expensive teeth. "We met Monika going in the entrance…"

Dom interrupted. "What time was this?"

Elliot shrugged, "I don't know. Ten? Ten: fifteen."

"Go on."

"Monika asked us to come up for a drink. So we did. When Dad was in the john, I told her I had the purse," Elliot whispered.

"Speak up."

"She was so nice. She said she'd take care of it. I gave her the shopping bag."

"You're telling me that the director of the Lemrow volunteered to hide an item taken from a crime scene?"

"It wasn't like that," Elliot whined. "She understood what I'd been through."

"Why would she do that?"

"She understood that I didn't want Dad to know about the purse. He was on my case about the mirror."

"Describe what the director did."

"She said she'd keep it in a safe place and give it to you. She said you'd understand."

Chapter 23

1:30 p.m. Friday, September 8

Monika and her lawyer were at the front desk. A few minutes later, a patrolman swung open the interview door.

"Monika Syka and Roger Atkins enter the room," Dom read the latter name from her cell as she spoke into the video's recorder. She checked that the correct time and date were scrolling along the bottom of the frame.

Elliot's lawyer stood up and shook hands with Monika's.

"Monika," Elliot whispered. His face was alight with hope.

Dom directed Monika to a chair at the end of the table where she faced Dom and the soundproofed booth. Steve watched Monika, dressed in perfectly pressed running gear, fold herself into the chair and place her small hands in her lap. The gesture suggested that she was only there as a responsible citizen.

Monika bestowed an enchanting smile on Elliot.

"Elliot, describe your actions last night, Thursday, September Seventh, when you and your father entered the Trident," Dom said.

"Monika asked us to come up for a drink. When Dad was in the john, I told her I had the purse." Elliot kept his eyes on Monika. "She was so nice. She said she'd take care of it. I gave her the shopping bag."

"You're telling me that the director of the Lemrow volunteered to hide an item taken from a crime scene?" Dom said.

"She understood what I'd been through." Elliot's eyes were beseeching Monika to agree with him.

"Why would you do that?" Dom looked at Monika.

Monika took her time. Finally, she shook her head. "Poor Elliot. I will do anything to help you, but I can't lie for you."

Elliot threw himself back in his chair so violently that it rocked.

"Director, describe what happened between you and Elliot."

"Nothing. He was rattled, but who wouldn't be after the day he'd had?"

"He didn't ask you to hide a Lemrow shopping bag?"

Monika shook her head.

Elliot crossed his arms tightly across his heaving chest. "You bitch," he exploded.

His lawyer put a warning hand on his arm.

"Director, describe what happened in your apartment."

"Elliot, Harry and I had a few drinks and then they left."

"What did you talk about?"

Monika hesitated. Dom drummed a ballpoint on the table.

"He was under terrible pressure." Monika avoided looking at Elliot. "So was his dad."

"What did you talk about?" Dom said.

"Well, they talked about you."

"Did you hide anything for him?"

"Of course not."

"How did the Lemrow shopping bag get into your closet?"

"I have no idea."

"Did you leave the living room?"

Monika thought. "I went into the kitchen, to the john."

"She understood that I didn't want Dad to know about the purse." Elliot rocked his chair. "He was on my case about the mirror."

"Did your dad talk about the mirror in front of the director?"

Elliot thought a moment. "No, Dad kept frowning and stomping around, but he didn't say anything."

"What did you think of Harry Ross's behavior, Monika?" Dom said.

"I thought they had both had – we all had – a terrible, terrible time and his behavior was perfectly understandable."

Dom said to Elliot, "Describe what the director did when your dad went to the bathroom."

"She said she'd keep the purse in a safe place and give it to you. She said you'd understand."

"Go on."

"I placed it in a cupboard."

"You placed it?" Dom said.

"Yeah. She held open the door and told me to."

"Poor Elliot," Monika said.

"Then what?"

Elliot shrugged his shoulders. "I don't remember. She shut the cupboard door, I guess. I was concentrating on Dad when he came out of the john."

Steve studied Monika watching Dom and Elliot. Her lovely face showed the ravages of the past two days. He was certain she was aware she was being observed.

"Director, did you take Phoebe's iPhone out of her purse?" Dom said.

"No, Lieutenant, I did not," Monika said, lowering her voice like the sexy defendant in a noir movie.

"You can leave, but don't leave the city," Dom said abruptly to the director.

Monika blushed. Steve figured it was out of anger not embarrassment. She stood up but didn't move.

Dom signaled to the officer in the soundproofed booth. Seconds later he entered the interview room and escorted out the director.

"I have some news for you, Elliot." Dom said. "We checked out the DNA of the fetus."

Elliot flinched.

"It's not your DNA."

The detectives and intern bumped heads leaning into the window.

Elliot sat in a daze, the recent revelations sweeping over him. Then he said, "I had dinner with her the night C. E. died. She was hinting, like she was pregnant but not by me."

"Go on."

"I didn't have the balls to break it off." He looked up. "We're broke."

Dom nodded.

"Did she tell you she was pregnant?"

"Like I said, she hinted. Talked about it like it was only her decision to get rid of it. That's when I knew the marriage wouldn't work."

"Did you tell her that?"

"I hinted, sort of."

"How did she react?"

"The minute Phoebe couldn't have something, she wanted it. So this kid wasn't mine?"

"Who else was she sleeping with?" Dom said.

Elliot shook his head, unable to speak.

"You get what's in the bank account."

Elliot sat a little straighter then slumped again.

"Ashamed, Elliot?"

"Of what?" he snarled.

"That the thought of everything in the joint bank account comforts you."

"No, I'm ashamed that I trusted that bitch."
He shook off his lawyer's hand.
"Does Dad know?"

"About what?" Dom said.

Elliot searched for words. "I mean about its
not being mine."

"You can tell him. I think it's time for a
coke. Don't you?" Dom said. The lawyer leaned
over the table and whispered to Dom.

The detectives stared at Dom's broad back,
Elliot's head resting on his arms on the interview
table and the lawyer talking in low, urgent tones
about community service.

"Busy locker room at the little old Lemrow,"
Rosaria said. "Who's interviewing the security
guard?"

"You? Needs a woman's touch," Steve said.
"What about Cristobel?"

King pointed to himself and then to Steve.
"And then Max."

"First I'm tagging along with Rosaria,"
Steve said.

"And then Max?" King said.

Steve nodded in agreement as he texted the
detective who'd interviewed Max about his cell
photos on Staff Day.

Rosaria texted this to Dom. The three
detectives watched Dom scan her Blackberry. Her
knife like scowl between her eyebrows appeared a
few times. Then she texted back, "What are you
waiting for?"

Chapter 24

3:15 p.m. Friday, September 8

A Reliable picked up Stasia, the security guard, at the Lemrow. When he brought her into the interview room she said in heart breaking, Middle European tones, "Thank you, Mr. Policeman." Then she stretched out her hand and tried to return the wet mushy ball that had once been his handkerchief.

"No thanks," he said brusquely and backed out of the room.

"Hi there." Rosaria's down home tone reminded Steve of the pregnant cop in *Fargo*. "Take a seat."

Stasia slid into the uncomfortable chair separated by the scar worn table from Rosaria and Steve.

"I'm legal." Stasia rooted through her maroon stud-infested bag.

"Whatcha lookin'for?" Rosaria said.

"My green card."

"That? Who cares about that?"

Stasia looked at her in horror.

"Deep breath. Oooom." Rosaria drew in air.

Steve thought he'd be scared shitless too.

"Listen to me, Stasia," Rosaria dropped all traces of Fargo, North Dakota. "Let's establish a few basic facts for our video and recorder. You've worked at the Lemrow Museum for how long?"

"Five years."

"How did you get the job?"

"Mr. C. E. got it for me." Stasia was trembling so much that her lopsided chair shook.

"C. E. Stowbridge? How did you know him?"

"I clean his apartment, after the Lemrow," Stasia added in a guilty tone. "My cousin goes back to Poland and gives me the job."

"So how did you start working at the Lemrow?"

"I need money. Don't we all? He gave me the Lemrow job."

Rosaria made a quick note to check with Lemrow employment. "You kept working for C. E. Stowbridge when you took the Lemrow job?"

"Sure. I go on Tuesday nights after my shift."

"What did you think about C. E.?"

"Mr. C. E.? He was funny. Always sending me out to buy booze and not tell Mr. Yoshi."

"You work for Maximillian Stowbridge now?"

"Maxi," she shook her head. The lopsided chair had stopped rocking. "He teases me, but he doesn't pay me. He smokes my cigarettes." Steve remembered the director described Max as a leech.

"We want you to tell us about what happened on the Staff Day." Rosaria pulled some 9" x 12" black and white photos out of a folder and placed them in front of Stasia.

"I was late. I never do it again." Stasia panted. She stared, wide eyed, at the shots Max had taken of her sneaking into the Lemrow on Staff Day.

"You were due at 10:15?"

"I know. I know. Max gives you this?" She stared heart broken at the photos.

"We examined Max's cell and found these." Steve scrolled through his Blackberry for the list of owners of confiscated cells. He didn't find her name. "Do you have a cell?"

"No! No!"

Talk about a tell. Steve smiled so he wouldn't laugh.

"Calm down," Rosaria said. "On Staff Day what time did you actually arrive?"

"10:30," she whispered.

"It says here you signed in at 10:14."

"I never, never, never do it again. I swear on the head of Pope John Paul."

"Excellent." Rosaria kept her eyes glued to Stasia's sweaty face. "So you arrive at the Lemrow at 10:30 a.m. Why are you opening the closet door on the Lemrow's museum floor?" Rosaria flapped the photo of Stasia opening the door.

Stasia hung her head. "Now I tell truth."

"Yes?"

"I sign in and I put my coat in main hall closet."

"So you sign in," Steve said, recalling the antiquated book near the Lemrow video room. "Why didn't you put your coat in your locker?"

"Because I was late," Stasia shrieked. "I run up stairs and put my coat in that closet. Quick. But mean Maxi takes a picture."

Before the interview, the detectives had discussed that anyone at the Staff Day could have seen Stasia shoving her coat into the closet.

"Max Stowbridge shot you coming in late. Right?" Steve said.

Stasia crumbled, then moaned, "I tell Maxi taking my picture in the coat gets me fired.

"Why did you put your coat in that closet?" Rosaria said.

"I tell you! Then no one knows I just come in," Stasia shrieked again.

"Smart," Rosaria said. "So what did you do all day? The public wasn't allowed in until noon."

"I do plenty. I take flowers away, take tables away. At noon I have lunch."

"You don't have a smoke?"

"No, only five a day," Stasia said with vehemence. "I promise myself a smoke on afternoon break."

The two detectives led her through her afternoon.

"What about your coat?" Steve said.

"Coat?"

"Your coat."

"My coat. Yes. I forget my coat in main hall closet."

"So your break is at 4:15?" Rosaria said. "Late time for a break, isn't it?"

Stasia nodded. "Late night open on Thursdays."

"So what did you do on your break?"

She shrugged. "What I always do. Smoke."

"Go on."

"I go to Locker Room."

"First time that day?"

"First time that day what?" Stasia said.

"That you went to the Locker Room."

"Yes. That reminds me. I have funny story to tell."

Rosaria plowed on. "You went by yourself to the Locker Room for the first time at what time?"

"With Maxi."

"Maximillian Stowbridge." Steve said for the benefit of the recorder.

"Does Maxi spend a lot of time at the Lemrow?" Rosaria said.

"He's always there." Stasia said. "Can I ask a little favor?"

"Such as?"

"A little cigarette?"

"In here? Impossible." Rosaria's tone suggested her lips had never touched tobacco.

Steve thought with longing that not long ago the air would have been thick with his smoke and Rosaria's.

"But we get through this, and you can smoke your heart out," Rosaria promised. "What time were you and Max in the Locker Room?"

"4:15? My break time."

"See anyone else in the Locker Room?"

Stasia thought a moment. "I tell you the funny story."

Rosaria opened her mouth. "Later. Tell us about the…"

"Tell us the story." Steve interrupted her.

"Max and me we go down to Locker Room."

"What stairs did you take, Stasia?" Steve said.

"The outside ones."

"You mean the outside stairs at the front of the building?" Rosaria said.

Stasia nodded. "I go to locker and remember my coat upstairs."

"And your cigarettes are in your coat pocket?"

Stasia nodded in agreement. "But – this is funny part – Theodora comes in Locker Room opens her locker and pulls out my coat."

"That is funny," Steve said. He and Rosaria were both thinking that someone took the coat out of the upstairs closet, returned it to the Locker Room and put it in the wrong locker.

"I ask her why she steal my coat, but she is nasty and leaves." Stasia smiled. "I told you funny story."

"Go on."

"So I take my cigarettes out of my coat and Maxi and me go outside and smoke."

"Nothing else, Stasia?" Steve said, willing her to say she saw Elliot Ross.

Stasia took a deep breath, cigarette deprivation written all over her face. "You never believe me. You believe I never have cell?"

"Cell?" Both detectives said, caught off guard.

"Maybe," Rosaria said. "Tell us, and you can smoke."

"I never steal anything in my whole life."

"We believe you," Steve said.

"Do you believe me?" Stasia said to Rosaria. Steve liked the way Stasia turned the tables.

"Yes, I believe," Rosaria said with a straight face.

"Guess what I find in my coat pocket?"

"No guessing. Tell us."

"A cell. A little phone. I never see it before."

"Where is this cell?" Rosaria said.

"Maxi take care of it."

Steve thought of Max shoving a cell into his pocket and King saying it looked like a disposable. He pulled out his own cell. "Look like this?"

"I don't know these things," Stasia moaned.

Steve texted Rosaria: Max: his own cell & disposable cell.

Rosaria glanced at her Blackberry. She had a wise look on her face as she taped a number into her Blackberry. After a few clicks someone said hello.

"Is this Mr. Stowbridge?" Rosaria said.

"Who is this?" Max demanded.

"Detective Hernandez. We had a glitch in our system. Just making sure my Blackberry is working. We'll get back to you." She clicked off and continued talking to Stasia.

"Okay, so you and Maxi are standing outside smoking. Did you see anyone else?"

"Only that boy Elliot who tries to hide from us. But Maxi say peek-a-boo I see you and Elliot marches past us."

"Anything else, Stasia?" All that talk about cigarettes had awakened Steve's urge to smoke.

Stasia hesitated.

"Come on, Stasia."

"I don't tell on Maxi."

Instantly alert, Rosaria said, "You want to smoke? You tell us now."

"Maxi drops a piece of paper. It says twins. He was so rude. When I say, twins, he says mind your own business."

"Now you can smoke."

Stasia was already out of her chair.

"But first, a detective will accompany you home and get the coat you wore that day."

Stasia moaned. "I can't afford it."

"We'll give you a receipt. You'll get it back."

"Promise?"

"I promise," Rosaria said.

"Promise you don't tell Maxi I was here."

"Sure."

Chapter 25

4:10 p.m. Friday, September 8

Dom said over the loud speaker into the interview room. "My office. Now."

"So you confirmed that Max has his own cell. That's the one you called, right?" King said to Rosaria as they entered the room. "I want Max's disposable."

"Question him about that paper that had the word twins on it," Rosaria said.

Steve joined them. The three of them had just finished watching the video of Stasia's interview.

They sat down and faced Dom across her desk.

"First I want to go over your interview with Theodora," Dom said. "She said that Phoebe told her there was a thief at the Lemrow?"

King nodded.

"What's with this Phoebe?" Dom said to Steve. "She told everybody in a fifty mile radius."

"Major guilt," Steve said. "She thought C. E. died because she'd broken their dinner date."

"Theodora claims Phoebe had a mark on her neck," King said. "She asked Phoebe about it and Phoebe claimed a boyfriend did it."

"Elliot?" Dom said.

King didn't say anything.

"Did you ask this Theodora if she meant Elliot?"

"No, boss."

"Jesus. Why do I have to do everything? I'm sick of this place." Dom directed this last remark at King. "I'll go to the Lemrow -- check out the internal stairs, the whole set up in the locker room. Steve, King get that cell from Max. Rosaria, you come with me."

Dom and Rosaria were accompanied by a patrolwoman who swung open the Lemrow's iron gate that was the employees' entrance. They walked down the outside area that led to the door. Both detectives nodded to a maintenance guy who was smoking a cigarette.

Inside, they showed their badges to the security guard who looked out at them through the window in the Video Room. Instead of continuing, Dom indicated she wanted to go into the room. The guard pressed a button, the door clicked and Rosaria pushed open the door and they were in the cage. Dom noticed that the guard's finger was pressing another button.

Dom was examining the wall of closed-circuit screens. "Where's the Locker Room?"

"Down the corridor."

"I mean on here." Dom pointed to the screens.

At that moment, an inner door opened and Kenny entered the room. "Ken O'Malley, head of security."

Rosaria had met him before and introduced him to Dom.

"The Locker Room's not monitored?" Dom said.

"We have problems with that. Sometimes the employees change in the locker room. We've told them not to, but the younger ones change anyway and we don't want any trouble about shooting people taking their clothes off," Kenny said.

"Any complaints about stealing in the locker room?" Dom said.

"No. They have locks."

Kenny indicated the main gallery monitor. "We keep the rooms on view that have the guests."

"Guests?" Dom said, honestly confused.

"The public," Kenny said.

Dom pulled a floor plan of the Lemrow out of her purse and studied the ground floor layout for a minute. "I go down that corridor and the Locker Room's there?"

"Correct."

"Say I'm upstairs in the museum, how do I get to the Locker Room from there?"

"Two ways – three ways, actually, but we'll come to that later." Kenny warmed to his theme. His index finger flew to the stair symbol on the first floor plan. "That's the internal route," he said. "Or you can take the external stairs which means you'd go out the main entrance, open the iron gate and go down to the locker room."

"We came through the iron gate off the street," Rosaria said to Dom. "What's the third way?"

"Take the elevator from the museum floor to the locker room on this, the ground floor."

"Thanks. Let's go," Dom said.

"I'll go with you," Kenny said.

"No, we'll find our own way," Dom said.

Kenny opened his mouth to protest, studied Dom's expression and closed it.

"Thanks," Rosaria said to Kenny's retreating form.

The two detectives and the patrolwoman walked to the Locker Room two times -- once using the internal stairs, then the external ones, and then finally getting into the elevator.

"The internal ones take a few seconds longer, but they're more private," Rosaria said.

"Stasia and Max took the external ones."

"Faster. They had only thirty minutes to smoke."

Dom and Rosaria had walked through the building yesterday, the day Phoebe died. In addition, Rosaria, from interviewing the staff, had become familiar with it. "We can take the elevator to talk to Theodora. She's in the research library."

"Who uses these lockers?" Dom said, looking around at the rows of lockers.

"The staff," Rosaria said.

"Names?" Dom said.

"Elliot's is here," Rosaria touched the olive metal door. She pointed across the room. "Cristobel's is across from his. Two down from hers is Theodora's. Stasia's is next to hers." As she said this, she thumped each locker.

"Does the director have a locker?" Dom said.

"Of course not." Rosaria was one of the few people who could answer Dom this way.

"Any one else in that category?"

"The curators and conservators."

"They have individual offices?"

Rosaria nodded in agreement. "And Kenny."

"How do we gain access to the elevators?" Dom said.

Rosaria held up her elevator card.

"Detective Hernandez and I need to discuss a few things." She swung the Locker Room's door back and forth, an open invitation for the patrolwoman to stand outside.

"Wait. What's this?" Rosaria pointed to a printout with a pointing finger and the message, "ITS EVERYBODIES RESPONSIBILITY Do you foul your own nest? Don't foul your work place." It was signed by Ken X. O'Malley.

"Get Kenny," Dom said to the patrolwoman.

Three minutes later, Kenny rushed into the Locker Room.

"What's this?" Rosaria jerked her thumb at the sign.

"After Staff Day, trash was on the floor, valuable equipment was left all over the museum."

"Still have this valuable equipment?"

Rosaria said.

"Yeah."

"Where's your office?" Rosaria said.

Kenny jerked his head in the direction of the corridor. "Down the hall, first door on the left."

"Stay there. I want to talk to you."

Kenny's face turned ashen white, a reaction Rosaria was used to. They watched his retreating figure scurry down the hall to his office.

"So Theodora found the security guard's coat in her locker," Dom said. "Why was the director in here if she doesn't have a locker?"

Rosaria thought this over. She shrugged.

"Listen, it's getting late. I want to speak to this Theodora. Check out that stuff with Kenny. I'll meet you in front of the building." Dom looked at the young police officer. "You come with me. Record the interview."

"Theodora's in a cubicle on the third floor, one floor above the museum collections and the reference library." Rosaria traced her finger on the floor plan.

"Lieutenant Leguizamo," the director said as she was getting out of the elevator and Dom and the police officer were getting in. "May I ask where you're headed?"

"Theodora's."

"Theodora's? How extraordinary." The director backed into the elevator. "She's odd and terribly shy. Perhaps I'd better come along."

Dom thought this over, weighing what she'd learned about Theodora and about the director. She studied Monika long enough to make her play with her pearl necklace.

"You don't mind, I hope." Without waiting for an answer, the director flashed her ID at a flashing light on a panel and pushed the third floor button. The elevator lurched upward.

Dom followed Monika to Theodora's cubicle. She was as aware of the other researchers as they were of her and the director.

"Theodora, this is Lieutenant Leguizamo," Monika said.

Dom indicated the front of Theodora's cubicle to the officer who stood at its entrance, facing the room. A thrilled hush settled over the already quiet room. Whether by covert glances or open stares, everyone kept looking at the young patrolwoman who stood like a poster marine with her legs apart in an inverted V and her hands over her groin.

In her cubicle, sitting at her desk, Theodora looked up at Dom the way kids stare at firemen during the St. Patrick's Day Parade. Dom had a hard time not staring back. Theodora's desk was crammed with papers, folders, and catalogues. Theodora had on a hat that would have been at home on a member of the Taliban and a pink blouse with lots of frills that ran up and down her ample bosom. Embedded within were various religious metals, almost as many as the ones hanging from the shelving over her desk.

Dom removed a mass of materials from the one other chair besides Theodora's and seated herself. She watched Theodora's eyes following the bundle of loose papers, folders and envelopes as she placed them on the window ledge. Quite nimbly for someone of her girth, Theodora sprinted forward and grabbed a thick envelope on the top of the pile and placed it on her desk under her hand.

"I'm Lieutenant Dom Leguizamo and I'd like to ask you a few questions." Dom's eyes roamed around Theodora's nest.

Theodora, unlike the rest of the population, thought Dom was asking her permission to speak to her. "I am busy. Could you come back another time?"

"I appreciate you want to get back to work. This won't take long." Dom smiled mechanically. At the station Dom was known for her interviewing skill with eccentrics.

"This is important, Theodora," Monika said sternly. Her critical eyes swept over the vast clutter that surrounded them. Then she excused herself to the officer standing in front of her, poked her head outside the cubicle, raised a well manicured hand and said, "Chair?"

Instantly, someone brought in a folding chair.

"Very well," sulky Theodora responded. She brightened up. "Are you finger printing me again?"

"No, but I am recording our interview."

"Can I have a copy?" Theodora said.

" 'Fraid not." Dom then added in a folksy tone, "Helps us keep track of things." Dom took a recorder out of her shoulder bag, handed it to the patrolwoman who placed it on the cluttered desk. After doing so, the patrolwoman said the relevant information about time, place and participants. Dom nodded to her to stand in front of the cubicle.

"On Tuesday around ten a.m., you and Phoebe met here?" Dom said to Theodora.

"How did you know?"

"Detective King told me."

"I don't think it's very nice to be giving away confidences."

"I'm his boss and this is a murder investigation," Dom said.

Theodora sniffed.

"Did Phoebe say anything about a scratch on her neck?"

"Yes."

"Tell me about that."

"Elliot didn't do it."

"How do you know that?"

"She told me."

"What did she say?" Dom was watching Theodora's pudgy hands. They fluttered around a manila envelope.

"She said another man did it."

"Did she describe him?"

"No, but I think she texted him."

"Go on," Dom thought that Theodora was a good snitch. Behind her the director clear her throat.

"I just happened to notice that she wrote something about some statues."

"Why did you think this was to the other man?"

"Because she told me." Theodora looked very pleased with herself.

"You and Phoebe were friends?" Looking at the Taliban hat and the outfit, it was hard for Dom to imagine the chic and lovely Phoebe giving this old bird the time of day.

"She trusted me."

"She often stopped by?"

"Sort of."

"Theodora, why did Phoebe visit you?"

"If you must know," there was a giant heave of the majestic bosom, "she wanted me to repair a pearl necklace she was wearing to her uncle's exhibit."

"Go on."

"Well, she was a mess," Theodora whispered.

Dom leaned closer. Noticing the director clenching her hands, Dom was pleased she'd followed her hunch and allowed Monika to accompany her to Theodora's cubicle.

"Phoebe was feeling very sad about the retired curator."

"C. E.?"

"He told her there was fraudulent activity at the museum."

"This is the usual rumor mill that is part of museum life," Monika interrupted. "Frankly, Theodora, I'm disappointed in you."

"I'm conducting an interview, Director. Leave if you can't remain quiet," Dom said.

Monika stiffened, not used to being talked to in this way. Outside the cubicle someone snickered.

"Gracious," Theodora said, planting her right hand on her frilly chest, momentarily not guarding the thick envelope.

"Did Phoebe pay you?"

"No."

"Did she offer to?"

"Oh, yes, but I wouldn't take money from her."

Dom studied Theodora's desk: the salt and pepper shakers in the shape of girl and boy snakes, the photos of royalty, the holy cards of various female saints being tortured genteelly.

"Did you take her photo?"

"How did you know that?" Theodora's right hand clutched the envelope.

Dom gestured to the magazine cut outs and photos that festooned Theodora's desk. "While you were fixing her necklace, did she use her iPhone?" She asked Theodora. Out of the corner of her eye, she noticed the director stiffen.

"Oh, yes," Theodora gushed. "She couldn't live without it."

"Who did she call or text?"

"Well, I was fastening her necklace around her neck," Theodora blabbed. "I couldn't see who she was texting, but she wrote 'statues'. What do you think that means?"

"It is against museum policy to examine another employees' personal possessions," the director said.

Ignoring the remark, Dom thought of something she wanted to ask the director about. Instead, she directed her question to Theodora.

"I want to ask you about the coat."

"The coat?" the director said.

Both Dom and Theodora turned and stared at her.

Monika kept clearing her throat. "Sorry, I must have picked up something." She cleared her throat again.

"Theodora, didn't you find a coat in the Locker Room?" Dom said.

"In my locker. That security guard accused me of stealing it."

"She probably placed it there by mistake," Monika said.

"Then why accuse me of stealing it?" Suddenly, Theodora smiled. "Were my finger prints on it?"

Instead of answering Theodora, Dom said, "That reminds me." She directed her glance at Monika. "Why were you in the Locker Room?"

"Me? In the Locker Room?" Monika said. "Oh, you mean yesterday. What a terrible day. Yes, I passed through it. I was on my way to the hospital."

"Director, why didn't you accompany Phoebe to the hospital?"

"Really, Lieutenant, I don't think this is the place…"

"Answer the question."

"If you must know I was in urgent need of a bathroom."

"Why didn't you go out the main entrance? Why go through the locker room?"

"Because, Lieutenant, I was distraught and didn't want to run into anyone."

She certainly sounds distraught, Dom thought. "Did you run into anyone?" Elliot had claimed he ran into the director in the Locker Room.

"I don't remember."

Dom turned her power look on Theodora.

"Theodora," Dom began. At the same time, she placed her hand on a mountain of papers, then let it slip. She watched Theodora slap her hand on the thick envelope, allowing everything else to drop around her.

"I am sorry," Dom said, as she stood up and awkwardly knocked against Theodora, while quickly sliding the envelope out from under Theodora's hand.

She opened the flap and pulled out a scrapbook.

"What's this?"

"It's my personal property," Theodora panted. "You heard what the director said. No one is supposed to examine your personal property."

"It's at the museum. We have a right to look at it. Let's see." Dom sat down in the chair and started turning the pages, filled with carefully mounted photos and coy inscriptions.

Ninety-nine percent of the pictures were of Phoebe Chen. "Did she ever take a bad photo?" Dom said.

"Never," Theodora said. She rolled her chair next to Dom's and looked on like a kid at a pajama party.

Dom was looking at a photo of Phoebe kissing a man in a discreet corner of a room. "What's this?"

Theodora looked mortified except for her slightly insane smile. "I think that was the man," she whispered.

"You mean the one who scratched her neck?"

"Yes, him. He was a curator, but he's not here anymore."

"Who's this man?" Dom looked over her shoulder at the director who had stood up to get a better view.

"Somebody who worked on the Chen exhibit. A friend of Wellington's. Theodora, if this is the way you spend your time, we should have a little chat."

"Does he have a name?" Dom said.

"Sami," Theodora cooed. "Good looking, isn't he? Such a handsome couple."

Behind them, the director retched.

"When did you take this photo?"

"Oh, I can answer that," Theodora looked pleased with herself. "Eight days ago -- last Thursday."

"Where was it taken?" Dom said.

"The Green Room. I was early for a Staff Day committee meeting. They jumped apart, but I got them."

"Did you take any other shots in the Green Room?"

"Oh, yes. We're coming to them."

Behind them, the director took deep breaths.

"Are you all right, Director?" Theodora said. "You sound awful."

"Theodora, I'm deeply disturbed about your lack of professionalism," Monika said between gritted teeth.

"Who else is on the Staff Day committee?" Dom continued flipping through the album, stopping briefly at the snapshot Theodora had taken when she repaired Phoebe's necklace.

"Hilda – she's the head librarian." Theodora paused, lowering her voice. "And Geoff, the photographer who died."

Dom grunted without taking her eyes off the Daily News shot of the hit and run scene. Grainy, murky details didn't lessen the impact of the tragedy.

"That's you," Theodora said, pointing to the director, "and that's your duffel bag and the sleeve of your jacket. Why would anyone carry a duffel bag while jogging?"

Monika sniffed, not deigning to answer her subordinate's question.

"Why did you do that?" Dom said, turning and looking at Monika.

"As I explained to one of the detectives, I don't carry it. I parked it behind a tree. I carry the usual stuff: a comb, a brush, lipstick. My only crime is vanity."

"And a jacket?"

"I chill down quickly."

Theodora piped up. "Then why didn't you put it on?"

The director tightened her lips and looked at her watch.

Dom was looking at the newspaper photo of the hit and run and focusing on the sleeve of the jacket. The techs had analyzed the photo, but all they could do was enlarge the blur. They'd analyzed Stasia's coat and found no fingerprints.

As if reading Dom's mind, Theodora said, looking at the director, "Is that the security guard's coat?"

"Theodora, I am not in the habit of borrowing clothing from security guards. Perhaps you'll be able to work for Lieutenant Leguizamo in the near future."

"What's this?" Dom had turned the page and was pointing at a photo of C. E. holding the Riccio statue, flanked by Monika and Sami.

"Nice, isn't it?" Theodora shifted her girth so Monika could see the photo. "Geoff said he didn't want it so he gave me a copy."

"Lovely," Monika said. She dabbed at her face with a tissue.

The lieutenant stared at the director. The cool, collected Monika was dripping like a faucet.

Dom then turned to the last page of the scrapbook and studied a photo. Red lip decals decorated the photo's borders. In the foreground three women were smiling – one sweetly, one gently and one insanely. In the background was a small statue on a table and a woman, wearing gloves, was standing next to it. In addition, there was a backpack and wrapping materials on the table.

"Who's this?" Dom pointed to the group in the foreground.

"Phoebe."

"I know that's Phoebe. Who's the other person?" Dom pointed to the sweetly smiling woman.

"My friend, Hilda, the head librarian." Theodora pointed to herself in the photo. "And that's me, of course."

"What's her story?" Dom pointed to the small woman standing near the statue.

"That's Mary Ratt. We called her the Mouse because she's so small and because of her last name."

"What's this?" Dom pointed to some stuff on the table.

"That's packing material," Theodora said.

"And that's a backpack." Dom moved her finger along the table in the photo. "And this?" She pointed to the statue.

"That's the Riccio," Theodora said. "At first I thought it was being packed up to go to the Met to be restored. They do all our bronzes, don't they, Director?"

"Yes, indeed," Monika said in a dead voice.

Courteously, Theodora waited while Monika got over clearing her throat again. "Maybe it's an allergy, Director. Remember the Mouse?"

"Of course, I remember Ms. Ratt." Monika said in crystal glass tones. "She was my personal assistant."

Theodora addressed Dom, "You've never met the Mouse? This was her last day. Maybe that's why she looks sad. She was such fun. Wasn't she, Director?"

Monika gulped. "Yes, indeed."

"Who took the photo?" Dom said.

"Geoff. He was such a nice young man. I don't care what others say."

"How did you get this?"

"He gave it to me. I love it, being in a photo with Phoebe."

"It was taken in the Green Room last Thursday?"

"Let me get this straight, Theodora. First, you took the photo of Phoebe and Sami. They didn't know it."

"That's right," Theodora said brightly.

"Second, Geoff took the photo of the director, C. E. holding the statue and Sami."

"No, no," Theodora said.

Behind her, the director was clearing her throat again.

Theodora pointed to the simple wooden table in the photo's background. "Ms. Ratt, the Mouse, came in. She was carrying the Riccio statue that she placed on the table and then she opened a cupboard and took out wrapping material."

"Did she say anything?"

"It was weird."

The director cleared her throat repeatedly like a car ignition that won't start.

"What was weird, Theodora?" Dom raised her voice. She glanced at the recorder to make sure it was working.

"The Mouse had on that backpack. I thought she was going out to lunch." Ever the lecturer, Theodora said. "Why bring it to the Green Room? She could take it out of her locker on the way out. She had to go through security."

Dom grunted, digesting this information.

"She seemed sad or grumpy. Didn't feel like talking." Theodora was enjoying her walk down memory lane. "I asked Geoff to take our picture. I figured it was the Mouse's last day and she'd like the photo, but she wouldn't leave the table -– afraid something might happen to the statue. So Geoff took my photo, the one here, with Phoebe and Hilda and the Mouse in the background. Then the director came in with Curator Stowbridge."

"That's C. E., the retired curator?" Dom said.

"Yes." Theodora and the director said in unison.

"Go on."

"Well, right after Geoff took our picture, Phoebe walked out. Didn't say anything," Theodora said. "That's when Curator Stowbridge pulled on some gloves, picked up the statue and asked Geoff to take his picture holding the statue. He told the director and Sami to smile. They were standing on either side of him."

"You agree with this?" Dom looked over her shoulder and addressed the director.

Monika paused before giving a stiff nod.

"The director told Curator Stowbridge not to be absurd, but Geoff shot them as she was talking," Theodora said.

"That is ridiculous, Theodora," Monika said.

Dom was studying the photo of Theodora, Phoebe and Hilda with grumpy Ms. Ratt standing in the background next to the table with the Riccio, the packing materials and the backpack.

"I'd like to see the Green Room," Dom said as she turned the last page of the scrapbook. Shoved into an envelope was another photo. She pulled it out. "What's this?"

Dom studied a photo of the director, Sami and CE. On the table in the background was Ms. Ratt standing next to the backpack.

"Where's the statue?" Dom said.

For the first time, Theodora looked very nervous. She glanced over her shoulder at the director who gave her a stony stare.

"Hilda and I could tell that they wanted us out of there and Geoff was taking photos so we couldn't have our meeting. Geoff left after he took the photo for Curator Stowbridge. I took this shot with my cell. No one noticed me." Theodora raised her eyebrows indicating the director behind her.

Dom studied the photo, obviously a candid shot. In it the director looked pissed off, Sami had put his right hand on her sleeve as if to restrain her and C. E. looked puzzled.

"Where's the statue?" Dom repeated.

"The Mouse put it into her backpack," Theodora whispered. "The only time objects are removed from the building is when they're loaned or restored and it's always done in the presence of a curator and insured guards."

The director said nothing.

Dom closed the scrapbook and looked Theodora in the eye. "I have to take this, but you'll get it back."

Tears came into Theodora's eyes. "Promise?"

She tucked the scrapbook into her briefcase. "Promise. We're done here, Officer Higgins." The patrolwoman had been facing the room outside Theodora's cubicle. She turned around and picked up the recorder.

"I'll take that," Dom said. She slipped the recorder into her shoulder bag and put out her hand. "And the cell, camera whatever you used to take these."

"I didn't bring it today."

"Theodora, don't lie to me."

"Honest. My mother sat on it. It's broken."

"An officer will accompany you. You bring that cell," she scrutinized Theodora who nodded obediently, "to the precinct now. Do not alter, change or delete any of the images. You are to hand it to the officer. Got it?"

"Got it."

Dom said to the officer who was standing in front of the cubicle. "Higgins, go with Theodora to her residence. Get her cell and bring it to me."

As Dom and the director headed toward the elevator, Monika said, "I told you Theodora was odd." She stretched out her hands, "Let me keep that silly, old scrapbook for you. You can pick it up when you leave."

"I'll keep it. No problem," As Dom pressed the elevator button she looked up and saw it was on the ground floor. She checked her watch, not bothering to hide her impatience.

Without saying another word, Dom flung open the fire door and ran down the stairs. Aside from the distant honk of horns, it was quiet for NYC.

She paused a moment, relieved to be alone. Dom had a buzz thinking about the scrapbook. She couldn't wait to show it to her team. If I hadn't been pissed off at King for not questioning Theodora about who scratched Phoebe's neck, I probably wouldn't have interviewed her and wouldn't have found the scrapbook. Dom checked her briefcase to make sure the scrapbook and recorder were safely tucked in it.

After she texted Rosaria that she was checking out the Green Room and to meet her at the Lemrow's entrance in twenty minutes, she tapped in the following words, "statues and Phoebe's iPhone". The whereabouts of the iPhone were bugging her. Behind her, Dom heard the fire door opening. She continued to stare at the word, iPhone. Where the hell is it was her last thought.

"My office. Now." Monika sat at her polished desk. Her eye ran over her computer's screen with the list of secretarial candidates, but she didn't see it. Instead, she examined two broken nails, then tucked a pair of latex gloves into her leather tote parked by her side.

Ten minutes later there was a tentative knock on her door.

"Come in."

She remained seated as Theodora crept across the room. The northern light streaming through the window in back of Monika cast a cruel searchlight on Theodora.

She had on a thrift shop coat four inches shorter than her dirndl skirt. Her Taliban hat was perched on her head like a deranged chef's toque.

The director looked at her as if she were a cockroach. "You have been busy, Theodora. Taking unauthorized photos, fixing jewelry, creeping around the museum and spying on people. Lieutenant Leguizamo wants you to give me your cell or camera or whatever you used to take those illegal photos."

"She can't. She was injured."

"What are you talking about?"

"The officer was escorting me to the elevator. We heard someone moaning in the stairwell. We found Lieutenant Leguizamo. The officer told me to wait in my cubby. When you called me, I thought you knew."

"The officer who was escorting you called me. She told me she wants you to give me that cell." Monica said through gritted teeth.

"I told you and the detective. I can't," Theodora moaned.

"What do you mean, you can't?"

"My mother sat on it."

Exasperated by a typical Theodora defense, the director said, "The officer said to remind you that what you have done is a criminal offense. She said you were not to mention it to anyone."

Theodora was about to sit down.

"Don't bother. I will accompany you to your house to get the cell," the director said. Her cell buzzed. She swung her chair around so that her back was to Theodora.

Theodora felt faint. The thought of going home with the director to search for the cell and of explaining it all to her mother in the early stages of Alzheimer's was too much to bear. She took a tissue from a box on the director's desk and blew her nose loudly. How could she tell Hilda she wouldn't be meeting her? She imagined her dearest friend wondering where she was.

Her keen ears picked up the director muttering into the phone.

"I told you we have an emergency and I'm not talking about the statues. They're the least of our problems." Monika glanced over her shoulder at Theodora before returning her attention to her smartphone.

Theodora looked to her left, then to her right for a wastebasket. She didn't see one, but she did see something on the floor. She bent over, picked it up and gasped. It was a scrap of the photo of the Mouse standing next to her backpack.

Theodora ran into the director's john and locked the door. She pressed her ear against the door and listened to the director.

"Oh, so, now it's *my* problem," Monika snarled into her cell. "Ratt has a fellowship to study at that so called museum and don't you forget it. And what's this shit about you ripping a necklace off precious Phoebe's neck?"

The director's cell buzzed again. She listened to the terse message, then responded, "This is horrible. Lieutenant Leguizamo has been injured? What can I do? I'll be right over."

Theodora turned on both faucets to their fullest extent and quietly opened the bathroom's other door that led to the corridor.

Monika snapped shut her cell and swung around expecting to see Theodora. Hearing the running water, she stood up and pounded on the john door. "Open this door immediately or I will fire you."

The director thought over what she had just said and realized it was better to keep a loose cannon like Theodora on a leash. She said over the faucets' cascade. "I will give you one more chance, Theodora. If you mention this to anyone you will be fired. No references, of course. And you will be sued. Come out of there immediately."

When there was no response, the director jiggled the door's handle. Then, breaking out in a sweat, she ran out of her office and into the corridor. The john door was open. She marched in and checked the space between the radiator and the wall. Breathing deeply, she steadied herself against the sink and splashed water on her face.

Chapter 26

6:00 p.m. Friday, September 8

Detective Rosaria checked her iPhone again. At seventeen: forty Dom had emailed her to meet in front of the Lemrow. For the past twenty minutes Rosaria had been standing near the entrance. It wasn't like Dom to be late.

Rosaria's cell rang. She checked the ID panel. "Yeah?" It was King. Max wasn't at his apartment. He and Steve were going in anyway.

"Whoa. He's walking toward me. Call you back." Rosaria stepped toward Max sauntering along as if he hadn't a care in the world. "Mr. Stowbridge?"

"Detective, please call me Max." As he came closer, the charm floated across to Rosaria like heavy perfume.

"Didn't you have an appointment with Detective Kulchek and Detective King?"

"You're right." Max slapped his forehead. "I have a little errand, and then I'm going right back."

"They're waiting for you."

"How thoughtful. If you'll excuse me."

Rosaria made a quick decision. If she told him to return immediately to his apartment, he might, and he might not.

"Where are you going?"

He glanced at the Lemrow. "Where else? My second home."

"Where exactly in the Lemrow?"

"I have an appointment."

"Who with?"

"That, dear Detective, is private," Max said so sweetly that Rosaria wanted to slap him. "Afterwards, the cafeteria. I'm parched and broke so will probably have to settle for a cup of tea. Join me?"

"No thanks." She eyed him. "One mystery meeting and a cup of tea."

"That's it, I'm afraid."

"Enjoy." Rosaria realized he was lying to her, but she went along with it. Then she texted King and Steve about Max being at the Lemrow.

Steve texted back that he and King were on their way. They were going to pick up Max at the Lemrow.

Rosaria figured that they would find out why Max was at the museum. If he didn't have the disposable cell with him they would accompany him back to his place to get it.

Her cell rang. It was the officer who had accompanied Dom to Theodora's cubicle. In between gasps, she reported finding Dom lying unconscious in a corner of a seldom used stairwell.

Rosaria did what she always did in an emergency. She became very quiet and very methodical, both to gather her wits and to reassure the younger members of the squad.

After kicking into standard procedure, Rosaria checked with the patrolwoman to make sure emergency services had been called. She raced into the building and up three flights to the library floor.

Nodding at the patrolwoman, Rosaria knelt down by her chief, slipped a pair of latex gloves out of her pocket and pulled them on. Then, she took off her own jacket and cushioned it under Dom's head. Blood covered Rosaria's gloved hands. She figured there was a nasty gash on the back of Dom's head. Dom's shoulder bag lay near her body. Rosaria reached into her backpack and pulled out a large evidence bag and slipped in the shoulder bag. Next, she put Dom's brief case into a larger bag.

The patrolwoman had already checked the area for a weapon and had found nothing. Also, she had cordoned off the corner.

Rosaria called the director and Kenny, the security guy, to tell them no one was to leave or enter the museum until further notice. She texted King and Steve to mobilize the squad and to join her immediately.

They arrived at the same time as Emergency Services.

The three detectives commandeered the adjacent library. Meanwhile, everyone else present at the museum was being escorted to the Music Room to be interviewed by the Reliables.

In the library, Cristobel and Hilda were asked to remain behind. They stood together, straight backed and silent.

Both women had heard the director's announcement over the seldom used public address system that an unfortunate incident had occurred, but both women realized it was more serious than an accident.

A young officer opened the library door, shut it and walked over to the three detectives.

Steve told Cristobel and Hilda to sit at the far end of the library.

"Officer Higgins," Rosaria said, "did you accompany Lieutenant Leguizamo to her interview with Theodora?"

"Yes, Sergeant."

"We want to ask you a few questions," King said.

"Did Lieutenant Leguizamo ask the director to sit in on the interview?"

"We ran into her as we were getting into the elevator. The director insisted on accompanying us."

"Was the interview recorded?"

"Yes. The lieutenant opened her shoulder bag, handed me her recorder and told me to set it up."

"What happened to it?"

The officer looked alarmed. "After the interview, Lieutenant Leguizamo placed it back in her shoulder bag. "

"You're sure?"

"Positive. I saw her."

"What was discussed?"

"I had my back to the cubicle. I was facing the room, but I heard them talking about photos of Phoebe and something about a Green Room."

Steve stopped himself from saying, *That fucking Green Room*.

"Did the lieutenant take anything else?"

"I don't know."

"Both her shoulder bag and brief case had been opened," Rosaria said.

The patrolwoman shook her head.

"Anything else, Officer?"

"There was a nosy guy who hung around the copier. It's next to Theodora's cubicle. Maybe he heard something."

"Get his name?" Rosaria said.

The young officer thought a moment. "No, Sergeant."

"Thank you, Officer. We'll get back to you if necessary," Steve said.

She left the library.

"We have to check out that Green Room." Steve looked past the library tables at Cristobel and Hilda. After weighing keeping them in the dark, he decided to tell them the truth. The three detectives approached them. "Lieutenant Leguizamo was attacked on the adjacent stairwell about forty minutes ago."

Both women turned to stone. The older one spoke first.

"How can we help you?" Hilda said.

"Did you notice or hear anything unusual?" King asked.

"No. We'd just opened," Cristobel said. "Fridays the reference library opens at one."

The three detectives checked their watches with the wall clock.

"No one was here?" Steve asked.

"No one we know of," Hilda said. "Curators, researchers might have been here."

"Cleaning staff?"

"The cleaners finish by eleven," Hilda said.

"Where were you?" King said.

"We were both in the lunchroom," Cristobel said.

"Wait here," King said to the women.

The three detectives walked to the other end of the library. A patrolman stationed himself between the two groups.

Rosaria said in a low tone, "Attacker was an insider. Her recorder's missing."

The three knew that Dom never went anywhere without her recorder. Steve and King grunted in agreement.

"What's the weapon?" she said.

"Something blunt," Steve said. "They're checking out the workmen's tools."

"Any ex-cons working here?" King said.

During her career, Dom had made enemies who would have taken a swipe at her. They all had.

Steve shook his head in the negative.

Several Reliables were searching the stacks behind the library.

"Where's Monika Syka?" Steve asked.

"In her office. Harry Ross wants an emergency board meeting, but I told him no one enters or exits until further notice," Rosaria said.

"Monika and Theodora were the last people to see Dom?" King said.

"Correct. Monika accompanied Dom to Theodora's cubicle. Monika claims Dom asked her to." Rosaria looked hard at her two partners.

"The officer who accompanied Dom contradicts that," King said. "Dom was attacked one flight down from the reference offices. So she was coming from there."

Steve dialed Kenny, the security guy. "Where's Theodora?"

He heard Kenny call over his shoulder, "Anyone see Theodora?" Kenny came back on the cell. "Nothing, Steve. I'm checking the sign out sheet." Steve heard him clicking his tongue against his teeth. "Hold it."

Steve heard someone in the background mention Max's name.

Kenny came on the line. "One of the security guys saw Theodora leave the building with Max Stowbridge. They left the building right before the shut down."

"What time?" Steve said.

"Theodora signed out at 6:18."

Steve figured that was about five minutes before he and King arrived at Dom's corner. He put his hand over his cell and said to Rosaria, "Get a BOLO out on Theodora and Max."

After issuing the Be On the Look Out bulletin, he turned his attention back to his phone.

"Steve," Kenny lowered his voice, "Mary L. Culpepper, that lady who's on the board, wants in." His voice was reduced to a deferential whisper. "Wellington Chen is with her."

Steve imagined Mary L. rapping on the security desk window, not used to being kept waiting for anything.

"Take them to the director's office, okay? Tell them they're not leaving." Steve said. "Check the whereabouts of Harry and Elliot Ross," Steve said.

"Harry's in the director's office," Kenny said.

"When did he come in?"

"This morning around 8:30, the same time as the director."

"Get back to me on Elliot. Good work, Kenny," Steve clicked off.

He signaled to a Reliable to approach him.

"You know Max Stowbridge's address?"

The Reliable tapped on his cell then nodded.

"Check Max's apartment. Then call me," Steve said.

"Max was up to something. Maybe Max had the disposable cell when I met him?" Rosaria said.

"To shake down someone," Steve said.

"Yeah." Rosaria called over a Reliable and told him to check out anyone who was present in the library since the museum opened that morning.

"I'm checking on Monika and the other people in her office," Rosaria said. "Then I'm going to Dom." She pointed her thumb in the direction of Cristobel and Hilda. "Don't forget the ladies."

"I'm interviewing Cristobel again," King said.

"Now?"

"Now. She's the only one who gave a shit about Geoff, but I think she was holding back on Rosaria." King went on. "We never found Geoff's Canon or his cell. Why not? Maybe he got rid of them before killing himself, but he didn't sound that organized. It's like he murdered himself, like he was goaded into it. Same thing with the old guy who had a second heart attack."

Steve and Rosaria thought over what King had just said.

"King's right. Those two deaths. CE's and Geoff's, are connected," Steve said. "Where's Theodora? She's the last person, besides Mon- the director – to see Dom. I'm checking out Theodora's cubicle."

"So why was Max coming here?" King said. "He knew he had an appointment with us." He'd learned from Steve to think aloud.

"More than a free cup of tea," Rosaria said. "He had a cagey look. Our Max was up to something."

"That disposable cell…" King started to say.

"Dom's conscious," Rosaria interrupted. She was staring at her phone. "I'm going over there now. Monika and her gang can wait."

"Why did Dom interview Theodora? You already had, right?" Steve said to King.

King blew out his cheeks, embarrassed. "She was pissed at me. Remember? I didn't question Theodora about which one of Phoebe's boyfriends hurt her neck."

"She wanted to interview Theodora, but she also wanted to check out the internal stairs set up and the locker room, but you're right. She was pissed at you," Rosaria said.

"So we'll meet Rosaria at Dom's after I check out Theodora's cubicle and you interview Cristobel?" Steve said, referring to Dom's hospital room.

King nodded and approached Cristobel and Hilda. He said to Hilda, "You're going to be escorted to the Music Room where everyone else is waiting."

"Detective, is Theodora there?" Hilda said.

"Theodora?" King said and called down the room to Steve. "This lady was asking about Theodora."

Steve walked past the empty library tables toward them. "You know her?"

Hilda said, "Oh, yes."

"Any idea where she is now?"

"I assume she's in the Music Room."

Steve studied the librarian's lady-like pearls of sweat popping out on her upper lip. Should he tackle her about Theodora being off the premises or get up stairs to Theodora's cubicle? Let her sweat some more, he thought.

King held up his hand to keep Hilda from leaving.

"Could somebody overhear what's going on in the cubicles?" he said, remembering the tight quarters from when he interviewed Theodora.

Hilda nodded her head vigorously.

"Anybody in particular?" King said.

"Jo-Jo Morales. What a snoop. His cubicle is on the same floor as Theodora's," Hilda said.

Steve studied his printout of the museum's employees. Jo-Jo Morales was listed as working in the same department as Theodora. He motioned to a patrolwoman who was coming through one of the fire doors. "Take this lady to the Music Room. Thanks, King. I'll see you guys." Steve pushed open the door leading to the stairs.

Rosaria headed for the elevator.

Chapter 27

7:30 p. m. Friday, September 8

"Where can we sit?" King said to Cristobel. She led him to a nearby table. After they were seated, an officer stationed nearby took out a recorder.

King took out his cell and did his 360 degree turn, taking photos of the room.

Then Cristobel led King to a table. After they sat down, King stated the time, date, location, his name and Cristobel's.

She looked up at him and smiled. Around her fair, smooth hair was a simple rose band. She looked about fourteen, nervous about the circumstances but completely at home in the surroundings.

King wanted her off balance.

"Phoebe was pregnant."

That wiped the gentle smile off her face.

"I didn't kill her," Cristobel blurted. "We didn't like each other, but the last time I saw her…"

"Where?"

"At the Staff Day I told her something and she was grateful, really grateful. I had a brief moment of regretting all the times I'd hated her."

"What did you tell her?"

"She was walking around with a framed photo, asking who had shot it."

"Describe the photo."

"C. E. was holding a bronze statue."

"The Riccio?" King pulled out a copy of the truncated photo of C. E. holding the statue.

Cristobel studied it. She looked up with her hand outstretched. King nodded his okay for her to touch it. She ran her index finger down the right side of the cropped shot, where the gloved fingers of an unknown person were stretched out toward the Riccio. "Someone who works here?"

"What did you tell Phoebe?" King repeated.

"I told her Geoff had taken it."

"How did you know?"

"He told me."

"When?" King said, wondering why she hadn't mentioned this in her previous interview with Rosaria.

Catching a whiff of his annoyance, she hesitated.

"I saw Geoff on Monday. I told him C. E. had died the night before."

"How did he react?"

"He didn't. He just said he'd given C. E. a printout of his picture with one of the bronzes."

"Did he know C. E.?" King asked.

"Geoff was hired about the same time C. E. had his first attack. They barely knew each other."

"Where was he shooting the bronzes?"

She thought.

"What are you thinking, Cristobel?"

"Sometimes he shot in the Green Room."

"Did he say when he gave the photo to C. E.?"

She thought a minute. "I think he said last Thursday."

"Eight days ago?"

Christobel nodded.

King thought: C. E. died three days later on Sunday and Geoff killed himself two days after that on Tuesday.

King said, "Tell me about Geoff."

"Why? Nobody's interested. I put up a notice about his family sitting shiva."

"Anybody from the museum show up?"

"Aside from me? No one."

"You were with him on Monday, the last day of his life. Let's go over that again."

She took a deep, painful breath.

"When I came to work, he told me he'd lost his camera and satchel. Not unusual. I told you he smoked pot, and his head was a mess."

"What day was this?"

"Monday, four days ago." Cristobel sighed, indicative of having been asked this many times before.

"About what time was this?"

"About 9:20. We're due at 9:30. That's when he told me about giving C. E. the Riccio printout."

"Where was this?" King knew, but he wanted her to paint him a picture and he wanted details.

"In that outside corridor that runs down to the Locker Room."

"In your last interview you said he was more nervous than usual."

Cristobel nodded in agreement. At the same time she looked surprised at King knowing that detail.

"Answer for the recorder, okay?" King said.

She turned her head toward the recorder and said, "Yes."

"The first time you saw him on Monday was at 9:20. Then when?"

"At lunch, around 1:30. He said there were some things he didn't want to talk about," Cristobel said. "Like he was hiding something."

"Then what happened?"

"He got a call."

"His reaction?"

"Immediate relief."

"Who was he talking to?"

"No idea."

"You didn't ask him?"

"No. I know it's weird but I didn't." She looked at King for an answer. "Why didn't I?"

"Why didn't you?"

Cristobel's expressive face was looking back to that Monday. "Hilda, our superior, called me. I was late for a meeting. So I ran out of the cafeteria before I could ask him. Anyway, I knew he was into stuff, but I didn't care." She swung her head defiantly.

"Was the call from inside the museum or outside?"

"I don't know."

"Guess."

"Maybe inside, but I'm not sure. He'd put up several lost notices but only in the employees' work area. No outsider could have seen them, but he could have called people. He was a great whiner."

King reached into his backpack, pulled out some photos and spread them in front of her.

Cristobel blushed but didn't take her eyes off the homoerotic photos. "Poor Geoff. No wonder he was scared. I guess these are the things he didn't want anybody to know about."

"They were scattered all over the Green Room," King said.

"Why would he leave them, why not destroy them? Geoff was a private guy. Put them away, okay?"

King tucked the photos back into his backpack.

"When was the last time you saw him?"

"Around four in the cafeteria."

King felt she wanted to say more. He waited. In the background he heard the Reliables in the next room and the muted sounds of Fifth Avenue traffic.

"How was he at four?" King said.

"Terrible. I've never seen him so bad. He was clinging to his ratty old satchel like a little kid.

That's when he said, why hate me so much?" She gulped. "I told him I didn't hate him."

"What did he say?"

"He said I don't mean you." She shook her head. "He was a wreck. He was sweating and kept saying, why hate me so much."

"This interview is the first time you're saying this."

"Would it have mattered?"

"Of course, it matters." King wanted to shout.

Instead, he said, keeping his tone and expression nonthreatening, "Who did he mean? Who hated him so much?"

"To drive him to suicide," she whispered.

He waited.

She said, "He left me a message."

"Can I hear it?" He kept his voice low, trying not to scare her.

Cristobel fiddled with her cell. Geoff's voice, quivering, said, "I can't go on. Please don't despise me, Cristobel. Bye."

King took the cell and checked the time and date. It was sent at 1:55 a.m., the Tuesday morning Geoff killed himself.

"When did you listen to it?"

"Tuesday morning."

"You didn't tell anyone? No one? No boy friend? No girl friend? Hilda?"

Cristobel swung her head back and forth. "No, I said."

Although pissed at her for holding back information, King thought maybe she had saved herself from being killed.

"You called him back five, six times?" King was scrolling through the messages sent on Cristobel's cell. "He never answered, obviously. How did you find out he was dead?"

"Hilda told me. She was very kind."

"On Tuesday you went to the Green Room?"

"I wanted to say good bye."

"You know I have to take this?" King said.

Cristobel's eyes followed King's hand sliding her cell into an evidence bag. "You'll return it?"

"Absolutely."

"Messages and everything? I don't want to lose his voice."

King put the evidence bag into his backpack. Then he consulted his notes. "You lost Elliot's car keys?"

"One minute they were in my purse, then they weren't."

To King she didn't sound guilty, she sounded puzzled.

"When was this?" King said.

"Thursday – Staff Day. Yesterday. God, it seems so long ago. I had a job interview at Sarah Lawrence. Elliot lent me his car keys."

"When did you last see the keys?" King said.

"At the staff day. Elliot handed them to me while the director was talking to the group. I put them into my purse."

"What kind of purse was it?"

"This one." She patted a little knitted pouch that hugged the table.

"Cristobel is handing me her purse," King said. He held out his hand.

He turned the fragile thing over and looked into it without touching any of the contents. "No zipper, no safety clasp," he said for the recorder. "Did you keep it with you at all times?"

"Yes. Your colleague already checked it."

"I know." So easy to slip your hand into it, King thought.

"When did you discover the keys were missing?" he said. Rosaria had covered this in her interview but since this girl was full of surprises, he wanted to double check.

"On the way to the park I looked in my purse and the keys were missing. That's when I called Elliot."

King went through a mental list about the person who ran over Phoebe: he or she took the keys, knew the keys were to Elliot's car and where to find them. King was convinced this person had to be an insider and had to be someone at Staff Day.

King was staring at Cristobel's purse, but he was recalling that the tech squad had found the Lexus' keys in Cristobel's locker.

"Why did they end up in your locker?"

Cristobel shrugged her shoulders. "Maybe someone found them and tossed them in? I haven't a clue."

A look of horror flooded Cristobel's face.

"What?" King said.

"You're not confiscating my purse?" She hugged it.

King was tempted to fool around. She was a cute girl. Then, he thought of all the deep shit Steve had gotten into.

"No," he said, handing it to her. "What happened to the job interview?"

"I canceled it. I'd changed my mind anyway."

"Why leave the Lemrow?" Studying her *Alice in Wonderland* face, King thought she couldn't stand working in the same place where her friend, Geoff, had killed himself.

"I deserved the Stowbridge scholarship and Phoebe got it. How dare they?" Cristobel threw back her head, more reminiscent of Lady Gaga than Alice. "I'm the one who researched most of the Kuan-yin exhibit."

King barked a laugh at his misjudgment.

Cristobel sat up straight. "What's so funny, Detective?"

"Nothing. You call it the Kuan-yin exhibit?"

"Yes, because that's what it is. Calling it the Wellington Chen exhibit is sucking up to the rich guy who sponsored it." Cristobel stood up. "Something's driving me crazy."

"What?"

"I'm turning into Hilda." She walked across the room toward the two dog statues. She put out her hands to adjust one of them. "This isn't placed right."

"Stop. Don't touch it." King was out of his chair and standing between her and the statue. "Tell me what's different."

"It's not facing the other dog."

"End of interview." King looked over at a patrolman. "Escort her to the Music Room." As soon as Cristobel was out of earshot, he said into his cell, "Get the tech squad in here."

Chapter 28

7:30 p.m. Friday, September 8

Steve closed the cushioned library door that led to the stairwell and skirted the police tape around the corner where Dom had been found. He climbed the two flights to Theodora's cubicle, his eyes automatically sweeping the immediate area. There was a hushed air when he entered the Lemrow offices. Rumors had been swirling about an accident. Everyone had heard the director's announcement that no one was to leave the museum until further notice and that all staff members were to wait in the Music Room. Several Reliables were escorting small groups downstairs. One of the 1930's elevators was being used by the police. No unauthorized personnel was allowed in the stairwell so the wait for the one other elevator, five people maximum, was a long one. The staff were on their cells making impromptu arrangements with spouses, partners and baby sitters.

Playing ignorant, Steve asked an office mate where Theodora was, but she didn't know.

Someone else said that Theodora had left the office about an hour ago, after receiving a phone call.

Maybe Hilda knows, someone else said, but Steve recalled that Hilda had asked him where Theodora was. He also remembered that Hilda had referred to Jo-Jo Morales as a snoop.

"Anything so far?" He said to a Reliable as he glanced over the detective's shoulder at his personnel list .

"This guy," Steve pointed to a name on his list. "Jo-Jo Morales."

"Jo-Jo Morales?" Steve walked over to the elevator line and said to a roly-poly man who seemed to be enjoying the confusion.

"You're speaking to him."

The inquisitive light in the young man's eyes told Steve that he'd landed the office gossip.

How was he going to play this? Keep Jo-Jo blabbing.

"Come with me." Steve led the way to Theodora's cubicle. "We need to know what was discussed in this cubicle. Tell me everything you overheard."

Jo-Jo pursed his lips and put his head to one side like a Central Park robin.

"Like Theodora talking to a detective?" Steve prompted.

"I couldn't help it. I was using the copier."

Steve stuck his head out of the cubicle and saw that the copier was adjacent to the flimsy partition separating Theodora's desk from the rest of the office.

"Take a seat and tell me what you heard." He sat down in Theodora's chair and gestured to a stool in the crowded space.

Jo-Jo picked up a batch of photos and perched them on the windowsill. Sitting down, he waved to someone in the outer room. Steve knew that anything he said would make the gossip rounds.

"What did you hear?"

"The director was very annoyed with Theodora. She's such a gossip." Jo-Jo stopped. "Theodora, not the director. And she had such a crush on Phoebe Chen. She's never stopped talking about the day she fixed Phoebe's necklace. So of course she told that detective."

"Which detective?"

"The one who was in the cubicle with them. Tight fit," Jo-Jo said, raising his eyebrows.

"Did Theodora talk about anything else?"

His eyes glistening, Jo-Jo lowered his voice. "Theodora said something about a thief at the museum. The director said she was very disappointed in her."

"You ever hear anything about a thief?"

"No." An expression of disappointment but a willingness to listen spread across Jo-Jo's face. "But that detective told the director – *the director* - she could leave if she didn't like something."

Steve kept his mouth shut and let Jo-Jo unravel.

"The detective asked about a man, like they were looking at a photo and she wanted him identified."

Not for the first time, Steve thought the Lemrow staff were very observant and very nosy.

"Anything else?"

Jo-Jo shook his head. Then he stopped. "That detective told Theodora she had to give her something, but I couldn't hear what." Jo-Jo grimaced. "I had to get back to work."

Steve kept the tone of his voice routine and his expression bored. "Here's my card. Call me if you think of anything else. Wait in the Music Room. And don't mention anything we talked about."

Jo-Jo backed out of the cubicle, visibly itching to prolong his fifteen minutes of fame. "There was something about Theodora's mom, but I couldn't hear what she said."

"Call me if you think of anything else," Steve repeated. He swung around Theodora's office chair, turning his back on Jo-Jo.

Steve scrutinized the treasure and trash stuffed into every available space. The crowded office reminded Steve of a Whitney installation his ex-girlfriend, the current Mrs. Holbrook, had dragged him to.

Steve's eyes swept over the visuals: the files stacked with photos, the postcards taped to the side of a cabinet, the snapshots of Theodora. At the same time he was running over what Jo-Jo had said.

He backed up. Why did Dom want to interview Theodora? He remembered. King had screwed up. He had forgotten to ask Theodora something about Phoebe's boyfriends.

Theodora. Steve motioned to a patrolwoman. "Get Hilda the librarian. She's in the Music Room."

Steve remembered Wellington Chen's recent phone call on his way to this morning's executive meeting. It was obvious from traffic noises that Wellington was calling from the street. It was also obvious from his guarded remarks that he couldn't talk freely, but he had something to tell Steve. He remembered that Mary L. and Wellington had entered the museum together.

Steve opened one drawer after another. Each was stuffed with papers, trinkets, photos and files.

"Detective?" A young patrolwoman said, standing outside the cubicle.

Hilda, shaken and pale, stood beside her. Steve nodded to the patrolwoman to join the Reliables.

Hilda was sweating bullets. Steve assumed it was because she was about to be questioned. He was wrong.

"I couldn't find Theodora in the Music Room." Her voice was quivering.

"You're close to her, right?"

How dare you, what business is that of yours surfaced in her eyes. Instead, broken, she said, "Yes."

Behind Hilda he saw the line edging toward the elevator. The nosy, excited faces were openly staring at them.

"Do you know where she is? I want to talk to her as much as you do. Help me and I'll help you," he said.

"She isn't dead, is she?" Hilda said.

"No, she isn't." Steve pulled open another drawer. "This is the way it usually is?"

"Oh, yes. She loves chaos. It's the only reason we couldn't live together." Hilda gulped, having shocked herself by her own indiscretion. She cast a loving look at the flowered sweater draped over the blue smock on the back of the ample office chair. "I expect her to walk in at any minute."

Steve followed Hilda's glance. Now she was running her eyes over the stuffed, opened cabinets, the overflowing drawers, the wrapped and unwrapped candy wrappers scattered near the computer decked out like a Sixties hippy van.

"Is anything different?" He said, sensing that she was searching for something.

Hilda was staring at a photo of Theodora in one of her homemade hats.

"Come on, Hilda. Anything missing?"

"Theodora's missing." She put her hands over her face and turned away from him.

Steve lowered his voice. "What else is missing?"

Hilda cried out, "I told her not to do it at work."

"Do what?"

Without answering, she yanked open the stuffed drawers, one after the other, running her hands over and under the bulging folders. Then she checked the overhead cabinets, ignoring the busts, the trinkets, salt and pepper shakers and religious photos.

"If it's not here, something's happened to her. She loved her like a daughter."

"Who?"

"Phoebe. Theodora has a scrapbook about her." Hilda continued searching through stacks of materials. "It's not here."

He stepped in front of her, blocking her access to the desk. He figured he'd have the police crew search for it.

"Maybe the folder is," Hilda said.

"Folder?"

"Theodora kept photos and articles about Phoebe in a folder. Then she mounts them in her scrapbook," Hilda said.

"Keep going." He stepped back.

She opened one packed drawer after another. When she tried to close them, Steve said, "Forget that. Keep looking."

Hilda rooted around in a bottom drawer. "It's here."

Steve leaned down and slid the folder out of Hilda's hands. He flipped through the cuttings.

Hilda was breathing fast. "Believe me, it's innocent."

"Did she take photos herself?"

"I told her not to."

Steve signaled to a Reliable. "Escort this lady back to the Music Room."

"Please, please let me know if you find Theodora."

Steve nodded, his eyes still on the folder. Then he looked down at her. "If you get a call from her, you tell one of us immediately. Got that?"

Dazed, she nodded as she was led away.

Chapter 29

9:10 p.m. Friday, September 8

Dom's steel plate in her head from another attack probably saved her life. After her doctor diagnosed Dom with a concussion he told her to rest, but she was too mad at herself to hear him.

Holbrook had visited her hospital room earlier that morning. After saying, "We don't want you dying on us," he told her he was assigning one of her team to take over.

"Who?"

Then came the surprise.

"Kulchek."

Maybe it wasn't a surprise. In spite of or because of the concussion, Dom thought, so Holbrook thinks this can't be solved and Steve goes down.

"You assign him," Holbrook said. He backed away from her hospital bed, gave her a hurried thumbs up and ran out the door.

Stuff was scattered all over her bed and the diagonal table that stretched across the bed. The team – King, Rosaria, Steve, and Dom were going over the recent report about the marble dog statue that King had the techs bag in the Lemrow library and cart off to the lab. The fingerprints were those of the cleaner who had not been in the library since the previous day. Two strands of hair turned out to be Dom's. Additional analysis of Dom's head revealed that it had been imbedded with minute marble particles.

"So we have the weapon," Dom said. "Good, King."

"It's an insider," Rosaria said. "Someone who knew where the library was and that it was empty. Someone who could lift twenty pounds."

"Why hit you?" King said to Dom.

Dom swung her head back and forth as if she were trying to shake something out of it. Then she sank back in her pillows in frustration.

"Anything about a scrapbook?" Steve said.

Dom looked anxious. Her strong hands clutched at her top sheet as she forced herself to concentrate.

"Rest, right?" The doctor gave Dom a thumbs up signal and threw a warning look to the team before he continued on his rounds. Steve, Rosaria and King waited for the door to shut before they pounced on her.

"Theodora collected photos, news clips, anything she could find about Phoebe. They were placed in this folder, then pasted in a scrapbook. It's missing."

Steve opened the folder he had found in Theodora's cubicle. He and the other detectives had examined it earlier. He gave a brief summary of his interview with Hilda.

He placed the folder on the horizontal table. Dom tried to open it. Her right hand slipped. Rosaria reached over and leafed through the folder, going slowly so Dom could inspect the contents. After she studied an item she'd nod and Rosaria would flip to the next page.

Her team watched her, looking for signs of life. The heavy medication had turned her into a robot.

"Theodora and Hilda are a couple?" Dom said.

Steve nodded. "Very defensive. Hilda kept reassuring me that Theodora thought of Phoebe as a daughter."

"Okay. I remember." Dom said in a subdued tone, one of the indications that she'd been injured. "I took Theodora's scrapbook. You didn't find it?"

The three detectives shook their heads and leaned in closer to hear Dom.

She took a deep breath obviously exhausted. None of them thought of giving her a break.

"There was a photo of Phoebe with Theodora and an older woman." Dom gulped then looked for something on the horizontal table. Rosaria guessing what she wanted, handed her a paper cup filled with water.

"Hilda?" Steve guessed.

Dom sipped the water, then said, "Find that scrapbook. The photo of the three women was on the back cover. That fucking statue was in it."

"The Riccio?" Steve said.

"That one. On a table."

"The scrapbook's missing," Rosaria said. "That's the reason you were conked on the head?"

"Maybe. Find it," Dom said.

"Who hit you? Theodora?"

Dom hunched her shoulders then winced. "Don't know."

"What's Theodora like?" Rosaria said. She looked at Steve since he had spent so much time at the Lemrow.

"I never met her." He thought a moment. "I remember seeing some weird old bird in crazy clothes."

"That's the one. Weird is right," King said.

"I took her scrapbook and told her to bring me something." Dom put her bandaged hands up to her bandaged head. "God, what was it? Where is she?"

"She left the museum with Max Stowbridge at 18:18. We put out a BOLO," Rosaria said.

"They got out of the museum?"

"Right before we found you."

"Where are the others?"

"The director, Mary L., Wellington, and Harry Ross are in the director's office."

"Who's in charge?" Dom said.

"I assigned Joe," Rosaria said, referring to the Reliable veteran. "His team is interviewing them. Elliot Ross is in the Music Room. Everyone in there is being interviewed by the Reliables," Rosaria said. She looked compassionately at Dom, but changed her expression when her boss glanced up.

"Shit. I can't remember what I told Theodora to bring me," Dom said. "Listen, I can't lead the team."

No one disagreed with her. She and they felt the tension, each detective wanting to be the lead.

Never one to mince words, Dom opened her mouth and looked at Rosaria.

Steve's cell phone buzzed. He listened for a moment. Then said to the team, "It's Wellington Chen."

"Wellington Chen?" Dom looked puzzled.

Steve switched his phone to a conference call.

"I found him," Wellington said.

"Who?"

"The man who impregnated Phoebe."

"Impregnated?" Dom said.

"Lieutenant, are you all right?" Wellington said. "I know you were attacked, but it's important that I speak to you or Steve Kulchek."

"Wellington, I'm here," Steve said. "We all are."

"We all are?"

"Dom, me, Rosaria, King – all members of the team. Conference call. All right?"

"Yes, of course." Wellington sounded deeply weary.

"We're in Lieutenant Leguizamo's hospital room," Steve said. Then, he looked at Dom and said slowly, "Wellington is in the director's office. He's being interviewed by Joe's team." Steve said to his cell. "Still there?"

"I can't." They all heard Wellington's superimposed casual tone.

"You can't speak?" Steve said.

"Correct."

"Joe's there? The detective?"

"Yes."

"We're calling him now to take you into the corridor." As Steve spoke, Rosaria was speaking to Joe.

A few seconds later, Steve said, "Wellington, you there?"

"I'm in the corridor."

"Talk."

"Sami is his name. I knew his father. We bought some property in Hong Kong twenty years ago. It didn't work out. Sami has a grudge against me. I found out he and Phoebe had an affair." He raised his voice. "I also found out ten minutes ago that Sami was at the Lemrow arranging my exhibit, touching my statues." His bitter voice morphed into international businessman mode. "That's settled then?"

"We're signing off," Steve said. He clicked off his cell.

Rosaria speed dialed Joe. "What's up?"

"The director stuck her head out the door," Joe said.

"Isn't a uniform guarding it?" Rosaria said.

"Yeah, she is, but the director came out another door."

"What the hell are you talking about?"

"Her bathroom has a door leading into the corridor. The uniform was standing in front of the main door to her office."

"Where's the director now?" King said.

"Back in her office," Joe said.

Steve said. "I'm coming there."

"You have to get over there," Dom agreed. "Steve's the lead. Don't let her con you."

They all knew Dom was referring to Monika.

"Don't fuck up, Steve," Dom said.

King nodded, accepting the decision. He'd figured as the youngest member of the team he had the least chance.

Rosaria stood stone still. A middle aged, fat, black, Latina woman. What did you expect, she said to herself.

"You're not bad for a white guy." She extended her hand.

Steve kept his face impassive, but he exhaled a deep contented breath.

King answered his cell. "Keep them there. I'm coming over." He signed off. "Theodora and Max are at his apartment."

"Where were they?"

"At Theodora's apartment."

"I want the Reliables in the pit in 45 minutes," Steve said to Rosaria. "I'm heading over to the Lemrow."

Twenty minutes later Steve was speaking to Joe in the corridor outside the director's office. "What's going on in there?"

"Wellington and the director keep eyeing each other," Joe said. "Harry and Mary L. are sitting together. The shit hit the fan when Mary L. said the Mouse had a crush on Sami."

"The Mouse?" Steve said.

"The director's ex-secretary, Mary Ratt."

"How so? What happened?"

"Wellington exploded. He wanted to know what Sami was doing at the Lemrow. He wanted to know why Sami's presence had been kept a secret from him. Monika said it wasn't a secret at all."

"Find the director's ex-secretary, Mary Ratt," Steve texted to Rosaria as he said to Joe, "Bring Wellington out here."

Two minutes later, Wellington appeared before him looking years older than when they had last met. There were bags under his eyes and he'd lost at least ten pounds, but his voice was firm.

"Sami's the son of one of my competitors. He's always skirted the law." The words fell out of his mouth, like lava erupting from a volcano. He added bitterly, "He was definitely involved with Phoebe. He was responsible for two of the Kuan-yin statues. They're fakes."

Steve recalled asking Monika for the provenance of two of the statues.

"The blue and white ceramic one and the cast iron one," Wellington said. "My team found out they were made near Hong Kong three years ago."

"C. E. and Monika were your consultants?"

"And trusted friends." Wellington took a deep breath. "That's not fair. C. E. was duped. I think he knew something. Maybe that's why he died."

Once again, Steve thought Wellington would have made a good detective.

"Sami's father has a private museum and Sami's one of the directors." Wellington looked straight at Steve. "Would my niece hurt me, Steve?"

"She was upset, wouldn't let go. Maybe Sami conned her."

"If only he'd killed her," Wellington said.

"What's that supposed to mean?" Steve studied Wellington's face, granite-like in its determination to find out who killed his niece and, in so doing, killed a part of him.

"It means he didn't kill her. He broke her heart, involved her in cheating me, but he didn't kill her."

"How did you find this out?"

"I took her iPhone."

Steve stared at Wellington. They'd never thought of him.

"Go on," Steve said.

"On Thursday we had lunch before I took the helicopter to Kennedy. I figured the best way to find out what was bugging her was to take her iPhone. She was always on it."

"What did you find?" The thought flashed through Steve's head that this vital information was being given in a corridor with no witnesses and nothing being recorded.

"Shots of her and Sami. So I hired a private detective to look into Sami's affairs. I…"

"Where's Phoebe's cell?" Steve interrupted.

"I have it."

"Give it to me."

"No." The businessman spoke. Clearly no deal.

"Why?"

"Unfinished business." The gentler Wellington emerged. "Not now, Steve. I have to check out something."

"Can I check it out with you?"

"I don't think so."

Nothing recorded and a stand off in the Lemrow corridor.

Steve looked into Wellington's wily eyes. "Ever been strip searched, Wellington?"

Joe the Reliable came up to Steve. From the expression on his face, Steve realized he'd heard the last remark.

"I don't have it here," Wellington said.

"For now, you're going to repeat to Joe what you just told me about Phoebe's iPhone and answer some questions about Sami. I'll get back to you." Behind Wellington's back, Joe lifted his eyebrows at Steve. In spite of himself, Steve laughed.

He watched Wellington shuffle back into the director's office.

Steve's cell buzzed. It was King calling from Max's apartment.

"Theodora picked up her cell at her apartment. She keeps saying she has to take it to the Lemrow to give to the director. Theodora claims that, according to the director, Dom wanted her to hand over her cell to Monika. Theodora gave me a scrap of paper she found in the director's office."

"Describe it."

"Mary Ratt is standing next to her backpack. Theodora claims it was torn off a photo in her scrap album."

"Listen, King," Steve leaned against the brocaded wall. Too nervous to remain still, he started pacing up and down the empty corridor as he outlined a plan. After he clicked off, he opened a door, looked around an empty business office and signaled to a patrolman. "I'm seeing the director in here. Bring her in."

Chapter 30

9:30 p.m. Friday, September 8

A Reliable opened the door and stood back so
Monika could enter.

She walked in and managed a brave little
smile on her freshly glossed lips. "Am I glad, no,
relieved to see you, Steve."

"Rough, huh?" Like a headwaiter, he held
out a chair for her to sit down.

She gave him a sweet, grateful look as she
folded into the chair, kicked off her heels and
tucked her legs under her.

The crush was over. Even so, he felt her
charm.

"What do you think happened?" Steve
perched on the edge of a desk.

"You mean to Lieutenant Leguizamo?"
Monika took a deep breath. "I hate to say it, but I
think it was someone who works here." She ran her
hands through her hair. He got a whiff of her gentle

lavender scent before she looked up. "Has she regained consciousness?"

Steve made a wavy sign with his left hand, indicating so-so.

"You think it's an insider?" he said.

"Only employees use that stairway."

"Why would anyone attack her?"

"I don't understand anything, Steve. What was she doing here?"

"She was interviewing one of your employees, Theodora."

"I know. I was with her."

"You were? Why?"

"I bumped into Lieutenant Leguizamo in the elevator and she asked me to join her."

"Go on."

"Some nonsense about some photos Theodora took or collected. She had a crush on Phoebe. I think it's time she leaves the Lemrow."

"When was the last time you saw Theodora?"

Monika thought. "I escorted the detective to Theodora's cubicle. In my opinion, the interview was a complete waste of time."

"Nothing discussed?"

"Just the nonsense about Theodora's crush on Phoebe."

"Anything about suspicious activity at the Lemrow?"

"God no. Why?"

The door opened and King came in. He said to the director, "Theodora claims you ordered her to bring this to you." He held up his hand, revealing a cell.

"Really? Must be her guilty conscience."

"You didn't tell her to give this to you?"

"I wish I had. I'm concerned that Theodora was spending her time spying on other employees and keeping a record of it." She put out her hand to take it. "Thank you, Detective King, for confiscating that."

King opened his backpack, pulled out an evidence bag and placed the cell in it. "We'll have to keep it for now. It's part of a crime scene."

"A crime scene?" Monika said.

"Assaulting a police officer is a crime," King said.

"Of course, I'm not thinking."

King reached into his briefcase and pulled out a plastic bag.

Aside from running her little red tongue over her lips, Monika seemed calm. She sat up straight, aware that Steve and King were watching her, put her feet on the floor, pushed them gracefully back into her heels and stood up in order to examine the transparent bag.

All three looked down at a smashed recorder.

"What's that?" Monika said.

"Lieutenant Leguizamo's recorder," King said.

"What happened to it?" Monika looked horrified by the destruction.

"It was smashed with something heavy and then thrown out a window." King didn't mention that particles had identified it as being destroyed with the same statue that injured Dom nor that it had been found under the Lemrow library's window.

King put the transparent bag back into his briefcase and pulled out another one. "The scrapbook."

"The scrapbook? That thing Theodora kept when she was supposed to be working? Where was it?"

"In your washroom."

"In my washroom?" Monika laughed. "That Theodora. She claimed she felt ill and I let her use it."

"When was that?" Steve said.

"Theodora came to my office after the interview with Detective Leguizamo."

"What time was that?"

"I'm not sure. Around 5:30?" She started to take out her cell. "I'll check it on my calendar."

"Not now. So that was the last time you saw her."

"Of course. I'm sorry. I forgot that I'd seen her after that ridiculous interview." Monika threw him a wary look, then settled back in her chair.

"Anybody else use your washroom?" Steve said.

"All the people who are now in my office. I did, of course."

While she was talking, King had slipped on a pair of latex gloves and pulled the scrapbook out of its protective sheaf.

"Let's take a look," King said.

"Sure." Steve stepped to one side so King could put the scrapbook on the desk.

Very gently, King placed the scrapbook on it.

"You'd make a good conservator," the director said, joining them.

Neither detective told Monika not to touch the scrapbook knowing she'd have the sense not to.

King leafed through the pages, mostly shots of Phoebe.

"She was so beautiful," Monika said softly.

"Hey, here's a shot of you," King said.

It was the Daily News photo of the hit and run scene. Grainy but still clear, Monika was trim in a running outfit. At her side was her work out bag.

"I still don't understand dragging that along when you're jogging," Steve said.

"My only crime is vanity." Monika threw up her hands in a pretty gesture. "And I didn't drag it with me. As I told you repeatedly, I parked it, as I have every day I've jogged, behind a tree."

"And that coat." King pointed to the sleeve sticking out of the work out bag.

"Well, as I've explained many times, I get chills quite easily and like to slip something on after a run."

"So why didn't you?" King said.

"Put my jacket on? Because I was too upset about Phoebe." She glanced at the photo. "Obviously."

Steve figured it was time to tell her something. "You know one of the guards' coats was missing?"

"I'm not involved with lost property. At least not the guards' property."

"We wondered if you'd taken her coat by mistake."

"Her?"

"The guard we're talking about is a woman."

"I'm not in the habit of taking other people's clothing."

"You know, just grabbed it. Maybe it looked like yours."

"I doubt that."

"What would you say if I told you we found your fingerprints on the guard's coat?"

Monika thought a moment. "I have to confess, blame it on my fussy nature, that I will pick up after others. If I saw that coat on the floor I probably picked it up and threw it into the nearest closet."

Both detectives knew this would play well in court.

King had continued to turn the pages.

He turned to the last page. Lipstick kisses and hearts framed a space where a photo had been ripped out.

For an instant, Monika looked relieved. King raised his eyebrows. He caught her look.

"Anything wrong, Director?" King said.

"No, no," she said.

"Maybe it's on Theodora's cell," Steve said.

"Maybe," Monika gave him a little smile.

"And here," Steve turned to the inside back cover and ran his finger along a jagged edge. "Another photo has been ripped off."

"Detectives, it's been an exhausting and horrible day. How much longer are you going to keep me?" She put up her little hands as if they were handcuffed, then laughed at herself.

Damn. She was enjoying this.

"A few more questions," Steve said.

"Who do you think attacked Detective Leguizamo?"

"How should I know?" She stretched her buffed core like a cat aware of its beauty.

"You think it's an insider, right?"

"I didn't want to say this before, but I think it was Theodora."

"Why?" Steve said.

"Because she's ashamed. She and Hilda have been a couple for God knows how long. Who knows what they got up to with Phoebe."

"Sexual abuse?"

"Who knows? Theodora's always been odd. There have been episodes."

"Give me an example."

"My personal assistant, Mary Ratt, resigned because of her."

"Are you saying that Theodora made sexual advances to your secretary?"

"Mary Ratt is very shy and wouldn't give me the real reason."

"Why did Theodora come to your office?" King said.

"I don't know how to say this without sounding ridiculous."

The detectives waited.

"She threatened me."

"Go on."

"She told me she'd reveal what Phoebe was up to."

What bull shit, Steve thought, but good bull shit.

"What was that?"

Monika slid her left hand down to a tiny pocket, pulled out a handkerchief and dabbed at her forehead.

"This will kill Wellington."

You wish, Steve thought.

"Go on."

"Phoebe was involved with a man from Hong Kong."

King flipped back a page in the scrapbook. "Is this him?" King pointed to a photo of Phoebe kissing a good-looking man.

Monika looked down at the photo of a couple kissing in a discrete corner of the library. "Yes. Wasn't Theodora busy?"

"Why was he at the Lemrow?"

"He's a curator of sorts. Against my better judgment, I gave him a temporary contract." She gulped. "God, this is hard. Phoebe begged me to persuade her uncle to buy two statues from him. She said he was Wellington's godson."

"For the Kuan-yin exhibit?" Steve said.

"Wellington arranged for Sami to work on the exhibit?"

"Not exactly," Monika said.

"Did he know anything at all about Sami's involvement with the exhibit?"

"I assumed he did."

"Didn't Mary L. tell him in your office about an hour ago that Sami was working at the Lemrow on the Chen exhibit?"

Monika froze.

"You okay?" Steve needled her.

"I'm fine."

"How did Wellington react?"

"He blamed me. He was furious that I hadn't told him." Monika looked sorrowful. "Does Wellington have to know?"

"Know what?" King said.

"That his beloved niece took advantage of him, allowed her lover to steal from him…" Monika said.

"Steal from him?"

"Two of the statues might be copies," Monika said.

"You let them in the exhibit?" King said, the outrage in his voice worthy of a Lemrow trustee.

"What could I do? The provenance papers seemed genuine to me and Detective Kulchek." She smiled smugly.

"Yeah," was Steve's reply to his brief appearance as a provenance guy. He looked at Monika. "Your reputation is on the line."

"I know." She reached across her desk, grabbed a tissue and dabbed at her forehead.

"Wellington paid how much?"

"I'm not sure."

"Make a guess."

"Two million for the porcelain?"

"Two million dollars?"

"Ming, sixteenth century," She caught his confused look. "A dynasty known for its wonderful art."

"Hot with collectors," Steve said. "Manufactured yesterday. What's the so-called provenance of the other fake statue?"

"A little beauty. It's the stone one from Manchuria – supposedly."

Steve changed the subject. "How did Theodora get involved?"

"Involved? You mean in the forgery? I think Phoebe said more than she meant to during their endless jewelry repair sessions."

"You can leave now," Steve said. He and King didn't bother to look at Monika knowing this would bug her.

King waited until the door closed. "She lied. Dom didn't ask her to accompany her to Theodora's cubicle. According to the patrolwoman, the director insisted on going with them."

Steve nodded. He looked down at the photo of Phoebe kissing Sami.

King studied the photo. "I know where I saw him – C. E.'s apartment. Remember, Max said to ask Monika about him."

"There's a photo of Sami in Monika's apartment. When I asked her about him, she pretended she barely knew him," Steve said. "I saw him during my first time at the Lemrow. He was leaving the Green Room with Monika and C. E. She looked pissed off. What's with this guy? Phoebe slept with him. Monika has a cagy relationship with him."

 Steve looked down at the scrap of the photo Theodora had given King. "This is Mary Ratt and her backpack."

King nodded. "Theodora claims that Mary Ratt wrapped up the statue and put it into her backpack."

"Let's talk to both of them."

Chapter 31

11:00 p.m. Friday, September 8

Steve pushed back the Reliables' meeting to nail down Theodora's and Mary Ratt's testimonies.

Both he and King had shoved their ties into their jackets and their jackets into their lockers hours ago. With rolled up sleeves and bristly chins, they were in sharp contrast to Theodora. She sat across the interview table from them, arrayed in pink frills topped by a felt hat with bright flowers circling the brim.

Five minutes ago Steve had formally met Theodora so he watched King handle her.

"We want to discuss what happened during your interview with Lieutenant Leguizamo today at around 5:00 p.m.," King said.

Theodora studied Steve with great interest. "Who's in charge now?"

Caught off guard, Steve said, "What?"

King suppressed a laugh.

"Since Lieutenant Leguizamo has been injured, someone has to take her place." Theodora said this kindly, tutoring her slow student.

"I'm in charge," Steve said. "Let's get back on track. What happened during the interview?"

"The lieutenant came to my cubicle and looked at the scrapbook. The director was there." In spite of the late hour, Theodora was gushing with delight over the attention.

King reached into his backpack and placed the scrapbook on the table. The tech department had swathed it in a protective covering.

"What's this?" cooed Theodora, eying the covering on her precious scrapbook.

"To protect it," King said.

"Make sure the fingerprints aren't smudged, you mean," Theodora said.

"What was in the scrapbook?" King said.

"Photos." Theodora's smile morphed to a frown. Her voice rose. "You said, 'was'. Does that mean all the photos have been destroyed?"

"No, not all," Steve said.

"We're going through the scrapbook. Describe the ones the lieutenant was interested in, Theodora," King said.

Without asking, Theodora ran her hand over the covering coating the cover. She flipped it open.

"Still here." She smiled down at a shot of Sami and Phoebe kissing. "I caught them in the Green Room."

"When was that?" Steve said.

"Last Thursday, August 31. The lieutenant was interested only in the photos shot in the Green Room that day."

King and Steve exchanged glances.

"Did you shoot all the photos in the album?" Steve said.

Theodora shook her head in the negative. "Geoff shot two. There's a Daily News clipping. I shot the rest. "

"As we go through the scrapbook, you'll identify who shot the photo and describe the ones that are missing." King kept his voice calm and low.

"Well, I took this one of Sami and Phoebe kissing."

"They knew you took it?"

"No, of course not. I'm very careful. No one knew about it until the lieutenant and the director saw it in the scrapbook." She whispered, "I didn't even tell Hilda."

The three of them looked down at the handsome couple who were oblivious to everything except themselves.

"Next," Steve said, breaking the spell.

King leaned across the narrow table and turned the page. He paused at a photo of Phoebe. She was touching a necklace around her neck.

King looked at Steve and then turned the page. A photo had been ripped from it. "What was here, Theodora?"

"C. E., the director, and Sami were standing together. On a table in the background Mary Ratt was standing next to her carrier."

King took a photo from the slim pile at his elbow.

"Is this a copy of that photo? It was taken from your cell."

"Yes," Theodora said.

"Why did you take the photo?" Steve said.

Steve read correctly her teacher/preacher expression.

"What's missing in the photo, Detective?" Theodora looked at King. "I'll give you a hint: You've seen the photos on my cell."

"You tell us what's missing, Theodora," King said. Steve could tell that King got a kick out of her.

"The Riccio statue." She paused dramatically before continuing, "The statue's in the carrier. That's why I took the photo."

Steve and King examined the red case. "It would fit," Steve said, meaning the statue. He looked at Theodora. "Explain yourself."

"It's highly irregular for an employee to put a museum object into her carrier even if it's wrapped and the director and a curator are present." Like a cat finding an imperfection in its coat, Theodora rubbed one of the numerous metals pinned to her frilly blouse.

"And that's what I found on the floor in the director's office." Theodora pointed to Mary Ratt.

"You mean this?' King slipped a remnant of paper in a protective, plastic covering from the pile next to him. It showed part of Mary Ratt's face and one side of a leather case.

Theodora studied it. "Yes."

Steve scribbled the word, backpack. "When did you take this photo?" he said.

"When I was leaving. No one saw me. I shielded myself behind Geoff and took it."

"Did you take any other photos in the Green Room on Thursday, August 31?"

"No."

"Who else took photos besides you?" King said.

"Geoff, of course." Theodora turned to the next page. One of the tabs that had held a photo fell onto the table. King picked it up and shoved it into an envelope.

"Describe the photo that was mounted here," Steve said.

"This one was of Hilda, Phoebe and me. Mary Ratt was standing at the table and next to her was the statue."

"This is in the Green Room last Thursday, August 31?" Steve said.

"Yes," Theodora said.

"Did Geoff give you this copy?"

"Oh, yes. I'm sorry you'll never see it. It's lovely except for Mary Ratt looking so grumpy."

Steve sighed deeply. He thought about Mary Ratt and her carrier. Sneaky, weird Theodora was a vital witness.

"Did Geoff take any other photos?" he said.

"We're coming to one." Theodora took the reins.

King exchanged a look with Steve as he turned to a blank page. The black background paper on which a photo had been mounted was darker than the surrounding borders.

"C. E. begged him to take one of him holding the Riccio. The director and Sami were standing on either side of C. E."

"How did you get a copy?"

"I asked Geoff for it."

"When was this?"

"Later that Thursday. I think it was at lunch. He said, 'Sure, why not? I can't use it.' Those were his exact words," Theodora said.

"Is this the photo that Geoff took?" He held up a copy of Max's copy.

"Yes," Theodora said. "Where did you get that?"

"I can't say," King said.

Theodora smiled smugly. Steve imagined her gushing this bit of cop secrecy to Hilda.

King recalled what Cristobel had said less than four hours ago. Geoff told her he'd given a copy of the same photo to C. E.

"Did Geoff take any other photos?" Steve repeated.

"Not while I was there. We were supposed to have a Staff Day meeting, but I saw it wasn't taking place so I went back to work."

Steve thought: And Geoff, the poor schmuck, was tormented to his death because he did C.E. the favor of giving him a photo Geoff himself couldn't use.

After King had promised Theodora that her scrapbook would be returned to her eventually, he told a patrolman to escort her home and remain outside her apartment.

He and Steve entered an observation space overlooking an interview room.

Mary Ratt, aka the Mouse, was seated at the table facing the observation space. With her porcelain skin and carefully made up face she reminded Steve of a doll his daughter never played with. Unlike Theodora, whose outfits were often ludicrous but always original, Mary Ratt was dressed like someone who pored over Life magazines from the 1950s. From the pair of gloves on the table to the little hat with a tiny veil perched on her finger-waved hair, she screamed vintage.

Rosaria had her back to the observation room. Steve spoke into her ear phones. In response, she put her right hand behind her back and flapped her thumb and fingers together, indicating that the Mouse was a chatterbox.

As soon as Mary Ratt's streetwise voice drew breath, Rosaria said, "What did you think about delivering the statue?"

"I told the director I didn't want to. She said did I expect Curator Stowbridge to carry it after his recent heart attack? You know, laying a guilt trip." The Mouse lifted her manicured hands to her veil, pushed it over the brim of her felt hat and shook her head in disgust.

In spite of the late hour and the regurgitated air from the a. c., her make up was bullet proof from sweat.

"I said why not have an insured carrier deliver it the way we always do. And that's when she said read this and handed me a great reference. Should I tear it up, she said."

"What date was this?"

"Like I said before, Thursday, August 31."

"What happened next?"

"I went to the Green Room. She -- "

"The director?"

"Who else? Yeah, the director told me to take the Riccio to the Green Room."

"Anyone see you do this? Doesn't anyone say anything when someone picks up a valuable sculpture?"

"The guards know me. I'm a trusted employee. I put a 'being restored" sign in the Riccio's place, yanked on those ridiculous gloves that destroyed my manicure and took it to the Green Room."

"You weren't afraid you'd be caught?"

"Doing what?"

"Removing a valuable object from a museum."

"The director told me to take it to the Green Room. She's the one who told me to put up the sign."

"What happened then?"

"The clowns on the Staff Day committee were meeting."

"Who are they?"

"Geoff, Theodora and Hilda."

"Anyone else present?"

"It was a regular Grand Central. Phoebe and Sami were there. Then her highness showed up with Curator Stowbridge. She told C. E. that I'd accompany him home after the statue was wrapped."

"Did you accompany him home?""

"Eventually. He sailed out of the Green Room with her and Sami. Per instructions, I went downstairs to the monitors. The director was there with Curator Stowbridge."

"Was your case checked?"

With an attempt at balletic grace, the Mouse fluffed up her voluminous skirt and crinolines.

"How did you carry the Riccio?" King said.

Miss Ratt's face turned red with resentment. "In my very valuable leather cosmetic case."

"Weren't you surprised to be taking an art work out of the museum?"

"Nothing surprises me about this place. The director made a big deal about seeing C. E. and me out the door."

Steve said into Rosaria's ear, "I bet she did."

The three detectives imagined the scene: The staff listening, without being noticed, to the director's and C. E.'s cultured chit-chat. The director giving the Mouse a sweet smile and resting her hand on the red case as she escorted C. E. and Mary Ratt to the outside door.

In the observation room, Steve made a note to check with Kenny who was working the security desk that Thursday afternoon.

Steve wired Rosaria: Ask her about Theodora.

"Are you close to Theodora?" Rosaria said.

"Theodora?" The Mouse twisted her fire engine red lips. "You're kidding. I avoid her."

"Why?"

"Wouldn't you? She's crazy."

"Give me an example."

"She sneaks around taking photos. She did it in the Green Room." Mary Ratt tapped her crimson, pointy nails on the table. "When she was leaving, she hid behind Geoff and snapped Curator Stowbridge, the director, Sami and me. I knew she was doing it. She does that stuff all the time."

"Did you say anything to her?"

"What's to say? She does whatever she wants."

"Did you decide to leave the Lemrow or were you pushed?"

"A little of both." Mary Ratt eyed Rosaria.

"Who wanted you out of the Lemrow?"

"Who do you think?"

"Answer the question."

"The director."

"She gave you your notice?" Rosaria said.

"She's more subtle than that."

Rosaria imagined Mary Ratt putting a cigarette holder to her crimson lips and blowing a smoke circle to emphasize her remark. "Why did she want you out of the Lemrow?"

"I knew too much."

"What did you know?"

For a second, Mary Ratt twisted her mouth into a secretive smirk.

"I'm not playing games with you, Mary. Answer the question."

"The director told me not to mention to Wellington Chen that Sami was working on his exhibit. Odd, huh?"

Rosaria wondered if the Mouse was a blackmailer. Maybe.

"This great opportunity came up in Hong Kong. It's a fellowship at a museum."

"Anything to do with Curator Sami?"

"I think he runs it."

"How did you learn about the position?"

"The director told me. She knew I wanted more museum work, less secretarial stuff."

"When are you supposed to start?"

"In a week, but I'm reconsidering," a wily expression spread over the Mouse's features.

Chapter 32

12:30 a.m. Saturday, September 9

The cesspool's bright, iridescent lights exposed the Reliables' determined, haggard faces. The attack on one of their own had stepped up the ante.

Rosaria perched on a nearby window ledge. Steve and King stood on either side of the bulletin board. In the top right corner the familiar images of C. E., Geoff and Phoebe were partitioned by black masking tape. Beneath them were photos of Elliot, Harry, Cristobel, Monika, Sami, Theodora, Max, Wellington and Stasia. A patrolwoman squeezed in photos of Mary Ratt and Yoshi.

Below the photos the detectives eyed the shots of the 72nd Street curb showing Elliot's Nikes, Phoebe's purse and the rearview mirror.

A blown up map of Central Park and Fifth Avenue between Sixty-fifth Street and Eighty-sixth Street was pinned in the middle of the bulletin board. To its right were shots of five numbered cell phones.

"Listen up. I'm heading the investigation until Dom is on her feet," Steve said.

The Reliables didn't react. The news of Steve replacing Dom had already spread throughout the ranks.

Steve pointed his thumb at King, "We interviewed Theodora. Look behind you."

All eyes in the room turned to three blowups on the back wall.

"These shots were taken in the Green Room on August 31 around 10:30," Steve said. "They're in chronological order."

Rosaria moved the pointer to the first shot. It was the familiar cropped photo of C. E. being handed the Riccio. On the right side of C. E. were the tips of four gloved fingers handing him the statue and on the left side was part of the shoulder of a man's jacket.

"This is C. E. holding the Riccio. According to Theodora's testimony, he's flanked by Monika and Sami," Rosaria said. "When King interviewed Cristobel she claimed that Geoff gave one copy of the photo to C.E. Max found the cropped copy after his brother's death and gave it to Phoebe, but he Xeroxed it before giving it to her. Our Steve took this copy from Max. Geoff also gave one to Theodora. King will cover that. Questions?"

The room started buzzing. A young Reliable said, "What did Max say about that piece of paper with twins written on it?"

"When I got the disposable cell from him, I asked him about that," King said. "He admitted he'd picked it off the floor after his brother died."

"His brother wrote twins?"

"Correct," King said. "He said his brother had gone to Scranton after his heart attack and referred to it."

"They were twins."

"So were Monika Syka and a sister who had died in a car crash," Steve said.

"C. E. and Max, Monika and her sister – two sets of twins from Scranton." Rosaria folded her arms across her massive chest. "C. E. pushed for Monika's appointment as Lemrow director."

"This twin thing keeps cropping up. What do we have on Monika's Scranton background?" Steve pointed at Joe, the oldest Reliable.

"Her family died in a car crash." Joe said from memory as he flipped through his notes. "She was the only survivor. Excellent student."

Steve shrugged. Something was edging around his memory. He nodded at a Reliable who had an eager look on his tired face.

"I checked out C. E.'s copy of this photo. The techs think C. E cropped it, cut out Sami and the director," a Reliable said. "According to Wellington Chen and Steve, the director wanted to borrow it for the Lemrow Newsletter, but no one in their media section knows anything about it. When I questioned the director, she claimed she didn't know what I was talking about."

"At the Staff Day I overheard the director thanking Phoebe for lending the Lemrow the cropped photo," Steve said. "Phoebe didn't want to. Her uncle forced her to."

"Let me get this straight," a young detective said. "This cropped photo shows that C. E. didn't hide or sneak it out of the Lemrow. Was Monika setting him up?"

"Yeah, we think so. If C. E. was stealing the statue why would he want a photo of himself holding it and flanked by Monika and Sami? This shot screwed her," Steve said. "I saw the director leaving the Green Room shortly after the photo was taken. She was furious."

"Cristobel told me that Geoff gave C. E. a copy of the shot," King said. "That's the one that disappeared after the director got her hands on it at Staff Day, but Geoff also gave one to Theodora."

"So the director didn't know Theodora had a copy?" a Reliable said.

"She found out when Dom went through Theodora's scrapbook," King said. "We think Monika destroyed it. Like Rosaria said, Steve grabbed this copy from Max." He paused before going on. "The director set up C. E. because C. E. figured there was something illegal going on at the Lemrow. Maybe he confronted her? Why did he go to Scranton, their hometown, after his heart attack?"

Steve glanced at his watch. "Let's keep moving. We're talking to Yoshi, C. E.'s boyfriend, who's in Tokyo, in ten minutes. Rosaria just finished an interview with Mary Ratt."

Usually, a name like Mary Ratt would have earned snorts and wise-ass remarks, but the Reliables were in obsessive hunter mode.

Rosaria flicked the pointer's red dot on the next blowup. "This is a fragment showing Mary Ratt's left side and a partial of her carryall. Theodora claims she picked it off the floor in the director's office. She's identified it as a section of a shot Geoff gave her. She claims it's a shot of her, Hilda and Phoebe. In the background Mary Ratt was standing next to a table. The Riccio was on the table next to the carryall. Except for this fragment, we have no record of this photo taken by Geoff. According to Theodora, it was ripped from her scrapbook. Mary Ratt remembers Geoff taking the photo. Finally, we do have this shot that sneaky Theodora took on her cell." Everyone's eyes followed the pointer to the third blowup, obviously, a candid shot. The director, Sami and C. E. were talking. In the background Mary Ratt was standing next to a table on which was the red carryall.

"What's in the case?" Rosaria answered her own question. "The Riccio."

"We'll run through some stuff till I speak to Yoshi," Steve said, glancing at his watch. "Phoebe's murderer and Dom's attacker. Same person?"

There was a unanimous grunt of assent.

Steve continued, tapping Elliot's photo on the bulletin board and pointing at a Reliable who'd been tailing Elliot.

The detectives knew the drill: motivation, pros, cons.

"This guy didn't kill her. He was standing on the curb when she was hit. He was at the Lemrow when Dom was hit."

Steve tapped on Harry's photo.

"Same thing," Another Reliable said. "He wouldn't kill Phoebe. She meant more to him alive. He was at the Lemrow for a meeting when Dom was hit."

Steve pointed at Cristobel's photo.

King spoke up. "Phoebe got Cristobel's guy, Elliot, and her scholarship. At the Staff Day on Tuesday, Cristobel borrows Elliot's car keys to go for a job interview, loses them and was in the park near 5th Avenue and 72nd Street where Phoebe was hit at fifteen:five. Cristobel found Elliot's keys in her locker. Cristobel was at the Lemrow when Dom was hit."

"These are the original suspects for Phoebe's murder. Now we have the complication of Dom's attack," Steve said.

Rosaria said, "Today Dom went to the Lemrow to interview Theodora. The director joined Dom for the interview. It took place at 17 hours this afternoon."

"The director claimed that Dom asked her to accompany her to Theodora's interview," Steve said. "Patrolwoman Higgins, who was with Dom, claims that the director insisted on coming along to the interview."

Rosaria tapped Theodora's photo. "Dom takes Theodora's scrapbook which has the August 31st photos in the Green Room. It was not found on her. Later, King found the scrapbook shoved behind a radiator in the Director's bathroom."

"So who hit Dom?"

"The weapon was a dog statue in the Lemrow library, weighing about twenty pounds. We figure it was done by an insider at around eighteen: thirty."

Steve tapped the photos of Elliot, Cristobel, Harry, Monika and Max. "These people were allowed to leave the Lemrow after being interviewed. Warned not to leave Manhattan."

"The director was allowed to leave?" A Reliable said, voicing the surprise of the rest of the group.

"Yeah," Steve said. "Suzie's keeping an eye on her." He named a seasoned detective.

"Joe is interviewing Wellington Chen now." Steve changed the subject. "King has a theory."

"Everything hinges on C. E. and Geoff," King said.

The Reliables studied the men's photos.

"We investigate their deaths again and we find our suspect," King continued. "Did C. E. have an induced heart attack? Why did Geoff kill himself? Were their deaths connected with Phoebe's and with Dom's attack?"

"Some of you know what's on these." Rosaria pointed to the photographs of the five numbered cell phones.

"Number One is a disposable, used last Sunday, 9/3, around nineteen: fifty. It was used to call C.E. Stowbridge who was holding the receiver of his landline when he died."

Everyone in the room knew a prepaid disposable meant you planned ahead -- premeditation -- and that you don't want to be traced. You want to hide something.

Rosaria continued, "The cell was found by Stasia, the security guard, in her coat. Thursday, 9/7, her coat was missing, then replaced in Theodora's locker." Rosaria tapped Stasia's photo and pointed to the hit and run scene and the sleeve hanging out of the director's workout bag. "Is this that coat? Stasia found the cell in her coat pocket and gave it to Maximillian Stowbridge, C. E.'s twin brother."

She indicated Max's photo.

Rosaria tapped on a photo of another cell. "Number 2: Elliot Ross's. On that Staff Day, 9/7, he sent a text message to Cristobel agreeing to lend her his car keys. Time: Eleven: ten."

King said, "On 9/4 Geoff told Cristobel he'd given the photo to C. E. He also told her his Canon and backpack were missing. That night he hung himself in the Green Room."

"We never found his Canon or backpack," a Reliable said.

King nodded in agreement and moved to the cell labeled Number 3. "Cristobel's. During my last interview with Cristobel about four hours ago, she said that Geoff gave C. E. a print of C. E. holding the Riccio. Geoff had taken the photo in the Green Room on Thursday, 8/31. The following Monday, 9/4, Geoff told Cristobel that his Canon and satchel were lost. Throughout that Monday, Geoff had a series of phone calls. The techs think they were from the disposable cell."

King pointed at the photo of the disposable cell and waited while the Reliables digested the new information. "According to Cristobel, that Monday

Geoff went from being relieved that someone had found his Canon and satchel to saying to Cristobel around sixteen hours, 'Why would anyone hate me so much?'"

This grabbed a lot of attention because the detectives hadn't heard it before.

"Who was calling him?"

"Geoff wouldn't tell Cristobel."

"At 1:55 a.m. Tuesday he left Cristobel a message, 'I can't go on. Please don't despise me, Cristobel. Bye.' She called him back six times but got no response. Like you said, we haven't found his Canon or his cell."

"Someone took his Canon on Monday, 9/4 but he had his cell on Tuesday," a Reliable said.

"Good point." King said.

"So who took his cell?"

"The director and that librarian found his body."

"Correct." King waited while the Reliables digested the information.

Rosaria pointed at Elliot's cell. "9/7, time: fifteen: ten. There's a texted message to his father telling him to come to Central Park."

A detective pointed to the photo of Elliot's Nikes on the curb, near the rear view mirror and Phoebe's purse.

The Reliables looked at the tattooed Chinese character around Elliot's right ankle. "So that's Elliot standing on the 72nd Street corner. He makes the call to his father from there or near there."

"Correct," Rosaria said.

King said, "Cristobel claims that Elliot's car keys were missing after the Staff Day."

"Someone inside the Lemrow swiped the keys on Staff Day that Thursday," a Reliable said. "So where did they end up?"

"In Cristobel's locker."

"The director was in the Locker Room," Rosaria said. "So were Elliot, Stasia and Max."

"On 9/7 there's a call made to Elliot at fifteen hours. Cristobel claims she told Elliot she'd lost the car keys and changed her mind about going for the job interview,"
Steve said. "Then she finds them in her locker. King, you want to summarize?"

King said, "We figure the director went to the locker room twice."

The Reliables buzzed like hornets.

"On 9/7 at sixteen: twenty-five Stasia and Max go to the Locker Room. They see the director who leaves by the internal stairs. Theodora passes her when she goes down to the Locker Room. Theodora takes Stasia's coat out of her locker and gives the coat to Stasia. When she leaves, Theodora sees the director near the internal stairs.

Sixteen: thirty-five: the director enters the Locker Room again. Elliot enters the Locker Room and sees the director leave by the internal stairs. He places the purse and the mirror in his locker. Sixteen: forty: Elliot leaves the Locker Room by the external stairs. He's seen by Max and Stasia."

A Reliable said, wrinkling his face in disbelief, "Didn't Monika say she was there because she was shocked over Phoebe?"

"She didn't want to run into anyone," Rosaria said, deadpan.

"King?" Steve said.

"We think she was returning Stasia's coat and put it in Theodora's locker by mistake."

No one said a word. The Reliables waited for the next remark.

"She came back a second time to put Elliot's car keys into Cristobel's locker."

The room was silent. Then the Reliables burst into applause, stomping their feet on the linoleum and high fiving each other.

As well as the three lead detectives shouting and laughing, listening to the conference call from her hospital bed, Dom was laughing too.

"Okay. Enough," Steve shouted.

After a few minutes of more backslapping and stomping, the detectives were quiet.

"So Monika is our killer?" a Reliable said.

"Now we have to prove it," Steve said.

Steve said. "King, you want to fill us in on Sami?"

"This guy," King directed a laser beam at Sami's photo, "is a Hong Kong curator who was in NYC to install the Chen exhibit. He and Monika have been professional associates a long time."

Steve interrupted. "Wellington didn't know Sami was working on his exhibit. Lots of bad blood between Wellington's family and Sami's. He's the last guy Wellington wanted near him or Phoebe."

"Sami was Phoebe's lover," King said. "He's probably the father of her child. Wellington Chen took Phoebe's cell."

The Reliables fell silent until someone said, "No shit?"

"He told me three hours ago." Steve said. "Questions?"

"So what's the connection between these photos and C. E. and Geoff's deaths?" a Reliable said.

"King, you want to answer that?" Steve said.

"We think C. E. altered the original shot of him holding the Riccio and standing in between Monika and Sami," King said. "The techs found some scraps of the altered photo at C. E.'s apartment and they match."

"Because he was pissed off?" a Reliable said.

"He'd drunk at least a bottle of wine. I can picture him thinking, but not too clearly, about shit going down at the museum. Then Phoebe cancels dinner. I can see him staring at the photo and cutting out the people he thinks are stealing from the Lemrow and betraying him personally."

"He backed Monika for her director's job and Wellington Chen was his best friend," Rosaria said.

"It could also have been his boyfriend, Yoshi. Don't forget. He found the body," a Reliable said.

"But he didn't know what was driving C. E. nuts. Remember, when we interviewed Yoshi that night he told us C. E. wanted to tell him something bad about the Lemrow?"

"We didn't take it any further because we thought C. E. had died from a natural heart attack,"

King said. "Don't forget he'd had his first heart attack a month before."

"Didn't Monika give Yoshi airfare to go to Japan?"

Heads nodded all over the room recalling the JAL one way ticket to Tokyo on Monika's credit card.

"Mary Ratt, the ex-secretary, leaves. Fired? Why?"

"She had to deliver the Riccio to C. E.'s apartment in her carryall. It was her last day."

"How about C. E.'s twin, Max. He could've cropped it."

King shook his head in disagreement. "Don't forget. Max gave the cropped photo to Phoebe. I think that C. E. did it."

Steve said, "On Staff Day, Monika wanted the cropped photo. Claimed it was for the members' newsletter. Wellington forced his niece to give the photo to Monika."

"So why is the altered photo so important?" A Reliable said. "Do you think it got Geoff killed?"

Rosaria flicked the pointer at the blowups. "The one on the left is Theodora's cell photo of C. E. holding the Riccio. He's flanked by Monika and Sami. The photo on the right is Geoff's. It's been cropped and shows only C. E.'s gloved hand, but by studying the details it's evident it was taken at the same time as the other photo."

"It looks like the director is handing C. E. the statue he's supposed to have stolen. So it's a set up," Rosaria said.

The Reliables nodded in agreement.

"C. E. knew something?" One of them said.

"He told Phoebe there was illegal activity at the museum," Steve said.

"Monika," several Reliables said.

"So Monika screws C. E. by telling him to examine the statue," King said.

"She told me he stole it and the museum wasn't saying anything," Steve said. "Claimed she didn't want Wellington canceling the exhibit, the bad publicity."

"Geoff takes an incriminating photo. And kills himself?" A Reliable said.

"Listen to this." King turned on the recorder. They listened to Cristobel's account of Geoff's last day.

After King snapped it off, he said, "Someone hounded him. And found the porn pictures on his camera."

"Geoff tops himself." Steve's cell buzzed. He checked the caller ID and stepped out of the room. "Yeah, Joe?"

"Something's funny. Wellington said the same old stuff."

"Nothing about Phoebe's cell and tracking down Sami?" Steve said.

"Denies it."

"We'll shake him up." Steve told Joe where to take Wellington.

"What time is it in Tokyo?" Steve adjusted the TV in Dom's office. He was used to Skype since he and his daughter used it when she was at school in Providence.

"1:30 p.m," Rosaria said after scanning her Blackberry.

Remembering how distraught Yoshi was at the Chen reception, Steve had decided that it was going to be one on one.

Rosaria and King were seated out of view and the interview was being taped.

Steve made sure he had a pleasant smile on his face as Yoshi, sitting in his office and dressed in black, came into view. After reciting the particulars about the case and that it was being recorded, he thanked Yoshi for helping with the investigation of Phoebe's death. Yoshi bowed his head in response to Steve's remarks.

"We think the three deaths are connected," Steve said.

"Three?"

"C. E.'s, Phoebe's and Geoff's, the photographer."

Yoshi thought a moment. "How is this so?"

"We don't think C. E.'s death was natural." Steve paused a moment, knowing this was a lot to ask C. E.'s lover to digest.

"What are you suggesting?" Yoshi said. "C. E. was very naughty. He ate and drank too much and never exercised."

"We think he was goaded into having a fatal heart attack because he knew something that could destroy someone's career." Steve paused, studying Yoshi's face. "What did you talk about during your phone conversation?"

"I'd been on a business trip and told him I was coming home that night. He was upset because

Phoebe had canceled their dinner date and made me promise that we'd discuss what was bothering him. Something to do with the Lemrow."

"Did he say what this activity was?"

Yoshi thought a moment. He shook his head in the negative.

"You mentioned that C. E. liked to eat and drink. Do you think he'd been drinking that evening?"

"Of course, he'd been drinking, but that didn't stop him from thinking logically."

"A cropped photo of C. E. holding a statue was found in the apartment."

"He told me about the photograph. The photographer gave it to him."

"Did you see the photo?"

"No. It was taken while I was on the business trip." Yoshi drew in his breath. "I did see it. When I found C. E. a ripped photo was near him. Was that it?"

Rosaria gave Steve a thumbs up.

"Do you know who else was in the photo besides C. E.?"

"No."

"What else did you discuss? Please think carefully. Your testimony is very important."

"I have tried to help you, but this is so painful." Yoshi was shaking his head. He looked up and stared at Steve, "I thought it odd that a Lemrow employee delivered the statue to C. E. He was holding it as we talked."

"Did he say the employee's name?"

"Something odd." Yoshi wrinkled his nose. "Ms. Souse? Ms. Mouse?"

Steve kept a straight face and was about to sign off, but Yoshi began speaking rapidly in a high, strained voice.

"C. E. and I were going through a hard time. I didn't have to go on the business trip. I wanted to get away, to think things over. After his heart attack, C. E. insisted on going to his hometown of Scranton. When he returned, he couldn't or wouldn't stop talking about it. If I hadn't gone, I could have protected him." Yoshi burst into tears, crying like a heart broken child. "I wish he had died from over eating. Now, you make me think I could have saved him." He wiped his eyes with his sleeve. "I go now." He leaned forward and pressed a button. His image faded away.

For a few seconds, the three detectives sat in silence. Finally, Rosaria said gruffly, "Good job, Steve."

Chapter 33

2:00 a.m. Saturday, September 9

"Tell me about Sami," Joe said. They were in a corner of the director's office at the Lemrow. The only other person in the room was a patrolman. Everything was being recorded and videoed. Except nothing was being said.

"Sami is the son of a business competitor," Wellington repeated, tired but patient. "That's all I know."

"Did Phoebe know him?"

"I don't know." Wellington didn't bother to lie with conviction.

"Did you take your niece's cell?"

"No."

"You told Detective Kulchek you did."

"He misunderstood."

"How does Monika Syka figure in all this?"

Wellington stared at Joe before saying, "A very good question."

Why didn't Wellington demand that his lawyer be present or that he wanted to leave?

Curious, Joe said, "Your bodyguards are downstairs?"

"They have the night off. I don't need them."

Steve and Rosaria arrived at the Trident. They spotted some guys from New York One TV. Not hard, considering they were sitting in their permanently unwashed, dingy white van with an antenna and rotating dish.

The detectives left a patrolman in the lobby so the doorman wouldn't alert Monika or Harry.

Up they went to the thirtieth floor. Usually, Rosaria gave a running commentary on the condos, townhouses, rentals, lofts they entered in the name of the law. Not tonight. Steve studied her determined look. "You okay?" he said, expecting a tough response.   Instead, she shook her head. "I don't know. Something's funny." Her comments were stopped by Steve ringing Monika's doorbell. They heard a click and assumed she was looking at them through the peep hole. Then the door opened.

Monika stood in front of them in an old plaid shirt, jeans and sneakers. Strained but composed, she said, "Isn't this late? It is for me."

She caught her breath and continued to block the entrance. The two detectives sidled around Monika and walked into the apartment.

"Come in," she said in a gently sarcastic tone. "Can't you do anything about New York One?"

"Like what?" Rosaria said.

"Tell them not to park in front of my building."

"It's not illegal and I'm not a traffic cop."

The place was a shambles. Boxes sat on tables. Open trunks, half full, were lined up against the terrace windows.

"Leaving?" Rosaria said.

"Too nervous to sleep, I'm rearranging everything."

"Get your coat, okay?" Steve said with a smile. "We want to go over a few things."

"At the station house?" Monika raised her eyebrows. "I'll call my lawyer."

"You can do it on the way." Steve opened the door while Monika grabbed a coat from a nearby sofa.

Down they went. Without saying a word to the doorman, they escorted her to a patrol car. Automatically, Rosaria put her right hand over Monika's head so she couldn't claim later that she banged her head on the doorframe.

As the patrolman pulled away from the front of the Trident, Monika texted her lawyer and told him to meet her at the station house.

Steve glanced back over his shoulder at the New York One van. It hadn't moved.

Reading his thoughts, Monika said, "They can harass Harry and Elliot. Good."

Her bitter tone hung in the Patrol car's stale air.

"We're making a detour," Steve said. "Brief stop at the Lemrow."

"I told my lawyer to meet me at the precinct.'

"Call him back."

Monika studied the Smartphone she'd been clutching. Then dropped it into her pocket.

At the museum they passed another media van and went down the ramp to the employees' entrance. Monika ignored the patrolman stationed near the door.

The night security staff, encased behind the glass partition, were silhouetted by the still images on the closed-circuit screens. Head of Security Kenny O'Malley's crumpled shirt was a white speck in the dark space.

The two detectives nodded to him. The director did nothing. Rosaria dropped behind. A patrolman took her place.

Steve kept going, slightly ahead of Monika. She didn't ask where they were headed. Behind them, the patrolman followed like a sheep dog.

They strode up the stairs and headed into the Water Court. The only sound was the padding of their sneakers on the marble floors. Steve looked up at the Triton sitting in the dry fountain and realized he missed its familiar splashing.

He nodded to the right, toward the Green Room. "You came out of the Green Room last Thursday – Remember?"

The director said nothing.

They turned right and stepped onto the oriental rugs placed in precision along the Renaissance Wing corridor. Instead of the usual muted lighting, adjusted to display the paintings and

sculpture, the gallery was as brightly lit as a
department store. They walked past Lemrow's
cherry wood desk and leather bound books.

Steve was familiar enough with the museum
to know they were approaching the eighteenth
century painting of the smiling girl. As they passed
it, he flinched, thinking of unfinished, personal
business.

He led Monika past a portrait of Judith
holding the head of Holofernes to the gnarled
walnut chest on which rested the Riccio. He looked
down at the statue of the lacquered angel, mystified
that this ugly thing had been the focus of countless
police hours.

Steve picked up the soft padding of steps
nearby. Inwardly, he cursed but managed to keep a
stern, impassive expression on his face. Had
Monika heard them? He studied her robotic stance,
standing straight, arms at her side, her face was
impassive as his, but her eyes were searching into
the Central Gallery shadows.

"Wondering why we're here?" Steve
cracked the silence. His voice too loud for his own
ears, he lowered it and repeated himself.

The intense lighting bleached Monika. She
resembled, in Steve's eyes, a faded photograph.

"Nothing surprises me," she said in a hollow
voice. Her fox eyes were peering into the Central
Gallery's darkness.

Steve listened hard for any sound from the
other galleries and heard none. He knew she'd
heard what – footsteps - a suppressed sneeze?

"Why would anybody steal this thing?" Steve looked down at the statue and put out his hand to touch it.

"Don't."

"Don't what? Don't con C. E. into taking this thing home and then accuse him of stealing it?"

She ignored him, saying for her invisible audience, "I should have alerted the Lemrow that C. E. stole the statue."

"Why didn't you?"

"Because he was a first rate curator who had one impulsive moment and stole the Riccio."

"Who told you he stole the Riccio?"

"Can't say." She turned toward him and said in a soft voice, "Steve, why have you changed toward me?" When he didn't answer, she raised her voice. "Early this morning you couldn't keep your hands off me."

The bitch is saying it for her audience.

"Why were you photographed handing him the Riccio?"

"Was I?" Monika reached up to her neck to fondle her missing pearls. "A publicity shot? How should I know?"

Steve reached into his breast pocket and pulled out the photo of Monika, C. E. and Sami. In the background Mary Ratt stood next to a table on which was her carryall. "Taken last Thursday."

"Isn't that packing stuff?" Steve referred to the bubble wrap on a table in the photo's background. "Did Geoff's suicide have anything to do with this photo?"

"How should I know?" She was catching her breath.

"Theodora…"

"Not Theodora." Her voice rose.

"Theodora and Phoebe saw you in the Green Room right after Geoff's body was discovered. Last Tuesday?"

"Of course, it was last Tuesday, How could I forget."

"You were wearing gloves."

"I've explained that I didn't want to damage the crime scene."

"Was it a crime scene? I thought he killed himself."

"How was I to know?" She shook her head. "I didn't want to disturb the scene, but I had to check Geoff. He was my employee."

"The guy was hanging from the ceiling. Who threw the photos of him jerking off around the room?"

"He did? I have no idea."

"Theodora remembers you were taking off your gloves, but when you saw her and Phoebe you pulled them back on. Why? Were you placing the photos to humiliate and discredit Geoff?"

"Don't be ridiculous." Monika managed to look bored.

"We know that he received phone calls the night he killed himself. He was searching for his Canon and satchel. He found his satchel. Keep the Canon, Monika? Remove his cell from his body?"

Monika looked defenseless and vulnerable. She turned her sweet, grave face to him. "Where's Theodora?"

"At the precinct. Some of those porn shots had your fingerprints on them."

"Impossible. Where's my lawyer?" She took out her Smartphone and punched in a message.

"Did you call C. E. Sunday night?"

"Of course not."

"Didn't anyone notice the Riccio was missing?"

"C. E. probably put a sign saying it was off view. If questioned he could claim he was examining it in his office. Not quite kosher, but he could get away with it."

"Does Wellington Chen know his college buddy stole the statue?"

"Of course not."

"So C. E.'s death, Geoff's suicide and Phoebe's murder have nothing to do with Wellington Chen?"

"I am the director. It's my responsibility to protect the Lemrow."

Steve marveled at Monika's sleight of hand: one minute the vulnerable maiden, the next minute the conscientious director of a major museum.

Monika continued in director mode. "Any breath of scandal and Wellington would have canceled the exhibit plans."

"I should have." The voice came out of the darkness.

Wellington emerged from the Central Gallery, flanked by Rosaria and Joe.

"I heard something," Monika said. "It was you."

Wellington stood stock-still. "Come to the exhibit, Monika." He ignored Steve, turned on his heel and led the way back through the dark hall. Rosaria pulled the flash light off her belt and flicked it on. Steve texted Kenny and ordered him to turn on full lighting in the Central Gallery and the Chen exhibit.

Rosaria and Wellington led the way, followed by Steve and Monika. They walked in formation past Van Dycks, Turners, and Duccios. When they got to the closed doors of the exhibit, Steve flashed his pass over a sensor and the two oak doors slid apart.

In the brightness of the overhead lights, the rectangular room's coppery wallpaper glowed like fire, but without the subtle lighting, the eight mounted statues were flat and the four pictures were faded.

Wellington looked only at Monika. "Why did you kill my Phoebe?"

Monika blanched. "How could you? How dare you? I protected her."

"Does it have anything to do with this?" Wellington walked up to the white and blue porcelain statue of Kuan-yin and touched it.

"Don't do that," Monika commanded.

"Why not? It's a fake like you."

Monika caught her breath but said nothing.

"Or this one?" Wellington touched the cast iron statue. Then he moved on to the sandal wood statue and grabbed it.

"Don't touch that one. It's genuine," she cried. "They all are, of course."

"Or this one?" Wellington's voice grew louder. This time he put his hands around the neck of the statue and wrung it. "I trusted you. When I wanted to investigate the man who hurt Phoebe you told me to stay out of it. What a fool I was."

"I protected Phoebe. She wanted the exhibit to please Sami."

Pain spread over Wellington's face like a rash.

"You're suffering, Wellington. I understand but don't turn against me. I'm your friend."

"I took Phoebe's iPhone."

Monika stood perfectly still.

"In Hong Kong, we traced her calls, her emails. My team spoke to Sami."

"I'm sorry she was involved with him."

"Don't give me that shit, Monika. You've worked with him for years. Import, export of only the finest forgeries."

Suddenly, Wellington grabbed the cast iron statue. For a second he stood facing Monika, angling the statue like a cricket bat. Monika spread out her arms, a futile gesture to protect the collection.

Wellington raised the iron statue over his head. Steve stepped between him and Monika. Wellington, tears coursing down his face, lowered the statue, then spotting the other forgery, raised the iron statue again and smashed it into the blue and white Kuan-yin. He rammed his left fist through the painting of the seated Kuan-yin, surrounded by magpies and storks. Steve grabbed him, pulled his arm gently out of the gaping canvas and held the sobbing man.

"They're mine." Tears raced down Wellington's face. "I can do what I want."

Chapter 34

6 p.m. Friday, November 25

"Go," Dom said. She was referring to a request from Monika Syka's lawyer that Steve interview Monika.

"All she does is flirt and lie." Steve knew he sounded dumb the minute he said it.

"No wonder she wants to see you."

"I have a shit load of cases. Come on," Steve said. "That guy at the Met who fell down the stairs, the baby in the garbage can, that guy at the school…"

"Stop whining. Get out of here."

After flinging his cigarette in the direction of the curb, Steve approached the Trident from Madison. His shoulders were hunched and his hands shoved into his pockets like a teenager being marched off to a hated school. Seeing the Fox News 7 truck parked at the corner of 79th Street and Fifth, he thought how the media had crowned Monika their evil darling. Cartoons depicting her as

Morticia and Cruella de Vil had blossomed in everything from the News to the New York Review of Books.

A hefty bail plus discrete surveillance – Steve spotted the Reliable in an unmarked Ford and couldn't resist tapping on the window – guaranteed they would meet in her apartment.

As he entered the Trident's vestibule, he hoped it was horrible for Monika to live in the same place as her alleged victim, Phoebe Chen. Did Monika run into Harry and Elliot Ross? How did they behave in the elevator - with stony silences or shrieks of ingratitude?

Monika opened the door on the first ring. She was wearing catalog jeans and an old sweater. She hugged herself and shivered slightly as she stepped to one side so he could enter. She reminded him of the way she'd looked in the ER the afternoon of Phoebe's death.

Act I, Steve figured.

"Lieutenant Leguizamo told me you wanted to see me." He determined to keep it business like.

Monika smiled her old smile then led the way into the bare living room. The sun's slanting rays fell across empty walls pockmarked with holes and dim outlines of removed frames. A few nails were scattered on the surface like ants. It reminded Steve of a war zone.

He sat on the sofa and studied the room's ordinary box-like shape. Gone were the custom made blond furniture and the slews of photographs celebrating Monika's rise in the art world.

Like the co-op, Monika was stripped down: no pearls, no jewelry at all, no thick silk scarf, no short shorts, no killer stilettos with red soles.

"Don't look so stern, Detective. Innocent until proven guilty."

"You sure you want to talk to me?" Steve listened for some cool jazz, a sound he associated with her. There was nothing.

"I coudda ben a contender," Monika said in a weak attempt at humor. Reading Steve's mind, Monika said, "Sold everything. How do you think I raised the bail? I can offer you three buck Chuck wine or coffee. What's it going to be?"

"Nothing. You know your rights?"

Steve knew she was loving the attention. He hated Dom for assigning him this interview. Recalling his five-minute crush, he felt his face grow red under the beard he was growing.

"I like it. The beard." Monika waited for a reaction. When she got none, she said,

"I wanted you to know before the media exploited it." She approached the bare window and looked down at the Fox 7 truck. Steve followed her moves. She really had lost weight.

Monica swung around. "I'm a twin."

Something stirred in Steve's memory. Max at the Opening had said that Monika was a twin like him and C. E.

"The two twins from Scranton. You and your sister and Max and C. E."

"Four twins, Detective," Monika said. The old, flirty tone asserted itself.

He watched her pretty, unmade up eyes open wider and heard a slight intake of breath. "You knew that the media has dug up stuff about my family?"

He shrugged, meaning, what else is new.

"They've found out that I forged my dead sister's college acceptance."

He shrugged again. What's her game, diminished responsibility? Showing off? Shock value?

"I didn't want you to get the wrong idea."

She's going on trial for killing Phoebe Chen, she's responsible for C. E.'s and Geoff's deaths and she's worried about my opinion? What else is new? She's a narcissist.

Unsound mind so she lands in Bedford Hills. Steve was thinking of the maximum security prison that was a who's who of infamous prisoners.

"Where did you get the idea?" Steve said. Maybe she wasn't original, but she was his first perp who was a mix of scholar, thief and murderer.

"You mean borrowing my sister's identity? After the car crash…"

"Who was driving?"

Monika froze, honestly confused. "You mean who was driving our car?"

Steve nodded.

"Dad. He was a lousy driver. It wasn't me. I didn't kill my family, if that's what you're thinking."

"So when did you think of stealing your sister's identity?"

"In the hospital. Monica was dead. I was smashed up and I saw an opportunity to get out of dear old Scranton." She smiled smugly and wrapped her sweater around her. "I've never returned."

"What's your real name?"

"Kitty. Doesn't have the style of Mo*ni*ka, does it?" Her old spiciness flickered in her eyes.

"Did Max …" Steve started to say.

"That little shit. Instead of persecuting me you should go after him for blackmail."

"He knew you weren't Monica?" Steve recalled that Max ran into Rosaria about the time Monika was bashing Dom. He said he had an appointment at the Lemrow. They had dismissed it as another of his lies, but figured he was up to something. Running into Theodora probably saved his life. "You had an appointment with Max the afternoon Lieutenant Leguizamo was attacked?"

Monika opened then closed her mouth resolutely. "You always were too easy to talk to."

Chapter 35

3 p.m. Saturday, December 1

Steve sat in the Metropolitan Museum of Art's Chinese wing. Overhead was a painting of a crane and birds that Steve recognized as magpies.

He was staring at a blue and white porcelain statue of the seated figure of Kuan-yin. It was labeled Ming. Steve wondered if it was authentic. He couldn't tell the difference between it and the forgery Wellington had smashed in the Chen exhibit. It didn't matter. The FBI had moved in on the forged statues.

Instead of attending Wellington's wedding today, Steve had come to the Met to wish his friend some contentment. He had refused the invitation, claiming a heavy workload. Privately, he admitted he was allergic to weddings.

He studied the harbingers of happiness and a long life of worthy pursuits. Steve thought that Wellington was crazy to be marrying for the fourth time a woman young enough to be his niece. He laughed aloud at its ludicrousness.

What a case. The media was having a field day with Monika Syka awaiting trial. New York One and the rest of the gang were in a lather over Monika's latest revelation that she had stolen her twin sister's identity. In high school she'd been a party girl and lousy student who had seen the opportunity to go to a prestigious college, courtesy of her dead sister's grades. She never looked back.

Harry Ross had informed him that Lemrow attendance was up. Mary L. said they were interviewing candidates for the director's position.

Cristobel and Elliot had not gotten back together. Steve suspected that she and King were seeing one another but keeping it quiet.

Dom was back at work, ignoring her doctors.

Holbrook conceded that the team, without mentioning Steve, had done a good job. For the moment, Steve was still in homicide, which was good, but working in the same unit as the guy who stole his girl, which was bad. He stared at a magpie without seeing it. Instead, he allowed himself a one minute daydream about Carmen.

In other jobs you got a bonus or a promotion for a successful job. In homicide, you were rewarded with more work.

Jessie, his daughter, was in New York for the Thanksgiving break. She had practically fainted when he asked her to meet him in the museum.

Steve glanced at his watch. His daughter was late. What else was new?

Steve's cell buzzed. It was Jessie. He listened. She was having man trouble with her boyfriend and begged off joining him.

"Dad, we'll go to a museum together real soon," she said.

"What a treat," Steve said.

THE END

Made in the USA
San Bernardino, CA
10 February 2014